Finding Cheer

BY

HEATHER SCHNEIDER

FINDING CHEER

Summary: The magical occurrences caused by Holly Claus's North Pole magic continue to impact Emerald Hollow, Oregon in this second book in the Magical Emerald Hollow series.

Editor: Red Adept Editing Services

Cover Design: Kylie Sek

ISBN: 979-8-9850507-4-5 (paperback)

ISBN: 979-8-9850507-5-2 (ebook)

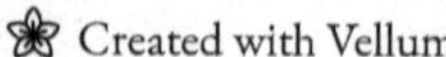 Created with Vellum

Finding Cheer

BY

HEATHER SCHNEIDER

To everyone who stops to smell the wildflowers.

Chapter One

SOFIA

As Sofia Reyes trudged through the snow, she remembered why she didn't like hiking, especially in the winter. A bit of the cold white substance that blanketed the ground had slipped inside her left boot, leaving her sock wet and her skin clammy. But she had an obligation to hike the trail through the woods on New Year's Eve. It was tradition, so she would suffer through.

The onslaught of snow had continued to fall since Christmas, and Sofia was hiking on packed powder that had to be three feet deep. She gave a little sigh, trying not to dream of spring. Snow was magical on Christmas, of course, but beyond that, she could do without it.

Snow meant shoveling her driveway. It meant helping her best friend, Ash, salt the walkways at the Emerald House. Snow meant road closures, trapping her in her little town of Emerald Hollow instead of giving her the freedom to shop in nearby cities. It meant no garden or blossoming flowers that lit her world with fragrance.

Flowers had been on her mind a lot lately, and she couldn't fully understand why. On Christmas Eve, a week ago, she'd had a dream that she was struggling to shake. It had felt so different from her other dreams, somehow more vivid despite her memories of it being unclear.

The Christmas Eve dream had involved flowers and jewelry, and though she couldn't quite remember the details, she'd woken up with a strong urge to take her jewelry business to the next level in the new year. Since then, she'd been tossing around ideas for a new collection, but nothing had stuck.

Her mind returned to the task at hand as her boots loudly crunched across the firm white ground. Sofia was nearly there. She would take in the view, say a few words of remembrance, then turn right back around for the comfort of the little electric fireplace in her living room.

Sofia's thoughts were broken when she spotted something on the path ahead, and she narrowed her eyes while reaching for the pepper spray clipped to her backpack.

"Oh my god," she breathed as a gray-and-blue lump, which was in stark contrast to the snow, came into focus. A man lay sprawled across the path.

Sofia's pulse pounded in her ears, and she ran to him and knelt to check for signs of bleeding. She didn't see any, but he appeared to be unconscious. She leaned her ear toward his mouth and listened to hear if he was breathing then watched for a rise and fall of his chest. Relieved, she let out a breath when she saw his jacket moving steadily up and down.

Thoughts bombarded her. *Okay, he's breathing. How long has he been out here lying in the snow? He seems to be dressed warmly enough, but hypothermia can set in quickly in these conditions.*

She shook him a little, and he jerked upright. The man looked around, his eyes wild.

Sofia stood and took a few steps back. "Sir, are you all right?"

He turned as if he was just seeing her, and his forehead crinkled in confusion. "Where am I?" His voice was deep and smooth, but his face signaled something between uncertainty and fear.

"You're in the woods outside of Emerald Hollow."

"Emerald Hollow?"

Sofia's brow pinched. "You haven't heard of it?"

"I... I don't think so."

Sofia tried not to bite the inside of her lip. While he seemed okay physically, something was clearly off. She stealthily pulled out her phone and sent Ash a quick text.

"Do you remember going out for a hike this morning? Where did you set out from?" Sofia was still keeping her distance. She'd put the pepper spray away when she saw that he was truly unconscious, but she was ready to grab it again if needed.

The man's forehead tightened again as if he was trying to remember. "I set out from... from..." He looked up at her then, and their eyes met. His were the palest brown, and they seemed to be searching for something as he looked at her. "I don't remember," he said at last.

As if on cue, thick, wet snow began to fall again. She tried not to roll her eyes at the circumstances, despite her concern and wariness. *This darned snow.* It was like something in a movie.

At the feel of a vibration, she checked her phone and relaxed a little. At least Ash had seen her text.

"Okay. I think you fell on your hike today, and you may have a concussion. We need to get you out of this cold. Are you okay to walk back? It's about a mile to the parking area."

How long was this man hiking? She hadn't seen any other cars when she'd parked, and the next natural entry point to the trail would have been five miles south. Every sense in Sofia's body was heightened, and a slight crackle in the distance, likely from a squirrel, made her jump.

The man slowly rose, and he seemed steady on his feet. Sofia finally realized how tall he was. Everyone was tall compared to her, but he had to be well over six feet. His blue hiking coat fit snugly on his trim frame.

"Yeah, I think so. I feel fine physically. I just don't..." He looked around again then reached near his shoulders as if feeling for something that should have been there. "I could have sworn I was wearing a backpack."

Oh good. He remembers something. "I'll follow you," Sofia said, stepping slightly off the trail so that he could pass her. If they were going to walk back together, she would at least be able to keep her eyes on him the whole way. Six years in the military had taught her something about basic situational awareness.

To her relief, he nodded and walked by her, shaking his arms and legs out a little to get the blood flowing. Sofia started walking a few paces behind him then turned her head to glance up toward the top of the hill. Guilt tugged at her chest like a thread of a sweater snagging on the back of a chair.

"Sorry, Mom," she whispered. "I'll try again next year."

Chapter Two

ASH

Ash was getting a guest settled into their room at the Emerald House, his bed-and-breakfast, when he got a text from Sofia. The words on the screen had him quickly bidding the guests farewell.

> SOS. Found an unconscious man on Lupin Trail.

He replied quickly.

> I'll be there in twenty.

Another text came through just as he was starting up his truck.

> He's up and walking. We're heading to the trailhead.

> Meet you there.

He fired up the heater in his truck and made a call to the hospital, letting them know to expect a patient soon. Sofia

5

hadn't provided a lot of information, but if the man had been unconscious in the snow when she found him, he at least needed to be checked by a doctor.

His mind snagged on something in her text. *Lupin Trail...*

Suddenly, it clicked. It was New Year's Eve. Sofia always hiked to Eagle's Peak to continue a tradition she'd shared with her mom. His heart ached, and he wondered whether she had encountered the man on the way up or down. She only pushed through that hike each year in honor of her mother, and adding a stressful event on top of it was likely to throw her off-kilter.

He cruised carefully along the highway, snow falling relentlessly and adding to the white mountains that already lined both sides of the road. He remembered a conversation with Holly, who thought that all the snow was probably her fault.

Thinking of Holly, he relaxed a little. She'd had business at the North Pole—or "Canada," as they referred to it to their friends in Emerald Hollow—the last few days, but she was coming back that afternoon. She'd said she couldn't miss decorating for her first Emerald Hollow New Year's Eve bash.

The smile that had unconsciously lit his face slipped away when he turned in to the dirt parking lot. Sofia and a tall man in a blue hiking jacket were making their way down the last stretch of the trail. Ash pulled his truck in next to Sofia's Subaru and left the engine running.

"Hey, Ash," Sofia called as they approached. "Thanks for coming."

"Of course. Is everything all right here?" He studied the man as he walked toward him and noted that there were no obvious signs of injury and he didn't appear to be carrying anything.

"Ash, this is Isaiah. He doesn't remember how he got onto the trail today. I think he needs to be checked out."

"I called the hospital, so they're expecting us." Ash stuck out a hand, and Isaiah took it and gave a firm shake, their eyes meeting. "I'm Ash."

"Isaiah. Thanks for meeting us. This kind of thing doesn't usually happen to me, I don't think."

Ash could hear the confusion in his voice. *Where did this man come from?* He wasn't local. Ash knew everyone in their small town. *Is he visiting Emerald Hollow?* Ash's eyes met Sofia's, and he could see from her expression that she had many of the same questions.

"Let's get you in the warm vehicle." Ash indicated his truck, and the three of them settled inside, with Sofia in the back seat.

Ash tried asking a few more questions on the way to the hospital, but the man, though he seemed friendly, couldn't answer much.

That has to be some nasty concussion. Ash peeked at Sofia in the rearview mirror and saw her clicking away on her phone.

They pulled into the small hospital, and an EMT Ash was friendly with met them at the door. He immediately escorted Isaiah into the building.

"I'm gonna go in," Sofia said suddenly, opening her door. "The doctor might have questions about what he was like when I found him."

Her voice quavered slightly. *Is this about the last time she was at the hospital? Or has the whole incident distressed her?*

"Do you want me to come with you?" Ash began to turn toward the hospital door.

But Sofia touched his arm. "No, it's fine. I'll see you at the party tonight. Thanks for picking us up." Her eyebrows suddenly rose, and she exclaimed, "Oh no! My car!"

In their hurry to get to the hospital, Sofia had jumped right into his truck, and they hadn't thought about her vehicle.

Her reaction to leaving her car behind confirmed she was wired from the whole experience.

"Don't worry. I'll take Tyler out, and we'll drop it off here. Keys?"

Looking relieved, she nodded. "You're a lifesaver, as usual." She tossed the keys to him.

"Good luck. Say hi to Dr. Margo for me."

Sofia hopped out of the truck and disappeared through the automatic hospital doors, and Ash, though he had no idea what was going on in her head, hoped that she would be okay. Despite the brave face and sassy snark Sofia typically showed the world, he'd always sensed that she wasn't as unbreakable as she led people to believe.

Chapter Three

SOFIA

Dr. Margo was already examining Isaiah when Sofia got to the room. Emerald Hollow had a tiny hospital, and Sofia knew her way around it like the back of her hand. She'd hurried through the hallways, not daring to look left or right, not wanting to remember, and kept her eyes moving from room number to room number until she reached her destination.

The nurse asked the doctor if Sofia could come in, and a moment later, Sofia was let inside the small room and ushered onto an extra chair. Isaiah had removed his jacket, and she couldn't help noticing the muscles under his long sleeves. She quickly turned away.

"Hi, Dr. Margo. Ash says hello."

"I should have known he was the driver Isaiah referenced. That man manages to be everywhere at once. So, can you tell me about finding Isaiah?"

Sofia repeated the encounter, sharing the story as if on autopilot, and Dr. Margo nodded along as she listened, though her forehead was slightly pinched.

"Well, we're running a scan just to be safe, but there are no physical bumps or indications of an injury to your skull, Isaiah. You really don't remember anything about this morning? How about yesterday? Where were you then?"

Sofia studied him. His light-brown skin had regained some of its warmth after being in Ash's truck. Sofia was surprised to realize she found him quite good-looking. But the thought quickly dislodged as he spoke, his forehead creased in confusion again.

"I'm sure it sounds strange, but I really don't know. I know my name is Isaiah. I can tell you the year and the president. But aspects of my identity are just... It's like they're locked away somewhere. I can feel them there, but I can't access them. It doesn't make any sense. Sorry, I probably sound crazy." He gave them both an apologetic look—his mouth squeezing together tightly as his eyebrows drew together—and Sofia struggled to keep her face unreadable. A feeling she couldn't quite place was building in her.

"So... what? You have amnesia or something?" she blurted out.

Dr. Margo gave her a look that quieted her again. "It seems so. Though amnesia isn't usually this complete. People typically remember who they are, but certain memories can become hard to keep track of. I'm thinking Isaiah here just needs a good rest. I'd like to keep him overnight for observation." She typed something into her computer.

Isaiah sighed but nodded. "Okay, if that's what you think is best."

Sofia wasn't sure why, but a sense of unease at the whole situation was creeping over her and getting stronger by the minute. She'd heard the doctor. Amnesia like he was supposedly experiencing wasn't really a thing. It only happened in movies. Suddenly, she wondered if Isaiah had an agenda he wasn't telling them about.

Sofia had been made to feel foolish by a man manipulating reality once before. She'd vowed to never let it happen again.

Her hands began to sweat despite the cold, and the harsh lights of the room made her dizzy. As her heart rate suddenly kicked up, she recognized the signs of an impending anxiety attack and tried to calm her breathing.

Sofia needed to get out of the room. She needed to get out of the hospital. Whatever was going on, it no longer needed to involve her. She stood up. "Well, if that's all you need from me, I'd better get going."

Dr. Margo stood up as if to follow her. Sofia gave one last glance at Isaiah sitting on the exam table, looking confused and vulnerable. His brow was still knitted, and the hair on top of his head was ruffled. Her heart rate sped up in a burst of compassion. *No. Nope.*

She peeled her gaze away from him and steeled herself. If that man was being anything less than truthful, she wasn't going to be around to fall for it.

"Sofia, just a moment," Dr. Margo said quietly, pulling the door gently closed behind her. "I'd like you to come back tomorrow if Isaiah hasn't gotten any better. You were the first person he saw when he woke up. Maybe you'll help trigger some memories for him."

Sofia took a step back and forced her voice into a whisper. "Doc, you can't be serious. Amnesia? Like, *Overboard* amnesia? From slipping on a hiking trail?"

Dr. Margo let out a sigh. "I don't know. We'll see what the scan shows. But until then, he's my patient, and I will assume what he says is true. Maybe someone will come looking for him by tomorrow."

Sofia nodded, latching on to that bit of information. Yes, one of his family members or friends would come searching for him. The hospital would be one of the first places they would check. And she would be off the hook for whatever was going on.

"You didn't find a cell phone or any identification along the trail?" Dr. Margo asked.

Sofia shook her head. "No, nothing on the way up, and there was nothing around him when I found him. He could have been coming from the other direction, though." She paused, considering. "Maybe I should go back up there and check farther up the trail."

"No, don't worry about it. I'll have the deputies send someone."

Sofia stiffened. *The deputies? Is Dr. Margo worried Isaiah's a criminal?*

Dr. Margo must have correctly interpreted the expression on Sofia's face, because she quickly added, "That's standard procedure in a case like this. We need to figure out who this man is to get his medical records and treat him appropriately before getting him home."

Sofia nodded, confusing emotions stirring in her. *Not every man is like Noah.* The words came to her as clearly as if her mother were in the hallway with her. *You can't distrust everyone just because one man didn't deserve your faith.*

And her mother was right. Ash was nothing like Noah. But Noah *had* existed. His betrayal had been real. What he'd done to her couldn't be erased, not completely. And if there was one person like Noah in the world, there could be others.

She closed her eyes for a moment, remembering what day it was. If there was any day she should take her mom's advice, it was her birthday. She opened her eyes to see Dr. Margo waiting patiently, as if she understood Sofia's hesitation.

"Leave your phone number at the reception desk if you're willing to come back tomorrow. I'll only call you if I think you're needed, okay? Otherwise, great job here. You did excellent work examining him on the trail and getting him out of the cold. Have fun at the party tonight."

Sofia nodded, said goodbye to Dr. Margo, and briefly stopped at the reception desk to leave her phone number. As she walked out the door, her phone buzzed, and she read the text message. Ash had let her know that he and Tyler had just dropped off her car. The keys were inside.

"Well, you're right about one thing, Dr. Margo. Ash does manage to be everywhere at once," she said to herself before leaving the hospital and not daring to look back.

Chapter Four

ASH

Ash pulled into the parking lot of the Emerald House, the anxiety he was feeling about Sofia melting into the background as he thought of the evening to come. Holly was on her way back to Emerald Hollow, and they would get to spend their first New Year's Eve together.

While Ash had been utterly awed by his tour of the North Pole—it was still hard to believe he'd met real-life elves and been in a flying sleigh pulled by reindeer—his favorite moments with Holly were still the magical ones they shared together in his hometown. And the only night that was possibly as magical and full of promise as Christmas Eve was New Years.

Comet raced to his side as he entered the Emerald House, the white streak across his black fur brighter than usual. Holly had given the dog a bath at the North Pole, and the clean evergreen smell refused to dissipate. At first, Ash had thought it was just lingering shampoo, but he'd begun to wonder if there was magic in the water at the North Pole. Ash reached down to scratch behind the dog's ears. "Hey, buddy."

A tall woman with curly black hair approached him, and

Ash grinned. "Esmeralda! How's everything looking for tonight?"

As president of the chamber of commerce, Esmeralda oversaw the New Year's Eve bash, and Ash was glad to see her.

"Nearly ready," she said, letting her eyes sweep over the coffee shop gathering area. "Holly is still planning to help with the decorations, yes?"

Ash tried to suppress a proud grin. Holly had become famous for her decorating capabilities after stunning the town at the fall festival and again at the Christmas Faire. None of them knew that she had the assistance of magic, and that was just fine by him. To him, Holly would be magical whether she was Ms. Claus or not.

"Yep. She should be getting into town any time."

"Excellent. A few of the chamber members will be here to help her, and the DJ should be showing up by seven. Are you and Enzo ready with the food and drinks?"

"All squared away."

Esmeralda clapped once. "All right, then. I think everything is in motion. Though we did sell more tickets than ever. I think we may need to look for a larger venue next year." There was reluctance in her voice, and her eyes held regret.

Ash understood where she was coming from. He'd had plans to build a larger conference space on the back side of the property, near the woods, but those plans hadn't come to fruition yet. *Could such a big project be completed in time for next year's New Year's Eve bash?*

"Normally, we cap it at sixty, but people were just clamoring for tickets this year. We ended up selling a hundred. It may have something to do with your Holly's party-planning skills. And it's hard to turn people away when the ticket sales go to support the animal shelter," Esmeralda continued.

Ash's head began to spin. *A hundred tickets? There are going to be one hundred people in my coffee shop?* In previous sold-out years, sixty had already made it feel like the space was ready to burst. He let out a soft whistle.

"I know, I know. Forgive me. But you and Holly are a dynamic duo with these things. If anyone could make this work, it's you two."

He relaxed at that. Esmeralda was right. Holly made it feel like nothing was impossible. Maybe it wouldn't be as overwhelming as he was expecting.

"Thanks, Es. I'd better get back to work. See you tonight."

Esmeralda gave his arm a little squeeze then left the Emerald House.

I hope you're ready for this, Holly, Ash thought. *Your first New Year's Eve in Emerald Hollow might be more than you bargained for.*

Chapter Five

SOFIA

Sofia drove straight to her house from the hospital and parked haphazardly. The snowplow had created a large berm where she normally parked, so she felt justified in placing her car wherever she could find room. All rules went out the window when snow blanketed their town.

She quickly scaled the porch steps and stepped inside then peeled off her hiking clothes as soon as she reached the bathroom. She let herself linger in the hot shower, the adrenaline crash from the day's events coming on in a wave. Once she'd erased all the cold from her bones, she settled down on the couch in front of the electric fireplace.

Her emotions were spiraling, and she reached for her tub of jewelry-making supplies in order to busy her hands. *Should I have gone back out to the trail and finished the hike? Would my mom be upset that I didn't?*

Sofia shook her head and brushed a tear from the corner of her eye. Her mom had been one of the most understanding people she had ever known. Sofia believed that she would have understood the situation and been glad that Sofia had chosen to help someone rather than complete their tradition. Still, unease tugged at the center of her sternum, and she wasn't sure if it was from leaving the hike early or for another reason.

Over the next hour, Sofia lost herself in the process of designing and making earrings. She smiled in delight as she held up the beaded champagne-glass earrings she'd made for herself then paused to contemplate what she should make for Holly.

Holly didn't usually wear jewelry, but she had worn the sparkly Santa hat pair Sofia created for her on Christmas Eve, and they'd made her look even more beautiful. Sofia would turn her friend into a jewelry wearer in no time. She thought for another moment, looking at her own champagne glass pair. Holly didn't drink alcohol. Sofia could say the glasses represented sparkling cider, but that didn't feel right.

An idea came to her, and she smiled as she resumed her work, humming to the music streaming from her phone. Jewelry making was her happy place—her escape. She'd just gotten into the rhythm of the music, most thoughts of the morning forgotten, when she was interrupted by her phone ringing.

"Hey, Ash," she answered, putting the call on speaker and continuing her beadwork. "What's up?"

"How'd everything go at the hospital?" Ash asked.

Oh, right. Isaiah, the man you found in the woods this morning. Reality snapped back into place.

"Dr. Margo says he has symptoms of amnesia. They sent some deputies to look for a phone or wallet on the trail to see if they can determine his identity. What a weird situation."

"Huh. Amnesia? I thought that kind of thing only happened in movies."

Sofia dropped the half-beaded earrings onto her lap. "Exactly! I think there's some other agenda going on." *Oops.* The words had just slipped out. She'd decided she wanted to be trusting of Isaiah to a degree, for her mom's sake, but if she couldn't voice her suspicions to her best friend, there was no one else she would be able to work through the situation with.

"What? You think he's faking it?" Ash always gave people the benefit of the doubt. It was one of the things the people of Emerald Hollow loved about him—one of the things *she* loved about him.

"Even Dr. Margo said amnesia doesn't normally present like that. It's not so complete. Especially when he had no signs of a head injury."

"He didn't?"

"They're running a scan, but on the surface, no."

The other side of the line was quiet for a moment, and Sofia wondered what Ash was thinking.

"Well, I hope they find out who he is and that the scans come back clean."

Sofia tried not to let out a sigh of exasperation. Ash was so *good*. He didn't have a hard time seeing the best in people. Sofia tried to remember whether she had been like that before everything had happened, but that felt like a lifetime ago.

"We'll see," she mumbled, eager to change the subject. "Is Holly back yet?"

"No. Anytime, though." Sofia could practically hear the smile in his voice. She didn't know what all had gone down on Christmas Eve, but those two were over the moon for each other. She smiled too. She couldn't think of anyone better for Ash than Holly, the woman who had mysteriously rolled into town the previous fall. It hadn't taken long for the entire town to fall in love with her.

"So, what exactly is the plan with you two now? Are you doing a long-distance-relationship thing? Or is she going to move to Emerald Hollow eventually?" Sofia's heart momentarily froze as another option occurred to her. *There isn't any chance Ash would move to Canada to be with Holly, is there?*

"We're still figuring it out, but she's decided to make Emerald Hollow her base camp for all her traveling."

Sofia sagged with relief. It seemed that, for the moment, at least, Ash wasn't entertaining the idea of moving away from their little town in Oregon. "But what about her home in Canada? Is she going to sell it? Rent it out?"

"She's keeping her place so that she can stay there when she needs to go home for work."

Sofia frowned, feeling like there was more to the situation than he was telling her. But she decided to let it go. Their relationship was their business, and as long as they were planning to stay together and spend most of their time in Emerald Hollow, she was happy with whatever arrangement they came up with. Things were still somewhat new between them, and if anyone was going to make a permanent move, there didn't need to be a rush to make that decision.

She changed the topic back to the New Year's Eve party. "What time do you want me there to make drinks tonight?"

"Doors open at seven thirty, so any time around then."

"You got it, boss. I'll have the champagne flowing when people walk in."

"See ya, Sof."

Sofia hung up and looked at the time. She still had a couple of hours before she needed to be at the Emerald House. She turned the music back on and resumed her work.

Chapter Six

HOLLY

Holly had been at the North Pole since Christmas day, helping the elves transition into Evergreen mode. The previous season was the first in recent memory that Christmas had almost fallen apart, and a week later, there was a palpable sense of relief in the air that things had worked out.

"Clementine, did you ask Auryn about those decorations?"

The Elf Mayor's ice-blond braids swung as she turned to Holly. "Yes, Ms. Claus. They should be in the sleigh already."

"Thanks, Clementine. I'll probably be gone for most of the cycle. Is that okay?" Holly was already buzzing at the thought of going back to Emerald Hollow. That time, she would be able to stay nearly a whole month. And when she had to head back to the North Pole to discharge her Cheer, Ash would know exactly what was going on.

The thought still made her giddy. Ash knew who she was. He knew about her magic, and he was okay with it. They had a lot of details to work out, but for the moment, she knew she would be spending a lot more time in Ash's hometown, a place she'd grown to love as much as he did.

She tried not to feel any guilt at the idea of taking up residence in Emerald Hollow. The elves were accustomed to her absence. After all, she used to spend most of each cycle traveling around the world. And she felt more connected to them since she was able to spend time with them while she was at the North Pole rather than being exhausted from her Cheer-collecting missions. She would still be gone a similar amount each month, but when she left to collect Cheer to power the North Pole, Emerald Hollow was the only place she needed to go.

"That's just fine, Ms. Claus. Everything is rosy here. Do you have any big plans to ring in the New Year?" Clementine asked, breaking Holly out of thoughts of her living situation.

"Emerald Hollow has an annual New Year's Eve bash. That's why I need the decor. How about you?" New Year's Eve wasn't traditionally celebrated at the North Pole. They partied heartily on Christmas Day, saying farewell to Advent season and ringing in Evergreen.

Still, human holidays weren't completely unknown to the elves, and a stray firework had occasionally been spotted against the backdrop of the Northern Lights on New Year's Eves past.

"I'm going skiing," Clementine said.

Holly's eyes widened. It was hard to picture her serious friend doing anything outside of her mayoral duties. But now that she thought of it, she could easily picture Clementine skiing. She was sure that the elf was an expert.

"That sounds like fun, Clementine. Do you need anything before I leave?"

"No, no. Everything is under control. Go soak us up some of that superpowered Cheer you've found in Oregon."

Holly grinned. She hadn't fully explained to the elves why her Cheer was so much brighter. They knew it had something to do with Ash, but otherwise, most were just happy that the North Post was back to full brightness and that the North Pole had all the power it needed. The past few months had been tense for them all, and elves were not accustomed to stress.

"Will do." She gave Clementine a little wave then made her way to the stables. Some of the Keyblar elves had readied four reindeer, and they stood waiting by the golden sleigh. Holly quickly peered into the back seat and noticed the large sack of decorations that had been carefully placed there.

Dancer, Willow, Butter, and Sprig were her reindeer crew that day. Ivy and Clove had begged to come—they were in love with the forests of Emerald Hollow—but Holly had been tipped off by Clementine that some of the other reindeer were starting to get jealous, so she'd asked for a fresh team.

While Ivy and Clove had been disappointed, Auryn, her elf assistant, had assured her they would be busy preparing for the reindeer games and would forget about Emerald Hollow in no time.

She climbed into the sleigh, settled herself, and lifted the delicate reins.

Emerald Hollow, Ash, here I come.

Chapter Seven

ASH

Ash sat at the desk in his office, reviewing paperwork. The vineyard deal he had been working on for months was finally being inked. The Emerald House would have exclusive sales rights to special varieties of two of the vineyard's most popular wines, and he was in the process of acquiring an old-fashioned trolley that could take people from Emerald Hollow out to the winery for tours.

They still had a few more details to work out, but he planned to debut the special wines at a Valentine's Day event at the Emerald House. Because of the success of that year's fall festival and Christmas Faire, Emerald Hollow was quickly becoming a holiday destination. Word was spreading that it was the place to be for anyone seeking a magical small-town experience.

They hadn't won the Hallmark competition, but that had always been a pipe dream. As he'd hoped, the publicity from it had generated a ton of buzz, and the last two weeks of both November and December were already completely booked at the Emerald House for the next year.

Ash thought of all the holidays up until then. Valentine's

Day, St. Patrick's Day, Easter, midsummer solstice, the Fourth of July… the opportunities were endless. He just had to find a way to put a special Emerald Hollow spin on each. And with Holly's help, they could make it happen.

Goose bumps rose on his arms, and he looked up to a soft knock on his office door.

"Come in!"

A grin split his face when he saw her. Snow floated on her dark-brown locks, and she was wearing his new favorite color —red.

"I thought I might find you here," Holly said, her voice as sweet and musical as he remembered. They'd only been apart for a few days, but it still took his breath away to see her.

He stood and crossed the room.

She gave a soft laugh as he slipped his arms around her and squeezed, lifting her slightly off the ground. She met his lips with hers, and a feeling that could best be described as spellbinding passed between them. For a moment, they just stood there, gazing at each other.

Finally, Ash broke the tension. "Sofia was asking about you. Well, about both of us. She wanted to know if we were going to do a long-distance relationship or if you had plans to move here."

Holly bit her bottom lip, and Ash wanted to kiss her again. But he stayed still and let her mind work. He couldn't stop studying her face. It was all so new, being with her and knowing the real her. He was blown away just being in her vicinity and would do whatever it took to hold on to her.

"It all looks a bit complicated from a human standpoint, doesn't it? I'm sure I will move here eventually, but that probably seems soon to everyone else, right? I feel so at home here already. And no matter where I live, I will always return to the North Pole at least once a month to discharge my Cheer. Maybe people could think we keep a vacation house in

Canada. Or that I'm traveling for work. Both are technically true."

Ash reached for her hand. "There was only one thing you said in all of that that matters."

She cocked her head, and he tugged her a little closer.

"You said you feel at home here." Ash couldn't even begin to explain what that meant to him. "The rest of it is just details. People can draw their own conclusions about where you live or how much time we spend together. They'll do that no matter what we do or say."

Holly nodded. "I guess you're right. And the elves don't seem to mind if I'm here most of the time. I know my parents resided at the North Pole, and they were used to that, but for years, I was gone almost every day, traveling around the world. If I'm here most of the month then spend a few days there, fully engaged, they're better off than they were before, aren't they?"

"Have you talked to Clementine about it?" Ash asked, the memory of the elf mayor's cool manner when she met him jumping into his mind.

Holly shook her head. "Not in much detail, no. She just seems relieved that the North Post is functioning again. As long as my Cheer meter is collecting Cheer, I think she'll be happy. And of course, I wanted to get back here to prepare for the New Year's Eve party. Speaking of the party, I've got the decorations. They're in the... shed."

"Shed" was their code word for "sleigh" in case anyone overheard them. References to a sleigh were fine around Christmastime, but it was almost January, and they'd agreed that Holly's secret would stay between the two of them. That was the way it had always been with North Pole magic, according to Holly.

"Great. Esmeralda asked about you too." Ash was on more solid ground discussing the party. He could handle the humans in Emerald Hollow, so long as Holly could handle the elves.

Holly laughed. "I'll have to decorate when no one is looking in order to make it really... you know." She raised her shoulders and shimmied a bit. *Magical.*

"The restaurant is closing early tonight, so that should be fine. But speaking of the restaurant..." Ash perched on the edge of the desk and told her his plans.

Chapter Eight

ISAIAH

saiah was sitting in his hospital bed, staring out the window at the snow, when a soft tap came on the other side of the door. Dr. Margo peeked in then stepped fully inside, an assistant a few steps behind her, poised to take notes.

"Hello, Isaiah. How are you feeling?" Dr. Margo's eyes were evaluating but had a softness behind them as well. He was grateful for that because he felt like a complete mental mess at that moment.

"About the same," he said, sitting up fully in the bed. "Physically, fine. I just can't figure out what happened to me."

Dr. Margo nodded and pursed her lips then looked at a paper on the clipboard she held. "Your scan results came in."

Isaiah's pulse quickened. *Am I finally going to get some answers?*

"Everything looks good. No swelling or other signs of internal injury. As far as we can tell, you didn't sustain a head injury."

Isaiah wasn't sure whether to feel relief or deeper confusion. A head injury was the only thing that explained why he couldn't remember anything about his life besides his name. *If I don't have a head injury, then what caused all this?*

"So what's wrong with me?" he asked, trying to tamp down the alarm he was experiencing. A cold sweat broke out on the back of his neck.

Dr. Margo sighed, but her eyes were still kind when she looked up at him again. "I'm not sure. The next step will be for you to see a psychiatrist. If there isn't a physical explanation for your memory loss, maybe there is something else that can explain it."

"A psychiatrist? You think I'm crazy?" Isaiah was more than alarmed. None of it made any sense. The monitor he was hooked up to beeped, and he realized his heart rate had spiked.

"That's not what I'm saying, Isaiah. I'm not a psychiatrist, but perhaps you experienced a traumatic event that caused you to temporarily forget who you are. Or maybe there's another explanation. But a psychiatrist will be better equipped to determine that. Do you understand?"

He took a deep breath. There was no reason to be upset with Dr. Margo. She was just trying to help him. Still, something deep inside told him a psychiatrist was not what he needed. Suddenly, he had the overwhelming urge to get back to the woods.

"I decline," he said abruptly.

Dr. Margo jerked her head back. "You... decline?"

"Yes. I'm physically fine. I haven't committed any crime. There is no further reason to hold me here. I'd like to leave." Isaiah unhooked himself from the monitor and stood.

Dr. Margo mirrored him. "I don't think that's the best idea, Isaiah. We should—"

"Thank you for your help, Dr. Margo, but I don't need anything else now. I need to get home."

Something flickered in Dr. Margo's eyes. "Home? Do you remember where it is?"

Isaiah had the feeling he wasn't the type of person who lied, because it didn't come naturally to him, but he was desperate. He said what she needed to hear to let him go. "Yes, it's all coming back now. I'll catch a bus home. Thanks again."

He'd already changed back into his pants and shirt after the scan, so he grabbed his coat from a chair by the door. Dr. Margo and her assistant seemed to be having some silent conversation at his side. *Are they going to stop me?*

The silent conversation appeared to continue as he backed out of the room. Only after he exited the hospital did he realize he had no idea how to get back to the trail where he'd been found.

His mind went to the tiny woman with caramel-colored hair and adorable freckles who had found him on the trail. *Sofia.* That had been her name. She'd seemed a little cautious of him—he was a stranger, after all—but otherwise, she'd been very helpful.

Maybe if he found Sofia, she could take him back to the trail. Something told him that was where he needed to be. But his current problem was how to find Sofia. He still had no idea where he was, let alone where she was.

He paused and thought about what he knew. Based on what he had seen on the drive to the hospital, he'd deduced they must be in a small town, not a big city. And Sofia had seemed familiar with the doctor, so clearly, people knew one another around the town. *Perhaps it isn't totally hopeless.*

Night had already fallen, and the air was cold as he exited the hospital. A convenience store sat across the street, its windows painted with winter scenes, and Isaiah crossed the road then went inside. He felt his pockets before dropping his hand. *Of course, no wallet.*

"Can I help you?" a woman called from the counter.

Isaiah racked his brain. *Should I ask her about Sofia? Would that seem too strange?* He didn't know the dynamics of the town. He thought back to the conversation Sofia had had with Dr.

Margo, which he'd barely been able to hear snippets of as they'd spoken outside his room.

Something in his short memory history clicked. Dr. Margo had said something about having fun at a party that night.

"I was invited to a party by a friend, but I'm not sure where it is." The lie felt unnatural again, and Isaiah stuck his hands in the pockets of his coat.

The cashier didn't look suspicious at all, though. "It's probably the one up at the Emerald House. Just continue straight up the hill here, and you'll run right into it. Who's your friend?"

"Ash," Isaiah said after a moment's hesitation, thinking of the man who had given him a ride to the hospital.

The cashier's face lit up. "Ah yeah. It's definitely at the Emerald House, then. Have fun. I've heard their New Year's Eve bash is a blast."

Isaiah's eyes widened with surprise, and he tried to quickly smooth his expression into one of excitement. *It's New Year's Eve? Could that have anything to do with my memory loss? If so, how?*

"I'm looking forward to it. Thanks for the information, ma'am."

The woman laughed. "I don't get called that too much around here. You're welcome, *sir.*"

She's surprised that I called her ma'am? Is that a clue to my identity? Do I come from somewhere where saying "ma'am" is common? Does that signal the South? No one had mentioned his having an accent. Though he supposed you could be from the South and not have an accent.

"Happy New Year," he said despite the barrage of questions her words had triggered. He brushed out the door, the chilly air barely registering as it hit his face. For the moment, he had a plan.

He was going to find the Emerald House and crash a New Year's Eve party.

Chapter Nine
SOFIA

"I know I've seen your work twice now, but wow, I still don't know how you do it," Sofia said appreciatively, giving Holly a quick hug as she surveyed the interior of the Emerald House.

The coffee shop had been entirely transformed with curtains of lights and tiny glittering silver disco balls, creating the illusion of dancing light and rainbows throughout the room.

She turned to her left and gasped. The whole restaurant was also alight, having been completely transfigured in the same classy-party style. Sofia momentarily imagined she was in a swanky New York City hotel, not in a small town in Oregon.

"You included the restaurant?" That had never been part of the New Year's Eve bash before.

"Esmeralda sold a hundred tickets this year," Ash said, raising his eyebrows.

"*What?* And she didn't consult with you first?"

"She said since it's a fundraiser for the animal shelter, we should just take it in stride, basically."

Sofia watched as Holly squeezed Ash's hand. *Ugh, they are cute.* Still, her temper flared at his words.

"Well, then, if Esmeralda says it, it must be so." She let out a deep breath, then a grin split her face, her irritation dissolving at the magic around her. "Holly, I'm so glad you made it to an Emerald Hollow New Year's Eve bash. The chamber goes all out on prizes for the silent auction. And I'll be making my favorite sparkling margaritas. Virgin for you, of course," Sofia added quickly, taking Holly's hand and pulling her away from Ash.

"Here. I made you something. I had no idea how perfect these would be until I walked in here." She reached into her clutch and handed Holly the sparkling disco ball earrings she'd made earlier that day.

"Sof, these are stunning!" Holly exclaimed, admiring them before expertly slipping them into her ears. They complemented the burgundy red dress she was wearing, and all the lights in the room seemed to reflect off them, making Holly appear more radiant than ever.

"You look fab. I bet Ash can't keep his hands off you," Sofia teased.

Holly flushed, but a soft smile played on her lips. "You look gorgeous too," she said, not rising to the bait.

Sofia had chosen to wear a sparkling floor-length silver-and-black gown and her highest heels. She still wasn't as tall as Holly, but she was inching closer. Sofia loved to dress up, and New Year's Eve was the perfect night for it. She was going to dance away all the stress and unwelcome memories that the morning had brought on. There was no better way to start fresh than welcoming in another trip around the sun.

~

THE SPARKLING MARGARITAS WERE AS POPULAR AS always, and Sofia decided to take a break from serving drinks to hit the dance floor again. Ash had done an excellent job choosing the DJ, and the party was already lively by ten o'clock.

Sofia tried not to let herself wonder how many of the party guests were couples who would be kissing at midnight as she danced through the crowded room. There she was for another year, surrounded by many people she loved but still feeling a little alone. Still, she wouldn't let it get her down. New Year's Eve was *not* just for lovers. It was about new beginnings and dreaming big, and that was her mantra for her business that year.

She stopped by the bar and made herself another sparkling margarita, smiling in satisfaction as she took a sip of the fizzy concoction. At least her drink-making skills had improved as she aged, she thought with a snort.

Holly gave her a quizzical look, and Sofia shook her head. She was glad to have a friend like Holly and more than glad that Ash had finally found someone. But there was no such magic for her. No world-traveling handsome man in market research who instantly fell in love with Emerald Hollow would fall out of the sky for her.

Besides, it would be easier for her to fall for someone she already knew, so she wouldn't have to question everything about their past and what they might be keeping from her. Unfortunately, pickings were slim in Emerald Hollow. She already knew everyone in the town, and none of the men was the one for her.

Park, a local who managed a sporting goods store, had been trying to dance with her all evening. She'd given in for a couple of songs but turned him down when he'd asked for a third. Sofia wasn't interested in the guy, and she didn't want to give him the wrong impression.

She wasn't entirely sure *why* she wasn't interested. He'd been divorced for two years, was conventionally attractive, and seemed nice enough, but there was no spark there. And Sofia knew enough about herself to know better than to waste their time if there wasn't one. *Though the last time there was a spark between me and a man, it ended in disaster,* she reminded herself.

Sofia took a big swig of her cocktail and pushed that thought away. Noah had already invaded her thoughts enough that day, after she'd gone months without thinking about him and what had happened. She'd thought she was making progress, but her reaction to the stranger, Isaiah, had shaken that notion.

She walked over to Holly and grabbed her wrists, pulling her onto the dance floor. The music continued to blare, the drinks continued to flow, and before Sofia knew it, it was eleven thirty. She swiped a flute of champagne from a tray, preparing for the toast at midnight.

She cruised by the silent auction near the lobby to see where she stood. She'd bid way too much on an overnight trip to Ashland and secretly hoped someone would outbid her. The cabin fever she was experiencing because of the snow had her dreaming of escape. She glanced at the sheet. *Darn.* She was still the top bid.

A rush of cold air hit her bare arms, and she turned to look at the front doors. Her eyes met those of the person who had just walked in, and she gasped, her fingers slipping from the stem of her glass.

The delicate champagne flute shattered as it hit the floor.

Chapter Ten

ISAIAH

Isaiah approached the Emerald House warily. He wasn't sure of the best way to initiate a conversation with Sofia. Though he didn't want to spook her, he needed the information about where he'd been hiking. Something told him he generally had a good sense of navigation, but he'd still been disoriented when they drove to the hospital, so he didn't think he could find the way back on his own.

The cashier at the convenience store had seemed to associate Ash with the Emerald House, so Isaiah guessed that Ash would be at the party. Maybe he could seek him out to ask about the trailhead and bypass Sofia altogether.

Isaiah heard raucous music as he approached the building, and he pulled open one of the large wood front doors, hoping to slip in unnoticed and find Ash.

But as soon as he stepped inside, his gaze landed on the woman who'd found him on the trail, and his pulse quickened. The smatterings of freckles across her nose were hard not to find endearing, and *wow*, she looked stunning in the sparkling dress she was wearing.

The warm sensation that had leaped into his veins at the

sight of her quickly evaporated as her eyes widened in shock and her glass slipped from her hand to shatter all over the floor. At least half the room turned to look in their direction.

So much for flying under the radar.

A beautiful woman in a deep-red dress approached Sofia and started to pat dry the floor with napkins. Isaiah took a step forward, wanting to help.

"Are you okay?" he asked, looking around for something to clean up the broken glass.

Sofia's eyes were narrowed, and she pointed a shaky finger at him. "You're supposed to be in the hospital." Her voice was a tad accusatory, and he took a step back.

"I was released," he said, deciding it was best to keep it simple. The woman didn't need to know any more about his medical history than she already did. There were HIPAA laws for that.

If possible, her eyes narrowed even further. "*Released?*" She said the word as if she were trying to sound it out. "Dr. Margo released you?"

Isaiah stood up straighter, looking around uncomfortably at the handful of people who seemed to be watching them. They quickly turned away when he made eye contact with them.

He swallowed. "I'm here, aren't I?" He hadn't meant to sound snarky, but he wondered why she didn't realize they shouldn't be having the conversation in front of everyone at the party.

A movement to the right pulled his eyes from Sofia's, and he noticed that the woman in the red dress had brought a broom and was surreptitiously cleaning up all the broken glass. Sofia took a few steps to the side, leaving her to it.

"Yeah, why exactly *are* you here?" She tilted her head as she studied him, and he couldn't read whatever was going on in her expression.

Isaiah took a deep breath again and let it out in a soft

whoosh. *Oh boy. This is going to be more challenging than I antic-ipated.* He looked around, trying to spot Ash.

"Did you hear me?" Her voice had his eyes snapping straight back to hers. Clearly, she thought he still had some kind of brain injury, and he didn't blame her.

"I came to find you," Isaiah said in exasperation. Maybe there was no way to finesse the situation. He would have to barrel through it, as Sofia seemed to insist on doing.

Her eyes widened. "*Me?* Why?"

"I need to get back to the trailhead, and I don't remember where it was."

"So your memories *haven't* come back?" Sofia pressed, her eyes still boring into him.

"I didn't say that. I just was a little confused when we made the drive into town, so I don't know how to get back to the trail."

Sofia stood there staring at him, crossing her arms and tapping one high-heeled shoe on the ground, and he realized she looked cute even when she was fired up. He let out a deep breath again and ran a hand through his hair, trying not to lean away from her.

Her eyes sparked like fireworks. Then ever so slightly, she shifted. The spark calmed just a little, and her shoulders relaxed almost imperceptibly.

"Fine. I'll take you to the trailhead. *Tomorrow.* You're not messing with my New Year's Eve even more than you already have."

Even more than I already have? Did I mess up her morning earlier on the trail? A loose curl was dangling from her forehead, and Sofia blew it to the side. Isaiah tried not to grin. He wondered what had her so wound up. *Or is she always like this?* She was direct—he would give her that. "Of course. Whenever you want."

Sofia was still studying him in a somehow intensely offhand

way, but he was relieved that she didn't seem to be about to change her mind. "Where are you staying tonight?" she asked.

Isaiah shifted his weight from one foot to the other. He hadn't thought that far ahead. He hadn't planned on staying overnight and had no money or identification. Running a hand through his hair, he tried to formulate a response.

Before he could open his mouth, the beautiful woman who had been cleaning up the glass straightened and looped her arm through Sofia's. "He can stay here at the Emerald House."

Sofia looked like she was about to protest but nodded after exchanging glances with the woman. "Fine. But I'm not responsible for him." She turned on her uber-high heels and pushed through the crowd, her dress shimmering as she marched away from him.

Isaiah let out a deep breath as he watched her go.

Chapter Eleven

SOFIA

Sofia was dancing her heart out when the DJ began the countdown to midnight. "Ten... Nine... Eight..." She glanced around her. Ash and Holly were nowhere in sight. She had a suspicion they'd slipped outside for their New Year's kiss. They were always slipping away during parties.

Throughout the room, people were beginning to pair up. There were couples who had been married for thirty-plus years and those who were newly together, like Ash and Holly. She spun in a circle, narrowing her eyes.

Why are there so few single people in this room? In past years, she'd had Ash to joke around with at midnight, poking light-hearted fun at the romance around them. This year, she felt like there was a neon sign above her reading "Hey! I don't have anyone to kiss at midnight! Feel bad for me!"

She saw Park, the owner of the sporting goods store, and she quickly averted her gaze. *Right.* She wasn't the only single person, but she also wasn't interested in encouraging the advances of any of the others.

I've done this to myself, she thought with a sigh, grabbing one last glass of sparkling champagne. She slipped into the kitchen just as shouts of "Happy New Year!" and the din of party horns being blown sounded from behind her.

Letting the door close, she leaned back against the stainless-steel counter. The cold seeped through her delicate gown. Sofia swirled the champagne glass for a moment then set it down on the counter. Her head was already fuzzy enough, and the day had been one for the confusing-as-heck history books.

Did I really discover an unconscious man on the hiking trail just this morning? A man who claimed to have lost all his memories but seems to be recovered and wants me to take him back to the trailhead?

She picked up the champagne glass again and wrapped her hands around it firmly. *Why does no one else see that the whole situation is as suspicious as an unaccompanied package at the airport? Am I destined to think poorly of new men for the rest of my life? Is it a defensive mechanism that will protect me, or will it turn me into a hardened shell of a person, as Mom warned me?*

She'd been grappling with those questions for years, and she felt like all her progress had been erased in minutes that day. *So maybe I haven't made any progress at all.* That realization hit her like a punch in the gut.

Her mind flashed to the conversation she'd had with Isaiah after she'd dropped the champagne flute. She'd agreed to take him back to the trailhead. *Why did I do that? There had to be some degree of allowing myself to trust involved in that, right? Or was I just trying to get rid of Isaiah as soon as possible, since he was threatening the precarious peace I've found for myself here?* She wasn't sure which motive should concern her more.

She pictured the moment. He'd been standing there in the doorway, a smile pulling at the corner of his mouth. He'd acted as if nothing the least bit strange had happened, as if not everyone in the room was wondering who the good-looking newcomer was.

How could a man who had an accident while hiking earlier

that day seem so... relaxed? Is he one of those men who is so confident in his looks and swagger that not even something like a possible head injury could deflate him? It was slightly infuriating.

Sofia considered her options, and her shoulders relaxed as she decided on one. She would just have to ask Ash to take him back to the trailhead, and she would never have to see him again.

"No more helping sexy strangers for me," she said, pouring the remainder of the champagne down the gleaming commercial sink.

"That's too bad. Are there a lot of sexy strangers stumbling into this town?"

The voice hit her like a glass of cold water to the face, and she jumped, just barely holding back a shout of surprise.

Unfortunately, her hands weren't as in control as her voice, and she dropped the champagne flute.

It shattered all over the sink.

~

"What are you doing in here?" Sofia breathed, taking a step back and trying to calm her heart rate. At least the broken glass was contained to the sink.

Isaiah put up his hands, and something that might have been concern flashed over his face. "Sorry, I didn't mean to scare you. I didn't know anyone would be back here. Your friend... Holly... She told me I could come find a meal in the fridge."

Sofia shook her head, flustered. *Of course Holly did.* She and Ash were going to let him stay the night at the Emerald House, and naturally, they were going to feed him too. That was their way. Sofia inwardly cringed that he'd heard her refer to him as "sexy." She decided the best course of action was to ignore it and distract him with something else.

She walked to the fridge and flung open the door then whipped her hand in front of it like she was the host of a game show. "Here it is. Take your pick. We always store extra food in here for employees to eat or take home."

Uncertainty filled his expression, and he didn't step toward the fridge.

"I'm sorry about the glass," he said, glancing toward the sink. "I guess that makes two of those I've made you break this evening."

Sofia pursed her lips. "*You* didn't make me break them," she said a moment later.

She noticed it again, that pull at the corner of his mouth. Her hands moved to her hips, the fridge door swinging closed. "You didn't!" she insisted.

"Okay, so you're always this careful with glassware?" He leaned casually against the counter—too casually. The kitchen was *her* place. *Why is he acting so comfortable here?* But she couldn't just ignore his teasing.

She took a step forward, moving closer and closer until she was nearly touching him. His eyes widened. Then she reached her arm past him to the cupboard behind him, pulling out a loaf of bread. She slid around him again for a cutting board and knife.

Without saying a single word, she continued to move quickly, reaching into the fridge for ingredients and whisking back to the counter. Within two minutes, she had crafted a gourmet sandwich with all the fixings. She slid the plate across the counter to him then leaned against the sink, crossing her arms.

"I don't have to be careful," she said at last as his eyes moved from the sandwich and back to her. "I'm just good at everything. Including breaking glasses."

His eyes sparked, and she tried to suppress a smile of satisfaction. "Enjoy your sandwich," she said then breezed past him and out of the kitchen.

Chapter Twelve

ISAIAH

Isaiah let out a deep breath as Sofia walked past him. *Good lord, that woman is a whirlwind.* When she'd stepped toward him, smelling like something spicy and floral, he stopped breathing for a moment.

Then she'd leaped into the sandwich making with the precision of a neurosurgeon. He swore the room was still ringing with the sound of the ceramic plate sliding across the stainless steel and stopping exactly in front of him.

Then she'd left, with all the intensity she'd worked with. *Does that woman ever cool off?* he wondered as he searched the cupboards for a glass. He needed a drink of water after that interaction. When he located one, he filled the glass and took a long, refreshing swig, then he bit into the sandwich. He studied it appreciatively. He might not have memories of any specific meals, but something told him it was the best sandwich he'd ever eaten.

~

Isaiah woke up with a sense of restlessness. He couldn't remember his dreams, but he knew they'd been active and disconcerting. Holly, the beautiful woman who had offered him a room in the Emerald House on New Year's Eve, had fixed him up with a very comfortable one, and he'd climbed into bed not long after midnight.

He'd fallen asleep quickly but tossed and turned all night. He wondered if the dreams were some of the memories he had lost on the hiking trail, trying to work their way back to him subconsciously.

Or maybe the visions of the fiery Sofia in her sparkling dress and untamed curls contributed to the vibrant dreams, he thought, shaking his head as he sat up.

He didn't want to dwell on that memory at the moment. His goal for the day was to get back to the hiking trail, go to the spot where she'd found him, and get his memories back.

Isaiah walked to the window and pulled aside one of the curtains. The sun was already halfway up the sky, and he spotted his hosts, Ash and Holly, walking toward the Emerald House from the woods, a black dog with a white streak down its back trotting along beside them. Snow was gently falling around them. The scene made Isaiah smile despite the circumstances. It looked like something in a postcard.

He turned away from the window and thought about the town. *How did I end up here in Emerald Hollow? Was I traveling here for some reason? Do I know people here? Is someone going to come forward today, looking for me excitedly? Someone who was expecting my arrival yesterday?*

Isaiah's brow furrowed. Something about that didn't feel right. It was a small town, and Ash seemed to know everyone. Ash hadn't heard of anyone looking for a missing friend or relative. If word hadn't gotten around by midnight, hours after he should have arrived, that likely wasn't the explanation for his being there.

No, the town was tight-knit. He could tell that much. If someone knew him, word would have gotten around already.

As his brain continued to wake up, he remembered something else that had happened the night before. Not long after Sofia had left him in a whirl and he'd eaten that delicious sandwich, he'd been cornered by a woman named Esmeralda who introduced herself as the president of the chamber of commerce. She'd explained that the New Year's Eve party was a fundraiser for the local animal shelter. Esmeralda had not so subtly encouraged him to bid on the silent auction, and since he couldn't exactly tell her he had no money to speak of, he'd agreed to volunteer at the animal shelter instead.

Why did I do that? With any luck, I'm leaving today. He got dressed in the previous day's clothes—Holly and Ash had given him some pajamas and underclothes when they showed him his room—and began to ready himself to meet up with Sofia and go to the trailhead.

He hadn't been able to stop thinking about her the night before—the sparkling dress, the fire in her eyes, the way she'd acted like shattering glass meant nothing at all, and those freckles and springy curls, which added a dose of softness to her otherwise fiery demeanor—it all seemed to run through his head like a movie. He wanted to know what was going on behind all that controlled chaos Sofia emanated.

He wondered if that was what happened when you lost your memories. Maybe you developed an unhealthy interest in the first person you met. *But what are the chances that person would be someone undeniably gorgeous and intriguing?*

He scrubbed a hand through his hair and told himself to forget the intense feelings from the encounter in the kitchen the night before and tried to focus on her attitude toward him instead. She clearly thought he was suspicious, and maybe she had every right to. He had no idea what kind of person he was, and that was the reality he needed to face that day.

He stepped out of his room into the hallway, where Ash was passing by with Comet. Ash paused to greet him, the dog wagging his tail and sniffing Isaiah.

"Good morning. Everything okay with your room?" Ash asked.

Isaiah nodded. "Slept like a log." Isaiah didn't mention the dreams he couldn't quite remember.

Ash laughed. "I hear that a lot. So, Sofia told me you're needing directions to the trailhead today. Holly and I thought we could tag along. Comet here hasn't been out there in a while, and he loves hiking."

Isaiah knelt and scratched the dog behind the ears. He thought he knew why Ash was offering to join them. He was worried about his female friend being out in the woods with a stranger. Isaiah certainly didn't blame him. He would feel the same in his shoes. "Absolutely. That'd be great."

Isaiah could sense Ash studying him, and he thought the man wanted to say something else. "Are you wondering if my memories came back?" Isaiah asked, thinking that Ash was too polite to ask what was going on and why he wanted to go back to the trail.

"I wasn't going to ask directly, but yes. None of us want to leave you out in the woods if you don't know where you're going."

Isaiah took a deep breath and decided it was best not to lie to a person who had been so kind as to put a roof over his head and a meal in his stomach, asking nothing in return.

"To tell you the truth, no. My memories aren't back. But I have a feeling that going back to the trailhead may trigger something for me. I can't really explain it, but... that's my only connection to what happened and who I am."

Ash nodded, and they continued down the hall together. "That makes sense. I hope things come back to you while we're out there."

Isaiah nodded in thanks, then his stomach grumbled as they emerged in the lobby, and he smelled eggs and bacon coming from the restaurant.

"Breakfast is included with your room. Just give them your room number," Ash said, then he disappeared into conversation with someone else before Isaiah could remind him that the room had been an act of kindness.

His hunger won out over his pride within seconds, and he eagerly took a seat at the counter in the restaurant. He ordered an omelet and was looking around the busy establishment when Holly appeared next to him. He smelled a hint of cinnamon and relaxed as she stepped near him.

"Make sure to order a hot chocolate," she said with a brilliant, soft smile.

"Oh, thanks. I don't really want to order too much. Ash told me the food comes with the room, but..."

Holly's green eyes shone. There was something about her, but he couldn't put his finger on it. She looked like she had stepped off a film set, and she had a little extra shine around her that didn't make sense based on the lighting in the room.

"Don't worry about that. There's plenty of food. Ash is happy to help you out. I know how you feel, though. I received similar kindness when I was a stranger here a few months ago."

Isaiah's eyes widened. "You were... You're not from here?" It was hard to imagine. She seemed integral to everything at the Emerald House.

"Nope. But this town took me in like I was one of their own. If you need something, you just have to ask." She smiled once more then walked away.

A few seconds later, the server brought Isaiah's omelet, and Isaiah remembered Holly's suggestion. "Could I get a hot chocolate?"

The server smiled and nodded. "Coming right up."

He dug into the omelet, wondering who had made it. He

didn't think it was Sofia. If she was taking him to the trail that morning, she probably wasn't working. He realized with a start that he didn't know for certain if she worked there at all. But the way she'd moved around that kitchen... She was deeply familiar with the place. He knew that much.

The server came back with the hot chocolate, and Isaiah absentmindedly took a sip. He looked down at the mug in wonder. It was *delicious*. He couldn't explain it, like so many aspects of his life at the moment, but something about the hot chocolate seemed almost unreal.

Maybe it's too good to be true.

Maybe Emerald Hollow was too good to be true. One didn't just lose their memory and end up in a place where everyone was willing to give them the shirt off their back.

He took another sip of the hot chocolate and tried not to wonder if it was all a dream.

Chapter Thirteen

SOFIA

Sofia parked her Subaru near the entrance to the Emerald House and began to psych herself up for the day's outing. *Get in, get Isaiah, and get out.* With any luck, he would be headed home that day, and the whole surreal experience would be over with.

"Here we go," she mumbled, pulling open the door to the Emerald House and hurrying inside. She spotted Ash immediately, doing something on the computer behind the check-in counter.

He looked up at her quickly before returning his gaze to the screen. "Be ready in just a minute. He's in the restaurant."

She let her gaze slide to the restaurant, and sure enough, there was Isaiah, seated at the counter, his thin blue puffer coat hanging over the back of the chair like he intended to be there all day.

That man thinks he's the reason I dropped two champagne glasses last night, she thought with a huff and a tinge of embarrassment. Ash and Holly had both teased her about that when they were cleaning up from the New Year's Eve party.

She'd made an effort to dress in drab clothes for the hike,

wanting to be in stark contrast to the flashy dress from the night before. *He definitely won't think I have any interest in him while I'm wearing this outfit.*

Sofia was just gearing up to go speak to him when Holly came through the door behind her. "Hey, Sof. I saw your Subaru while I was outside. I'll go grab Comet."

Sofia nodded at her then refocused on Isaiah. He was drinking out of a white mug—hot chocolate, she assumed. From the way he tilted the mug back all the way, it looked like he was enjoying every last drop. *Well, at least he has good taste.* If he didn't like their hot chocolate, she might think he was an alien.

He turned in her direction then, spinning casually on his chair, and she tried to keep her expression neutral. *Damn.* She'd wanted to be the one to surprise him that morning, not the other way around. And she definitely didn't want him to think she'd been watching him. She had, but he didn't need to know that. She straightened her shoulders.

Isaiah stood, nodded to Tyler, who was working behind the counter, and scooped up his jacket, that confident, easy swagger apparent in his every move.

"Good morning, Wrecker," he said with a grin as he came up beside her.

"Wrecker?" She arched an eyebrow. She hadn't been intending to spar with him, but if he was going to start it, she would.

"I thought about 'Shatterer,' but that word just doesn't sound right."

Sofia snorted. "Well, if I'm 'Wrecker,' then you're 'Malingerer.'" The word sounded weird to her ears, and she made a face, instantly wishing she'd kept silent.

"Malingerer?" His mouth still held a hint of a smile, but confusion filled his eyes.

Sofia racked her brain for a way not to make herself look like she'd been thinking about him the previous night. The truth was she'd gone home and googled "someone faking amnesia" and had stumbled across the term "malingering amnesia."

"Lingerer. Because you've been lingering around Emerald Hollow like Ash lingers over details." Sofia hoped he would think he'd misheard her the first time around.

"Ouch," Ash said, suddenly appearing at her side. "She managed to burn both of us in one sentence."

Isaiah laughed. "Is she always this hostile to strangers?"

Sofia noticed the smile that pulled at the corner of Isaiah's mouth again, which was more persistent than ever.

"Not always," Holly said, joining the group and linking her arm through Sofia's. "Why are you two picking on Sof?" Holly's voice was sweet and soothing, breaking the faux tension.

"Oh, I'm sure she started it," Ash said, putting his hand on the small of Holly's back. "Shall we?"

The four exited the Emerald House and piled into Sofia's Subaru, Comet jumping in the back with Ash and Isaiah.

"He's such a sweet dog," Isaiah said, running his hand over Comet's white streak. "Have you had him since he was a puppy?"

"Yep. He was a rescue from the local shelter, the place we were having the fundraiser for last night, actually."

"Oh, right. About that... A woman named Esmeralda asked me to volunteer. I think I might have agreed."

Sofia had been watching them both surreptitiously in the mirror while she drove, and she snorted.

Holly glanced at her curiously then turned around to look at Isaiah. "I'm sure they'd appreciate the help, if you end up staying around Emerald Hollow for a while, that is."

Sofia glared at her, but Holly was as serene and sweet as ever.

When they reached the dirt road that led to the trailhead, Sofia turned. A few minutes later, they parked and began the hike up to where Sofia had found Isaiah. Ash and Isaiah walked together with Comet, while Sofia and Holly walked slightly behind.

Once they had all fallen into a rhythm, Holly gently touched Sofia's arm. "Is everything okay with..." She darted her eyes toward Isaiah then looked back at Sofia.

Frustrated, Sofia huffed a breath. She didn't like to keep things from Holly, but she wasn't quite sure how to explain what she was feeling. She'd never told anyone except her mom about Noah. She was unfairly putting some of those suspicions on Isaiah, but she couldn't stop herself. "Don't you think this whole amnesia thing is a little... suspicious?"

"Suspicious how?"

"I don't know. It's just that Dr. Margo said complete amnesia like this is rare. And there was no head injury. So what happened?"

"I'm sure Isaiah would like to know as much as you."

"So you believe him? That he can't remember anything?"

"I believe that he believes that."

"Oh lord! One of your psychoanalysis answers. Are you sure you're in market research?" Sofia laughed. She'd lightly grilled Holly on that topic before.

Sometimes it was hard for Sofia to picture her serene friend in a corporate global-marketing job, but other times, it seemed a perfect fit. She had a feeling there was a lot about Holly she still didn't know after so many months, but Holly had brought a friendship into her life she hadn't known she'd needed. And that was good enough for her for the moment. If Holly wanted to open up to her more in the future, Sofia would be all ears.

Holly smiled softly. "Maybe something will come back to him on the trail today. That's his hope, right? There must be some explanation."

They both fell quiet then, lost in thought and listening to the soft crunch of the snow underneath their feet and the occasional deep laugh coming from farther up the trail.

Chapter Fourteen

ISAIAH

"I think we're getting close to the spot, but Sofia would probably know better than me," Isaiah said, stopping and turning toward the two women. Sofia's tiny fur-lined boots were leaving little imprints in the snow inside his and Ash's prints, while Holly seemed to float across the surface, as if her boots were built for Northern Alaska.

"Was it near here?" Ash asked once Holly and Sofia caught up to them.

Isaiah caught the spicy floral scent from the night before coming from Sofia when she stepped next to him.

Sofia nodded and pointed farther up the trail. "See that huge pine? He was right near there." Her eyes met Isaiah's briefly, then they quickly flitted back to Ash.

"Okay. Let's go see," Ash said, then the four of them walked the few hundred yards to the tree.

Sofia, Holly, and Ash hung back while Isaiah stopped and looked around. Isaiah hadn't realized how much he was relying on the plan to work until he was standing there, facing the massive pine tree. *What will I do if this doesn't trigger any memories?*

Isaiah turned a little farther so that they couldn't see his face and closed his eyes. He inhaled deeply, reaching for anything familiar.

Then he felt something. A little tingle ran up his spine, into the base of his neck. And he heard a voice.

His eyes snapped open, and he looked around in surprise, but nothing in the scenery had changed. Holly had taken a step toward him, a concerned expression on her face. Sofia's eyebrows were pulled together, and Ash was watching Holly.

Isaiah sighed. "I thought I heard something, but... it must have just been the breeze." He shook his head. He could have sworn he had heard a voice. *It almost sounded like... singing.*

"Do you want some more time?" Ash asked. "We can walk back down the trail and give you some space."

Isaiah turned toward the tree again, furrowing his brow. He closed his eyes once more and waited.

That time, there was no tingle.

"No, I think I was just imagining things. We can go back." A terrifyingly heavy weight settled on his chest. It was all becoming too real. He had amnesia, and there didn't appear to be a quick fix. A slew of questions ran through his brain, one after the other in rapid succession. *Who am I? What was I doing on this trail on New Year's Day? Are there people looking for me? When will my memories come back?*

He tried to wrestle the dread and mold it into a sense of direction. They were living in modern times. There was internet. Surely, if he was a missing person, they could find out. There had to be a reasonable explanation.

Doesn't there?

AFTER IT BECAME CLEAR THAT ISAIAH WASN'T GOING to have an epiphany by the large pine tree, the group turned back down the trail. Isaiah fell behind them that time, staying silent. He heard soft voices in front of him as the three friends conversed quietly, but he couldn't focus. The walk passed in a blur, and he was surprised when he looked up and found himself back at the trailhead.

Before they got back into Sofia's car, Ash turned toward him. "You're welcome to stay at the Emerald House as long as you need. Did Dr. Margo give you any recommendations on things to try?"

Isaiah tried not to wince. He didn't want to tell them she had recommended he see a psychiatrist. Steeling himself, he replied, "Not much, but how hard can it be to figure out a missing identity these days? Is there a library in Emerald Hollow? Can you drop me off there? I'm sure if I do some research, I can have this figured out in a day or two, tops."

Ash nodded. "That's a good idea. And there is a library, but we also have internet at the Emerald House, if you want to use one of the work computers."

Isaiah shook his head. "No, I don't want to put you out more than I already have. The library will be great."

They all climbed into the car again, and Sofia drove them back to town, turning on a different street from the one that would take them to the Emerald House. He noticed her eyes flick to him in the rearview mirror, and he wished he could read her mind.

Isaiah was quickly gaining a sense of direction in the small town. They passed a park, then Sofia pulled into the small lot of a quaint building shaped like an old English cottage. The sign in the snow-covered ground read Emerald Hollow Community Library.

"New Year's Day is a holiday, so they're not normally open now, but I'm on the library board, so I have a key," Ash said, climbing out of the car.

He looked like he was debating something, and Holly

climbed out of the car and put her hand on the keys. "I can go in with him if you need to get back to work," she offered.

The two seemed to have a silent conversation.

Then Sofia jumped out of the car, a large canvas bag slung over her shoulder. "All right, I'll wait with him. It's my day off, and it's not like I have anything better to do." Isaiah could hear the playful sarcasm in her voice. She jaunted between Ash and Holly and swiped the library key. "But you two are going to have to walk back to the House."

Ash nodded. "Okay, call if you need anything," he said to Sofia then turned to Isaiah. "Good luck."

Holly gave Isaiah a sweet smile, then the two linked hands and started to walk up the road, Comet swishing his tail as he followed them.

"Ready to do this?" Sofia asked, not waiting for his response as she strode to the library door and unlocked it.

"Are you sure?" He suddenly felt bad about teasing her earlier. It was possible he owed his life to her—he had no idea what would have happened if she hadn't stopped to check on him when he was unconscious on the trail—and she was giving up even more time on her day off to help him.

Sofia rolled her eyes. "Did you think you were the only one with business at the library? You're lucky this was already on my agenda for the week." She pushed the door to the cottage open with her hip and nodded toward the inside.

With a grin he didn't bother to suppress, he joined her.

Chapter Fifteen
SOFIA

Sofia kept one eye on Isaiah as he sat down at a computer and followed the guest log-in instructions. Once he'd managed to get on the internet, she went into another room, navigated to the business aisle, and scanned the shelves slowly.

The library was a converted old house, which had been marked as a historical landmark by the city because of its classic English village style. From the outside, it looked like a quaint cottage, and inside, each room was lined with floor-to-ceiling bookshelves.

Different rooms had different themes, and Sofia stood in what used to be the kitchen but functioned as the nonfiction section. Isaiah and the computers were in the old sitting room.

Sofia was looking for books on developing a business plan. She wanted something motivational but not too preachy, something that would give her a clear outline but that wasn't too structured either. Her hazy dream from Christmas Eve that had inspired her to take her business to the next level hadn't left her.

While Sofia knew it would be easy to keep going along as she had been for the past few years, working at the Emerald House and doing her jewelry business in her limited free time, something urged her to do things differently. She wasn't sure whether it was the dream that had been the catalyst for her motivation, or if it had something to do with Isaiah's arrival and the shock of someone being so completely lost.

Isaiah was physically lost, as were his memories, but Sofia wondered if she'd been lost in a different way—lost in the ease of time passing in a comfortable manner and not wanting to rock the boat. The events of the past few days had made her realize that if she wasn't deliberate, her business would never be what she'd once hoped it might become.

Is that something I could live with ten years down the road? Twenty? And what would my mom think? She always encouraged me to follow my dreams.

Ten minutes later, she let out a sigh, as she hadn't found exactly what she felt she was looking for. She circled back to a few books she'd eyed earlier and snagged them then set them on the large kitchen island and reached into her bag for her notebook. "Make your own magic" was emblazoned across the front in gold foil lettering, and she smiled a little. That was exactly what she was trying to do. *And this is going to be my year to do it.*

For the next forty-five minutes, Sofia worked in near silence on a barstool at the kitchen island, occasionally murmuring a *yep* or *hmm*. Her big vision goal was to vastly increase the online sales of her jewelry and expand into new products. Small-town festivals made up the bulk of her sales, but she didn't want to be completely reliant on those.

As much as she appreciated Ash's giving her the job at the Emerald House when her mom was sick, it was her dream to be a business owner. She craved the creative independence it could give her, but she'd also seen how Ash tended to work twenty-four seven, on the verge of burning himself out all the time. At least, he had until Holly arrived.

Sofia wanted to have a sustainable business plan. She wanted something that was *just enough*.

After an hour in the library, she'd fleshed out four pages of notes. She had three clearly defined next steps to act on for the online leg of her business, and she scheduled those tasks on her calendar for her next day off.

At the sound of a frustrated sigh, Sofia looked up. She'd nearly forgotten Isaiah was in the library, too, just a room away. She quickly closed her notebook and stood.

"Having any luck?" Sofia called, poking her head around the corner to the sitting room.

Isaiah turned toward her then stood and stretched. He shook his head. "I couldn't find anything about a missing man named Isaiah recently."

Sofia's brow furrowed. "Maybe it's like in the TV shows. People can't report you missing for at least forty-eight hours."

Isaiah was looking past her, his gaze unfocused, and something unclenched in her chest. She worried she'd come off a little harsh by being so suspicious of him at first. Clearly, the situation was harder on him than anyone else.

"Yeah, that could be it," he murmured, his voice quieter than she was used to.

"So, it's really only been twenty-four hours. Or even less. If someone thought you were out hiking, they might not have expected you back for hours. We can try again tomorrow and the next day."

Watching the little spark of hope in his eyes, Sofia was glad she'd tried to reassure him. If this was all a ruse, he was playing his part like an Oscar-worthy actor.

"Maybe we should go back to the House and have some lunch. I could use a break," she suggested, gathering the books she'd been looking through.

"Okay," he said simply, turning back to the computer.

Sofia returned to the kitchen to reshelve the books and pack up her notebook. By the time she was done, Isaiah had logged off the computer and was waiting by the front door.

"After you," he said, holding it open for her. The slight smile was on his face again, that cocky charisma back in place.

How would I conduct myself if I didn't have any memories? Sofia wondered, locking the library behind them. *Would I trust people who were offering help? Or would I push them away? Then again, what choice would I have?*

"So, what were you researching while I was trying to find myself?" Isaiah asked once they were in the Subaru, a teasing note in his voice.

Sofia glanced at him before returning her eyes to the snowy road. She wasn't sure if she should tell him. She barely knew the man and, even though her suspicions had softened during her hyperfocused research session, she still didn't know if she should trust him. Then again, maybe that made it a low-risk share. Within a few days, she would never see him again. In that case, it wouldn't matter if he thought her plans were silly.

"I was working on a business plan."

"What kind of business?"

Sofia thought she detected a note of surprise in his voice and wondered what that meant. She twisted her earring inadvertently and forced herself to stay focused on his question.

"I make jewelry," she began then quickly added, "but I'm hoping to expand into other handmade gifts as well. I've been tinkering with suncatchers, beaded plant holders... things like that."

"That's amazing. I'm not very artistic."

Sofia turned to him in surprise. "You remember that?"

Isaiah's eyes widened. "Not exactly. It's like, when something comes up, I instinctively know whether I'm good at it or whether it's something I like or dislike, but I don't have any specific memories attached. It's weird. I can't really explain it."

"So, for example, you know that you're not artistic, that

you're a shameless flirt, that you like to hike—" The words were out of Sofia's mouth before she'd fully formed her thoughts.

"Whoa!" Isaiah cut in, latching onto the barb she'd tried to sandwich between two other facts. "Who says I'm a shameless flirt?"

"Oh, come on. That little half grin you're always doing? The teasing? The way all the women at the New Year's Eve party were looking at you? I've known men like you. It's in your DNA or something." It was like the words were spilling out of her. She'd never been good at controlling what she said, and Isaiah's proximity seemed to amplify her natural instinct to spout her thoughts like a fountain.

Isaiah's jaw dropped, but Sofia was relieved to see amusement on his face. "You've known men like me? Other amnesiacs?" He grinned at her. "And what other women at the New Year's Eve party? I was blinded by this one in a sparkly dress."

Sofia rolled her eyes, but a little thrill rolled through her stomach. She shook her head and chalked it up to the excitement of sparring. Once they pulled into the parking lot of the Emerald House, she put the car in park and turned to him. She opened her mouth to say something, preparing to punish him further, but he cut her off.

"So, does your business have a name?"

Sofia sat back in surprise but responded automatically. "Sofia's Creations."

"Hmm."

"Hmm what?" Sofia narrowed her eyes.

"Isn't that a little... nondescript? With a business, you want a memorable name, right? Something that makes you stand out?"

Sofia had actually been considering a new name, but nothing she'd thought about had stuck. "Fine. What do you suggest?"

"Tell me more about the themes of your work."

"The themes of my work? I think you might be a writing professor in your real life."

Isaiah laughed but waited for her to continue.

"I draw on things that inspire me here in Emerald Hollow."

"There you go. Maybe Emerald Hollow should be part of your brand."

"What? Like the Emerald House? That's Ash's thing." Sofia shook her head.

"Does Ash own the town?" Isaiah's voice wasn't harsh. Sofia thought it was surprisingly gentle.

Sofia contemplated his remark for a moment. She hated to admit it, but he was right. And with the way Emerald Hollow had been starting to get national fame as a festival destination, Sofia agreed that maybe it could be a good marketing tactic.

"I'll think about it," she said, not wanting the idea to go to his head. For a man who didn't know who he was, he sure was confident.

Their eyes met for a moment, and Sofia realized they'd been sitting in her car for a few minutes as they talked. She quickly opened her door, breaking their eye contact. "I don't know about you, but all that research made me hungry."

"Same," Isaiah said, closing the passenger door carefully. "I'd offer to buy you lunch for babysitting me at the library, but..." He indicated his empty pockets.

Sofia laughed. "Well, it's a good thing I work here, and Ash said your meals are on the house until we figure out who you are. So it looks like neither of us has to buy."

"About that," Isaiah began, following Sofia up the steps of the Emerald House. "I feel bad. They're being really generous. I don't know what my financial situation is, but I'll pay them back."

Sofia waved a hand. "Ash loves to help people like this. Holly too. They have big hearts. I find it's best not to rain on their parade and just say 'Thank you.'"

Isaiah nodded. "Okay. Welcome generosity. Thanks for the

tip." He opened the door for her and held his hand out as if he were a butler ushering her into his castle.

Sofia shook her head, but something in her chest relaxed ever so slightly.

Chapter Sixteen

ISAIAH

Over lunch, Isaiah couldn't help dwelling on Sofia's comment about being a shameless flirt. *Is that true? Or do I just enjoy flirting with* her?

They ate lunch at the counter in the Emerald House restaurant, Sofia stealing a fry off his plate, since she'd ordered a side salad instead. The tiny intimacy delighted him.

"So, let's talk about Esmeralda. That woman is like a shark. If you told her you'd volunteer at the animal shelter, she's going to collect."

Isaiah rolled his shoulders back and spun on his bar chair, angling himself toward her. Their knees brushed slightly, and Sofia twisted away.

"I guess I don't have anything else to do around here. Aside from researching at the library. I might as well find something productive to fill my time."

"Well, don't you sound saintly," Sofia said, stealing another fry.

He grinned. "What? Do you have something against animals?"

Sofia looked aghast. "Absolutely not. I had a dog until a

couple of years ago, but... Well, I haven't wanted to make that commitment again yet. Comet is like a community dog here at the Emerald House, though. So I can get my canine fix with him."

Isaiah's heart lurched as he realized her dog must have died. That was one of the hardest things about having animals. Their lifespans were just so short compared to humans'. Isaiah wondered if he had a dog or other pet at home, wherever home was. The thought made his heart sink. Sofia looked like she could sense what he was thinking.

"Maybe working at the animal shelter is a good idea after all. Perhaps it will spark your memories. Anything that has a chance of doing that is a good thing, right?"

"True," Isaiah admitted then ate the last bite of his club sandwich. He was trying not to be disappointed at the lack of results from the library, telling himself that Sofia was probably right. He hadn't even been in Emerald Hollow for forty-eight hours. Something would pop up online in the next day or two, at most.

"Well," Sofia began, standing up and stacking her dishes. "My shift's about to start. Oh, and look who just arrived."

Isaiah followed her gaze toward the lobby, where he recognized Esmeralda, president of the chamber of commerce.

"Good luck, Saint."

Isaiah grinned but didn't comment on the nickname. He much preferred Saint to Lingerer.

"Don't need it, Wrecker."

Sofia raised her eyebrows then swiped his empty plate, stacked it on top of her own, and disappeared into the kitchen. Isaiah watched her go, the floral spicy scent not quite disappearing with her.

Chapter Seventeen

SOFIA

Sofia sat on her couch that night, her legs crisscrossed and her notebook on her lap. She'd glanced at some of the previous name-change ideas she'd had and struck each through with a firm swipe of her purple pen.

Next, she scrawled *Emerald Hollow* across the top and began to ideate. After just a few minutes, a smile crossed her lips. She'd come up with a name and knew in her heart that it was right. She practiced a few taglines then got to work on her computer, designing a new logo.

When that was taken care of, she bought a new website domain and began to move over her inventory. It took hours, but the work allowed her to zone out as reruns of her favorite TV show played in the background.

When all that was done, she began sketching earring ideas for a new line. Isaiah was on her mind, and she thought of their conversations over lunch. She tried not to dwell on the moment their knees had briefly touched. A little thrill had passed through her at the contact, and she'd turned away instantly.

What would it be like to have no memories of your life? To be completely dependent on others and at the same time trying to figure out the reality of your life? Her hands began to work almost on their own.

She made the first pair of earrings for the new line, which she decided to tentatively call the WanderLost Collection. She took a picture of the earrings and posted it on her social media as a teaser.

Well after midnight, Sofia shut down her laptop and silenced her phone. Her sparkly New Year's Eve dress was still draped over the back of the chair, waiting for her to drop it at the dry cleaner's. When she lay in bed that night, there was a smile on her lips.

SOFIA WOKE UP THE NEXT MORNING WELL AFTER TEN, glad, as usual, that she didn't work the morning shift at the House. She wrapped a blanket around herself and cranked up her electric heater immediately. As the house started to warm up, she poured some coffee and sprinkled a few chunks of granola on yogurt then unplugged her phone.

Her eyes widened at the number of notifications on her screen. She quickly unlocked the phone. There was a slew of comments on her social media post with the sneak peek of her new WanderLost Collection.

LOVE the name.

Those earrings are incredible. When can I buy them?

I need these for my next trip! How much?

The comments and likes had stacked up all night, it seemed. The post had gotten more traction than any others had before. She sat down on the skinny barstool at her counter, taking a scoop of her yogurt. *Why did this post take off? Did the idea of WanderLost resonate with people?*

Her mind drifted to Isaiah, the inspiration for the name, as she scrolled through the comments. *What is he doing this morning at the Emerald House, with no memories and no plans for the future other than trying to get those memories back? She remembered Esmeralda showing up at the restaurant just as her shift was starting.* Maybe she'd already set him up with volunteering at the animal shelter.

Sofia tried to rid her mind of Isaiah by replying to a few comments as she finished her coffee and breakfast. She looked around the living room at her jewelry-making supplies. She still had a few hours before work. Perhaps the WanderLost Collection could use a few new designs.

Chapter Eighteen

ISAIAH

Isaiah sought out Ash immediately after he woke up the next morning. The owner of the Emerald House was in his office, the door open halfway, and Isaiah knocked softly.

Ash glanced up and smiled. "Isaiah. Come in." He motioned for Isaiah to take a seat at the chair facing his desk.

Isaiah sat, scooting the chair back slightly to accommodate his long legs. "Hi, Ash. You know I struck out yesterday at the trail, and I'm not sure if Sofia told you, but I haven't had any luck at the library yet either. I'm sure I'll figure something out within the next week, but until then, I'd like you to put me to work. I can work in the restaurant, or if you have projects going around the building, I think I'm pretty handy." He paused, meeting Ash's eyes. "What I'm saying is I want to earn my keep."

Ash studied him for a moment then nodded. "That's nice of you to offer. Would you prefer to work outside or inside? I always need extra hands in the restaurant, but the forest has some brush that needs cleaning up after some big storms not too long ago. Does either of those sound like something you'd like to do?"

Isaiah's mind flashed to Sofia. His brain replayed watching

her prepare that sandwich like it was a dance. *If I worked in the restaurant, would we be on the same shift? He quickly shoved the idea away.* He got the impression she was being forced to spend more time with him than she wanted already.

And Isaiah did have a sense that he would like working outside. After all, he'd been out for a hike in the woods when he lost his memories. He made his decision. "The forest work. Just point me in the right direction, and I'll get started."

Ash stood and extended a hand. "Welcome to the Emerald House officially."

Isaiah took the hand, and they shook firmly. For the first time since he'd left the trailhead the previous day, with nothing but a strange tingle and a phantom of a voice to show for it, Isaiah thought that maybe things would work out all right.

He'd made a plan with Esmeralda to walk dogs at the animal shelter each morning, and he would be able to do some manual work on the Emerald House grounds until Sofia's break, when they went to the library. His time in Emerald Hollow didn't have to be completely useless. He could contribute.

At least until I figure out who I am and what happened to me.

Chapter Nineteen

SOFIA

Sofia clocked in for her shift then slipped her apron around her neck. She'd been receiving notifications and fulfillment requests for the first few designs on her WanderLost Collection all morning. Her brain was full of potential new designs—earrings, necklaces, rings—as she poured the first cup of early-afternoon coffee for a customer.

The first few hours of her shift went by quickly, and by the time her "lunch" break rolled around at four, she'd forgotten all about her offer to take Isaiah to the library again.

She jumped when she saw him sliding into a seat at the counter, tugging off a pair of leather work gloves. She narrowed her eyes. *Now what is he up to?*

"Hey, Wrecker," he said when he spotted her.

She blew a curl out of her face and glowered.

His grin broadened.

"What are those?" She inclined her head toward the gloves.

"I'm doing some work in the forest for Ash. Earning my keep."

"I see." She swished by him and filled the water glasses of a couple sitting at the counter near Isaiah.

"Ash told me your lunch break was now. I don't know if the offer still stands but..." He shrugged nonchalantly, even though the library visits were possibly his only means of getting home.

"I'm not rescinding my offer, if that's what you're asking."

Isaiah raised an eyebrow at her, that smile still pulling at the side of his mouth.

She turned away, slipping the apron over her head. "Jenn, I'm heading out for lunch," she called through the kitchen doors.

Sofia grabbed her coat and bag off the hook, feeling Isaiah's eyes on her back. "Well, are we going or not?"

She didn't look back as she walked out to her car.

THE LUNCH HOUR PASSED WAY TOO QUICKLY FOR Sofia's liking. She had been working on updating her online store on her laptop, and she was just getting into the flow of things when it was time to close her computer and head back to the restaurant.

She glanced over at Isaiah—they were both working in the sitting room—and saw that he was logging off the computer. The modern devices were in stark contrast to the cozy vintage design of the room, where a bright-green pothos plant trailed up the wall and around the bright window.

"Any luck?" she asked.

He shook his head. "I guess we'll be back tomorrow."

They stood and walked toward the door, Sofia waving goodbye to the librarian shelving books in the hallway.

"You know, now that I'm visiting the library during normal visitor hours, I could just walk here from the Emerald House. You don't have to supervise." His tone was playful, but Sofia thought she sensed something else underneath it. *What is he asking?*

She was surprised that his words summoned a little twist in her stomach. Coming to the library at lunch was a great use of her time. Normally, she just sat around in the café or outside in the gazebo, scrolling on her phone until she was back on shift. While the lunch break had felt too short, she had to admit she'd been productive.

"What? And let you loose on Emerald Hollow all by yourself? I don't think so." She pushed the door open with her hip, and the cool air assaulted her face. "When is this cold spell going to end?" she mumbled.

"Not a fan of the cold?"

Sofia sighed. "It's complicated. I love the snow at Christmas and all the coziness. But now, after new year, I'm just biding my time until spring."

"Is spring your favorite season?"

Sofia was surprised by the question, but she didn't have to think about it. "By far. The flowers here are incredible. Everything just feels so full of..." Sofia paused, searching for the right word. "Optimism."

"So are you an optimist, then?"

Sofia glanced at him. The rapid-fire questions were throwing her off. She whipped the car onto the road that led back to the Emerald House. "Not really. I would say Ash and Holly both are. I'm more of a realist. But in spring, things are more magical..." She caught herself, wondering why she was being so open.

"And what's your favorite flower here?" Isaiah asked, and she wondered if he sensed she felt like she was saying too much.

"Tulips." The answer came without hesitation. "The colors are insane. It's like a painting when you see a bunch of them together."

"When do they start blooming?"

"March or April. So still a little while."

"Well, I hope this tulip season is off the charts. And let's hope I've figured out who I am by then."

Sofia parked at the Emerald House and killed the engine. "By then? I'm sure we will. By next week, probably." She thought about mentioning her new WanderLost collection but wasn't sure how Isaiah would take it. *Would he assume that he was the inspiration?* He had been, but it was way too personal to admit that aloud. Despite their few afternoons together and the sparring that came so easily between them, he was still essentially a stranger.

"And you said you weren't an optimist." He grinned. "I hope you're right."

Sofia made a sarcastic *ha ha* face, but internally, she was trying to suppress a genuine smile. *He doesn't miss a beat.*

"Well, good luck with your forest cleanup," she said glibly, throwing a glance over her shoulder at him as she yanked open the front door to the Emerald House.

"Good luck with those sandwiches," he said, holding her gaze a moment too long, the corner of his mouth twitching.

She had a flash to New Year's Eve, when she'd sidled up way too close to him and reached past him to prepare the sandwich. They'd been within an inch of each other. The moment was frozen in her mind.

So he felt it too.

"I don't need luck," Sofia said, letting the door close behind her.

Chapter Twenty

SOFIA

Four weeks went by, and there was still no word on a missing person named Isaiah. Sofia had taken him to the library on her lunch break each day during her work week, but it never amounted to anything. She'd even done a little searching herself at home at night, wondering if his research skills just weren't up to par, but she'd come up empty-handed too.

They'd called a few local police stations to ask about missing persons, but there were no reports. Sofia pondered the problem as she turned on the lights in her kitchen. *What are we supposed to do? Call every police station in Oregon? In the country?* They had no idea where Isaiah had come from.

The mystery of it all vexed and perplexed Sofia. Part of her was still slightly suspicious of the circumstances. If Isaiah truly was a missing person, someone should have reported him. *What does that say about him?*

But lately, as they spent more and more time together on her lunch breaks and occasionally bumped into each other in the Emerald House in the evening—Isaiah had a pesky tendency to sit in her section when she was working—she had to admit that she felt much more concern than suspicion. *What would it be like, not knowing who you were for a whole month? And even worse, does Isaiah wonder if he has no one to look for him?*

It had crossed Sofia's mind early on that Isaiah could be married—though he hadn't been wearing a ring when he was found—or in a serious relationship. But the way he seemed so sure of his likes and dislikes, skills, and weaknesses, she thought he would probably sense if he had a great love on the other side of... *Whatever all this is.* But she couldn't know that for certain.

Sofia tried to shake all the thoughts from her mind. It was a new month, and she'd set some big goals for her WanderLost jewelry collection, which was growing steadily. She flipped her motivational-quotes wall calendar to February then started her coffee pot.

When she pulled open the front curtains, she gasped. All the snow had melted overnight.

Sofia shook her head in disbelief. She turned around and walked to get a cup of coffee to clear her mind then returned to the window, staring at the bare ground. The previous night, there had still easily been a foot of snow.

Questions flew through her mind as she scanned the dry ground. *Why did it all suddenly melt? Am I free from the snow at last? Are we in for an early spring?*

She picked up her phone and called Ash.

"Hey, Sof. What's up?"

"All the snow is melted at my place!"

"Here too. It just vanished overnight."

Sofia took another sip of her coffee. "Do you think this means I can put away my snow boots for the season?" She knew what his answer would be but couldn't resist asking.

"I wouldn't. Remember that year we got hit with a storm in May?"

Sofia groaned. "Don't remind me. Is Holly around?"

"Sure. One second."

Sofia heard Ash say something away from the receiver, then the sweet, musical voice of Holly came over the line. "Hey, Sofia. I bet you're loving the weather this morning."

"It's heavenly." Sofia cracked open the door, letting the late-morning sunshine fall on her face. She took a deep breath and could have sworn she smelled spring in the air. "Want to go to the concert at the Emerald House tonight? All The Kates is playing."

"I'd love to."

Once they finished the conversation, the two hung up, and Sofia hummed as she headed to her laptop. It had been too long since she and Holly had had a girls' night. She needed to fill her in on the latest on her business and catch up with Holly since her most recent trip to Canada.

And she would have to put a bug in Ash's ear about Valentine's Day. She didn't think he would forget, but it was the first year he'd been in a serious relationship since Sofia had moved to Emerald Hollow, and she felt it was her duty as his best friend not to let him slip up.

Valentine's Day. It was one of those necessary evils in her world. She knew she was a romantic at heart—her perfect night involved a bubble bath, fresh flowers, and a rom-com—but she didn't believe that there was love out there for her anymore. It was something some people got lucky with, like Holly and Ash. But for others, like her, one big crash and burn was enough to ruin their illusions for a lifetime.

"Well, at least the snow's melted, and if I want to take a day trip out of town, I can," she said as she went to get dressed. It was her day off, and the sun was shining. Sofia was going to enjoy it.

Chapter Twenty-One

ISAIAH

Isaiah was surprised to wake up to bright sunshine streaming through the space between the curtains in his room at the Emerald House. The mounds of snow that had blanketed Emerald Hollow since he'd arrived were gone.

He decided to head to the animal shelter first thing. He'd been volunteering there most mornings, and the dogs would enjoy the weather as much as the human residents.

He bumped into Ash in the lobby on his way out.

"Good morning," Ash said, giving him a quick wave.

"Hey, Ash. Headed to the shelter. How long do you think the sun will hold out?"

Ash looked up and peered at the window. "Hard to say, but honestly, I don't think it's going anywhere."

Isaiah knew what Ash meant as soon as he stepped outside. The temperature was perfectly springlike, not warm but definitely not cold like it had been. The town was like a different place. He could see little details that had been buried or overshadowed by the snow, such as the planter boxes that lined the Emerald House and most of the buildings around town.

His mind went to Sofia, as it did most mornings, and he

wondered if she'd seen it yet. They hadn't exactly discussed it, but he'd gotten the sense that she wasn't an early riser.

Isaiah picked up three dogs—which he'd learned was the most he could comfortably walk at a time—and took them to the park near the library.

As much as he was enjoying the weather, something about the change in temperature had made him acutely aware of the passing of time. He had been in Emerald Hollow for a month, and he'd made no progress on getting back home. *Where is home?* he thought for the millionth time.

He was at ease in Emerald Hollow and wondered if he was from a small town. Though he also realized it could just be that it wasn't hard to feel at ease there. Someone from a city would probably settle right into Emerald Hollow as well.

He tried to review what he knew, running through the information like it was an old police file he was scanning as a cold case detective.

He'd been found on a hiking trail outside of town. Though he didn't know what his stamina was, he was pretty sure that meant he hadn't started his hike more than ten to fifteen miles away, at most. He and Sofia had called all the nearby towns, asking if any abandoned cars had been reported at trailheads, but they'd come up empty-handed.

The local deputies who'd gone searching for identification had hiked the trail both ways for a while and hadn't come across any sort of backpack or other gear, so it was unlikely he'd been camping.

Questions plagued him. *How did I get onto the trail that day? Did someone drop me off? If so, wouldn't they have had plans to pick me back up, and wouldn't they have reported me missing when I didn't show at the scheduled time?*

None of it made any sense, and he wasn't sure what to do next. He'd been trying to make himself useful in Emerald

Hollow, doing physical work around the Emerald House and helping at the animal shelter.

But he couldn't live like that forever. *I can't go the rest of my life not knowing who I am, can I?*

He tugged the leashes gently to direct the dogs onto another trail, trying not to let his mind go the only other place it went besides trying to figure out who he was. *Sofia.*

He didn't know why she was still being kind enough to go with him to the library on all her lunch breaks, even though she claimed it had nothing to do with him. He loved sitting in her section for dinner. She worked as if there were always energy bubbling under the surface, and her face was more expressive than she probably realized. It made for decent entertainment, and she hadn't kicked him out yet.

Twice, he'd witnessed a local man, Park, trying unsuccessfully to flirt with Sofia. It was obvious to Isaiah what was going on, and even though Sofia was giving the man what seemed like clear signals that she was not interested, Park didn't seem to be giving up. Isaiah's jaw tensed a little at that, but then he relaxed. Sofia could handle herself. She was a kind, funny server, but she put rude patrons in their place if necessary.

And she liked to tease him relentlessly.

And he liked to tease her right back.

He hadn't found any excuses to hang out with her outside of those times, and he forced himself to be okay with that. Someday —soon, he hoped—his situation would be resolved, and he would be going home. And Sofia would still be in Emerald Hollow, breaking hearts and taking names.

The relaxed smile that had slipped onto his face as he thought of her slowly fell. He whistled to the dogs that it was time to turn around, and the trio followed his lead. All that time, he'd been looking forward to the moment he discovered who he was and where he was from. *But what will happen when it's time to go?*

Chapter Twenty-Two

SOFIA

Sofia and Holly met for live music in the café at the Emerald House. The past few weeks had passed in a blur between working at the restaurant, developing her business in every spare hour, taking Isaiah to the library at lunch, and all the other little tasks of life. She couldn't wait to debrief everything with Holly.

The weather had also completely elevated her mood. The fog of sadness that always descended on her mom's birthday and clung throughout the early days of January had been cleared by the bright sun and first sight of something green on the ground.

Holly walked into the café wearing a beautiful snow-white sweater and jeans, and they took their usual spots at the counter, where they could face the window to the front of the building or the band, depending on which way they swiveled their chairs.

Sofia stood up and hugged her. "Hey, gorgeous! I'm so happy to see you. It feels like it's been forever."

Holly gave Sofia that sweet, poised smile that was so unique to her, and Sofia took that as her sign to rush right in.

"We have so much to catch up on. I told you about my new

jewelry collection, WanderLost, right? It's been doing well these past few weeks."

"That's wonderful, Sof. You've really been working hard on your business lately. Did anything inspire it, or has this always been your plan?"

Sofia thought for a moment. "Actually, something did inspire it. I had a dream on Christmas Eve. I don't remember all the details, but I woke up with a really strong desire to scale my business this year. It was kind of strange. I've never sensed a goal quite that clearly before."

Holly choked a little on her drink, and Sofia patted her back.

"Sorry," Holly said when she stopped coughing. "That's interesting. It must have been some dream."

"Right? I was tempted to believe the dream had been sent straight to me from my mom, if I believed in that sort of thing."

"Maybe it was," Holly said casually.

Sofia nodded without arguing the point. She was ready to get to the next topic of conversation.

"Can you believe we haven't discovered what's up with Isaiah yet?"

Holly's smooth forehead furrowed slightly. "It does seem strange. It's been a month, so it's unlikely he's being seen as a missing person where he comes from. I wonder if we've been going about this the wrong way."

"What do you mean?" Sofia took a sip of the wine she'd ordered before Holly arrived. She'd gotten a Shirley Temple for her friend.

"We'd need to run it by Isaiah first, of course, but maybe we need to share his picture somehow. Is there a way to do that?"

Sofia nearly laughed. She tended to forget how un-tech savvy her friend was, which was surprising for someone who worked in corporate marketing. Sofia had never even seen her use a cell phone.

"I'm sure the police could do that or a local media outlet

but…" Sofia leaned in closer to Holly. "I've seen TV shows like this. There are weirdos out there. Someone might claim to know him. You know, say they're his girlfriend or something, and how would he know if it was true?"

Holly's eyes widened. "I hadn't thought of that. Do you think people would do that?"

Sofia raised an eyebrow. "Are you kidding? Isaiah's a good-looking guy. Spreading it out there to a bunch of strangers that he's lost his memory is just asking for trouble."

Holly sat up straighter. "We wouldn't have to include the information that he's lost his memory. There could be another reason we're searching for people who know him."

Sofia shook her head. "The only reasons that would be plausible for the news would be that he's a criminal on the loose or that he was injured in an accident and police need help identifying him. Like he's in a coma or something. Either way, we invite bad actors." Sofia bit her lip.

Holly sighed. "You're right. It could be risky. It seems like he's doing fine here for now. I'm sure you two will have to come across a lead at some point. Have you still been going with him to the library every day?"

Sofia nodded. "Yep. Just keeping an eye on him. He's a stranger in our town, after all. Bad actors, you know."

Holly pursed her lips in a knowing smile. "Don't think I didn't catch that you called him 'good-looking' a minute ago."

Sofia choked on her wine then smiled. "What? It's objectively true. The definition of tall, dark, and handsome. But in my experience, that combination spells trouble."

"So he's permanently under suspicion, then?"

"Just between you and me, I've been getting pretty comfortable around him. But while I feel like I'm starting to trust him on a personal level, the circumstances are still suspicious." She turned her attention briefly to the band.

"Maybe we need to get to know some more details about him," Holly suggested.

"How? The man doesn't remember anything about himself." Though as soon as she'd said it, Sofia realized that wasn't entirely true. While Isaiah couldn't spout his autobiography, if anyone asked him if he liked something or had experience with it, he could usually say yes or no. It was like there were certain instincts in him so ingrained that they hadn't been wiped away with his memory.

Sofia wasn't convinced of the accuracy of those feelings, but she was willing to go with it for the moment. They had only been tested on small, unimportant things, so the stakes were low if his instincts were off.

"We don't need to know all about who he was to know who he is now. I can sense... goodness about him. Maybe we get a chance to know who is here, right now, in Emerald Hollow."

Sofia thought about it. Part of her—a part she didn't want to acknowledge—wanted to take Holly up on that. She wanted to spend more time with him outside of the hours they spent working separately in the library or throwing barbs at each other during her dinner shift, though it was against her better judgment.

At that moment, the band quieted between songs, and Sofia glanced toward the lobby to see Isaiah there, fist bumping with Ash as he came out of the hallway. Isaiah turned and caught her eye, and a smile pulled at the corner of his mouth. For a moment, it was like they were the only two people in the room.

Then the music started again, and Isaiah turned away from her toward the restaurant.

Sofia leaned closer to Holly, her mind made up as she watched him disappear. "What do you suggest?"

Chapter Twenty-Three

HOLLY

The next morning, after an evening spent laughing and listening to music in Sofia's company, Holly took one of her two daily walks out to the little clearing in the forest, where her reindeer liked to meet her. She gave them each a treat snuck from the Emerald House and watched as Sprig and Comet chased each other in circles.

The conversation with Sofia had concerned her more than she'd let on. *How do we still have no leads on who Isaiah is after a whole month?*

Holly thought back to the moment when they'd all returned to the trail where Isaiah had been found. She thought she'd seen something in his expression that day, but she couldn't put her finger on what exactly it was.

She whistled to Comet, who stopped playing and ran over to her side. "See you all later," she called to the reindeer.

Holly walked back to the Emerald House to find Ash waiting for them just outside the back door.

"Are those hummingbirds?" Ash asked, looking at something over her shoulder.

She turned around, and sure enough, a pair of iridescent-blue-and-green hummingbirds was whizzing around near the gazebo.

"Gorgeous. That's the first time I've seen those here. Are they common in this area?"

"They used to be, but I feel like I haven't seen any in a few years. It could just be that I was too busy to notice, though."

"And now you have me, so you have time to stop and smell the sugarberries?" Holly asked, and Ash smiled. She wondered if he would ever get used to her North Pole expressions.

"Exactly." He planted a kiss on her forehead. "I wish Sof were out here to see this with us. I think hummingbirds were a symbol of good luck in her family. I feel like she could use a little boost right now. Isaiah has her wound tighter than I've ever seen her."

Holly looked over her shoulder again just in time to see the hummingbirds dash off into the distance. Ash's mention of Isaiah had reminded her of what she'd sought him out for.

"Can I borrow the truck?"

He'd been teaching her how to drive over the past few weeks, and she'd picked it up quickly. She'd officially been granted her driver's license the previous week.

Her magic must have wanted her to have one, because humans needed official government identification to obtain a driver's license, and she didn't have any. The woman at the DMV had simply smiled, let her take the driving tests, which Holly had passed with flying colors, then taken her picture. Holly didn't even remember filling out any paperwork.

Ash pulled the keys from his pocket and tossed them to her. "Where are you headed?"

"I just want to stretch my legs."

He paused and studied her more closely. "Going hiking? By yourself?"

"Just a short outing. Don't worry. It's a well-worn trail."

Ash didn't look one hundred percent convinced, but he just

pulled her in again, lifting her chin with his hand. "Dinner date in the gazebo tonight?"

Holly smiled. It was one of her favorite things. "Can we invite Sofia?" She paused for a moment, thinking about her suggestion to Sofia the night before. "And Isaiah?"

Ash didn't even hesitate. "Of course. I'll ask them today. Six o'clock?"

"I'll be there."

They embraced once more, Holly taking in the scent of evergreen that was Ash's aftershave. She would never get tired of it.

$\sim$

THIRTY MINUTES LATER, HOLLY WAS AT THE trailhead. The forest looked different with all the snow melted. The first signs of spring were already appearing, though she'd been warned by Ash that it was probably a false spring. Still, her eyes caught on the sage and lime colors that sprang up in such stark contrast to the bright white they'd had for the last month.

Before long, she approached the tall tree Sofia had indicated a month before. Holly walked to it and stood where Isaiah had, closing her eyes.

She nearly let out a yelp as a tingle shot up her spine and down her arms. The sensation seemed to wrap around her wrist, encircling the watch where she stored Cheer for the North Pole.

Holly looked around quickly, but the trail and forest were quiet. "What in the stars...?"

She suddenly had a thought and took a deep breath, trying not to panic. Slowly, she inhaled the fresh mountain air as she considered her options. She could either wait for her upcoming trip to the North Pole to chase down the idea that had taken root, or she could use her watch to call Clementine. Once they'd discovered the form of magical communication the previous year, Holly and Clementine had agreed to use the system to touch base if urgently needed.

Holly held the watch up to her ear and listened to the soft chiming pattern, which changed constantly. Once she caught the rhythm, she tapped along. *Tick, tick, tick. Tick, tick. Tick.*

The watch started to glow, and a few minutes later, Holly glimpsed the serious face and ice-blond braids of Clementine.

"Ms. Claus. Is everything all right?"

Holly remembered the last time she had called, when they had been on the brink of a full-blown Christmas emergency. She rushed to assure Clementine. "Everything's fine, I think. But I've experienced something... strange. I was hoping to talk to Lumi Kringle."

Clementine nodded, her golden eyes glinting on the surface of the watch like liquid amber. "I'll send Auryn for her. Be right back."

Holly stood to the side of the path as she waited.

Five minutes passed then ten.

Finally, Clementine reappeared on the watch face, breathless. "I'm so sorry, Ms. Claus. I'm afraid Lumi is nowhere to be found. And I couldn't find Auryn either." Clementine's normally smooth face was scrunched in concern.

Holly thought she had a pretty good idea where Lumi Kringle—the oldest elf—might be. Most likely, she was in Finland, living her alter-ego life as a human operating a café.

But Auryn's being missing seemed strange. He had never left the North Pole in his life.

"He's probably at the ski park," Clementine said.

Holly's shoulders relaxed. It was the offseason for the elves, after all.

"Okay. Thanks, Clementine. I'll get in touch with Lumi. Everything okay there?"

"All's gooey. Are you and Ash coming for the reindeer games next cycle?"

"Wouldn't miss it," Holly said, smiling at the thought. Ash hadn't been back to the North Pole since his first time there on Christmas Eve. She couldn't wait to see his reaction to the reindeer games.

Holly broke the connection on her watch and took one last look around the trail. Something was definitely off. She just hoped it wasn't what she thought it might be.

She started back down the trail, her pace a little quicker that time. Yes, she would get in touch with Lumi. She decided that the conversation warranted more than a phone call. Neither she nor Lumi was very skilled with phones anyway. At some point in the near future, she was going to have to go to Finland.

Chapter Twenty-Four

ISAIAH

Isaiah entered the lobby a few minutes before six, preparing to eat in the Emerald House restaurant. Ash had extended an invite for dinner, and he had accepted without hesitation.

Holly appeared beside him and looped her arm through his before he could enter the restaurant. "Not in there," she said with a grin.

Isaiah raised an eyebrow and walked with her through the front door.

"We have a little tradition here of ordering to go then eating in the gazebo in the back gardens. Seemed like the perfect night for it now that it's warmed up so much."

"Yeah. What's with that? Is that normal for here?"

"Actually—"

But Holly stopped speaking as they rounded the corner to see the gazebo, which was lit up bright with white lights. Ash was already inside it, setting the table. He moved slightly to the left, and Isaiah's heart rate kicked up as he spotted Sofia.

"Sofia thought it would be funny to surprise you," Holly whispered, apparently noticing the expression on his face, which he thought he had masked. "She likes to keep people on their toes."

Isaiah barked out a laugh. "I've noticed."

Holly grinned, seeming to relax at his reaction. He followed her up the few steps, shook hands with Ash, then turned to Sofia.

"So, is this you welcoming me into the fold? Letting me in on an Emerald Hollow tradition?"

Sofia scowled, but there was a twinkle in her eyes. "Don't be too excited. We're making you do all the dishes."

"Not true," Holly said quickly, though she was smiling too.

They all took a seat, Holly next to Ash and Isaiah and Sofia across from them. Ash began to open the picnic basket and pull out the food, which Isaiah thought smelled amazing. He couldn't get enough of the food at the Emerald House. Ash gave Holly a quick kiss on the lips as he set a roll in front of her.

"So, how long have you two been together?" Isaiah asked.

"Oh, they're not together," Sofia said.

Isaiah nearly choked.

Ash took a roll and threw it at her. "Geez, Sof. Don't you think the man has been through enough without you ribbing him? Sorry, Isaiah. She learned all that in the military."

"You were in the military?" Isaiah turned toward her, sensing an opportunity. He'd been curious about her personal life for weeks, but their conversations had always remained surface level, Sofia deflecting most of his questions with humor and sarcasm.

"Yep." Sofia didn't make eye contact with him as she pulled the roll out of her lap and placed it on her plate. "Six years."

"Which branch?"

"Air Force."

"Were you a pilot?"

Sofia laughed. "You say Air Force, and people automatically assume pilot. No. I was enlisted. Working dog handler."

Isaiah's eyebrows rose, and something flickered in the back

of his memory. *Didn't she say something about having a dog before?* "What was that like?"

"I enjoyed it for a while. Those dogs are amazing. I got to keep mine when he retired. He passed away a couple years ago. I haven't been able to get a dog since." Her voice was softer than he'd ever heard it, and he wondered if he'd been wrong to ask for details. But before he could shift gears, she spoke again. "Good thing we have Comet around for us all to spoil rotten."

They all laughed as Comet poked his head up from under the table then, placing his nose squarely in her lap.

"See what I mean?"

"So, why'd you get out?" Isaiah asked, still curious about her time in the military and what the transition had been like for her when she left.

Sofia's eyes dropped to the table for a moment. "Family reasons. My mom was sick."

"Ah, sorry to hear that." He could tell by the tone of her voice that her mom had never gotten better, and his heart ached for her.

Holly spoke up then. "So, Isaiah, we thought it was about time we got to know you a little better. We know you don't have your memories, but it's clear you're great at all the handy tasks around the House that Ash has you doing, and we've heard you're a natural with the dogs at the shelter too. Have you redis-covered any other interests since you've been here?"

Isaiah was grateful for the change in conversation, even if for Sofia's sake more than his. He contemplated Holly's question. Her soothing voice had seemed to change the atmosphere, his heart rate slowing and his shoulders relaxing. The evening sunlight was glistening on her hair like she was on the cover of a photoshopped magazine, and he had to force himself to refocus on her question.

"You know, it's interesting, because sometimes, I see some-thing, and I just know that I'm into it. Other things, I know I'm not a fan of. But I can't explain it beyond that. At the library a couple of weeks ago, I pulled up some maps of the area. I was exploring the trail where Sofia found me, trying to figure out where I might have been coming from. When I started sorting through the maps, it all felt familiar. Not the places, unfortunately, but the maps. I knew what all the symbols meant, how to interpret topography. I had a clear sense of direction. It made me think I was—or am—into maps or navigation or something."

Ash stopped slicing his steak and studied Isaiah for a moment. "That is pretty interesting. Maybe you were a Boy Scout."

Sofia laughed. "Wouldn't that be a perfect headline? 'Former Boy Scout gets lost in the woods and loses his memory.'"

Holly gasped. "Sofia!"

But Isaiah grinned. "It would be pretty ironic."

"Well, I think that's a good sign that the maps felt familiar. Maybe eventually, you'll bump into something else familiar that will be even more of a clue," Ash offered.

"I hope so. I'm not sure what else to do at this point. I can't live on all your hospitality forever."

"It won't be forever. I'm sure it will get sorted out soon. But as long as you need. You've been a huge help around here."

Isaiah nodded and took a bite of his baked potato, the hot, buttery taste sharp on his tongue. He glanced at Sofia out of the corner of his eye and caught her watching him. She jumped ever so slightly, and her face did a funny little dance as she tried to change her expression, then she turned and struck up a conversation with Holly. A smile tugged at the corner of his mouth.

As much as he wanted to know what was going on in his own head to recover his memories, he was also dying to know what was going on in hers.

Chapter Twenty-Five

SOFIA

Ash pulled out a coconut cream pie and passed a piece to everyone. Sofia gave him the stink eye. He knew she couldn't resist coconut cream and the thick layer of homemade whipped cream that topped it.

"So, Sof, what's new with you?" he asked, ignoring her expression as he handed her a small piece.

Sofia sat up a little straighter. She was glad the topic of conversation had moved on from her military days. Remembering that period of her life inevitably led her to thoughts of Noah, and as always, she was angry that he had soured all memories of that time.

She tugged on an earring. "Well, since you ask, my business has been going really well lately."

"Was it a particular product that started taking off, or have sales ticked up across the board?" Ash asked.

Isaiah turned toward her, waiting to hear the answer. She avoided looking at him, suddenly unexpectedly and uncharacteristically self-conscious. "Actually, I launched a new line, and it's been surprisingly popular. Also..." She swallowed, seeing Isaiah shift slightly in his seat out of the corner of her eye. "I changed my business name."

"What did you change it to?" Ash asked, a note of surprise in his voice.

"Emerald Hollow Artisanal. The tagline is 'Quirky jewelry, gifts, and more. Handmade in Emerald Hollow, Oregon.'"

"That's brilliant," Ash said.

"It's beautiful, Sof!" Holly said, reaching across the table and giving her hand a squeeze.

"A name change. What an interesting idea," Isaiah said slowly, his voice full of humor.

Sofia rolled her eyes up to the sky. "Fine! It was Isaiah's idea. And a very good one."

"Hey, you came up with the name, not me. And I agree with Ash and Holly. It's brilliant. And beautiful."

Sofia, who never blushed, felt heat creeping up her neck. She shoved a piece of the coconut cream pie into her mouth, determinedly not looking at Isaiah.

"Damn, this pie is good," Isaiah said after following her lead and trying a bite. "Are you sure there aren't some magic elves cooking in your kitchen?"

Holly choked, a very un-Holly-like move, Sofia thought, and Ash put his hand on her back.

"Just talented employees and old family recipes," he said, sharing looks with Holly.

What was that about? Sofia wondered. But her mind quickly returned to Isaiah. He was sitting inches from her on the bench, and she had felt his presence too strongly for her liking the whole evening.

"It was crazy that the snow just disappeared overnight like that. Is that normal for here?" Isaiah asked.

Ash shrugged. "The weather varies a lot in the late winter. But that was kind of unusual."

"I'm sure we'll have another snowstorm this week," Sofia said, disappointment rippling through her at the thought.

"Nah, I don't think so. This feels like real spring. I think the warmer weather's here to stay," Isaiah asserted.

Sofia turned to him, raising an eyebrow. "So, you, a man with no memory of this town as far as you know, think you know better than a local?"

Isaiah raised his large hands, that annoying, tantalizing smile pulling at the corner of his mouth. "I'm just saying. I know spring when I feel it. Maybe I'm a weatherman."

Sofia shook her head.

"How about we make a wager out of it?" Isaiah suggested, and Sofia tried not to roll her eyes.

"What are we betting? You don't have any money or personal belongings."

Isaiah paused to think, and Ash jumped in. "Loser has to sing at Valentine's karaoke night."

Sofia gasped, giving Ash a look of horror.

Isaiah whipped his head toward her, his eyes sparking. "What? You don't like to sing?"

Sofia glanced at him for a moment before turning dagger eyes back to Ash. She couldn't believe he would betray her like that. A smile played on his lips.

"No. I don't." Her mind flashed to a party the previous December when she'd done a little singing. It was the one and only time she'd sung in public since she was a kid. She had to admit that party had been one of the best nights she'd had in recent memory. But she hadn't been experiencing her normal insecurities. It was like she had been hypnotized or something.

Sofia peeled her eyes away from Ash and rolled her shoulders back, putting on an air of confidence. She knew that it was going to snow again, probably within the week. That was how things always went in Emerald Hollow. Unfortunately, winter liked to cling all the way through February and often well into March. There was no way Isaiah could know better than her.

"Fine. You're on. If it snows again by Valentine's Day, you sing a song..." She paused, looking Isaiah directly in the eyes and trying not to focus on the crinkles at the corners or the thick, dark eyelashes. "Of my choosing at karaoke night. If it doesn't, I'll sing."

"A song of *my* choosing," Isaiah added, sticking out his hand.

They shook on it, Isaiah's large, warm hand holding hers a second too long, and Ash rubbed his hands together with a grin at Holly.

"This should be interesting. May the best forecaster win."

Sofia smirked, all worries gone. She had it in the bag.

The next morning was Groundhog Day, and Sofia and Isaiah were seated on a couch in the café at the Emerald House, their eyes glued to the TV in the corner. Neither of them had brought up the bet they'd forged the night before, but Sofia was sure it was as top of mind for Isaiah as it was for her.

A handful of other people were there, watching with rapt attention as a reporter in Pennsylvania waited for a groundhog to join them.

"It's time for the big moment, folks. Is spring here to stay, or will we be having six more weeks of winter?"

In the café, patrons shouted their predictions. A voting area had been set up the week before on the café counter, with a glass jar painted in colorful flowers labeled Spring Is Here and another painted with snowflakes that read 6 More Weeks of Winter.

With the sudden snow melt and appearance of green grass and shrubs, most of the residents of Emerald Hollow had voted that spring was there to stay. That box was stuffed full of raffle tickets. There were only a few in the box Sofia had placed her vote in. As much as she would love for spring to stay put, she was still convinced that winter was coming back and that they would see a late-season snowstorm.

Cheers erupted on screen as a man in a black suit and top hat moved to the front of the group in Pennsylvania, carrying a groundhog who rested on his arm. A man beside them read from an old-fashioned scroll.

"Hear ye! Hear ye! This February second..." He continued with an introduction of the groundhog and his oracle-like abilities. Then, at a moment of peak anticipation of the crowd both on screen and in the café, his voice rose to nearly a shout, and the crowd erupted as he said, "There is no shadow to be cast, and early spring is my forecast!"

"I knew it!" Isaiah shouted.

Sofia jumped a little. "It's just a groundhog." She rolled her eyes, but she couldn't keep the smile off her face at his juvenile joy.

"Isaiah, do you want to choose the raffle winner?" Ash asked, holding up the flower-painted jar, which contained the names of everyone who had cast their votes for an early spring.

"Don't mind if I do." Isaiah cast a mischievous look at Sofia before sauntering over to the counter. She met his gaze unflinchingly. *So what if a groundhog predicted an early spring across the country? This is Emerald Hollow. We're on our own seasonal cycle.*

Isaiah reached into the jar of tickets and swirled his large hand around, pretending to take his time choosing. Sofia already knew that year's prize. The winner would get a gift certificate for dinner for two at Enzo's Italian restaurant on Main Street. It was tradition that whoever won the certificate got to take a date of their choice.

"Get on with it!" Sofia shouted, and Isaiah finally snagged a ticket. He unfolded it then read the name.

"I swear this wasn't rigged," Isaiah said faux sheepishly as he handed the raffle ticket to Ash.

Ash let out a soft laugh. "It looks like Emerald Hollow's

newest guest is our winner. Congrats, Isaiah." The two fist-bumped, then Ash spoke to Isaiah as he turned back to the small crowd. "So, who are you taking with you to dinner at Enzo's?"

Isaiah turned, a grin tugging at the sides of his mouth, and locked eyes on Sofia. "It's only fair to treat the loser to dinner, right?"

The crowd cheered and whistled, and a few people congratulated her, but Sofia's eyes were narrowed on Isaiah. *What are you up to?* she wondered as her heart raced.

~

SOFIA WOKE UP LATE THE NEXT MORNING, AS USUAL. Her mind was on the Groundhog Day events as soon as she opened her eyes. She and Isaiah would be going to a fancy Italian dinner together at the time of his choosing. It wouldn't be so bad except that she couldn't figure out how she felt about it.

She wanted to be irritated, but instead, when he'd called her out of the crowd, she'd been thrilled. *That was probably just my ego acting up,* she chided herself.

Pulling open the living room curtains, she gasped as her eyes processed what she was seeing. All her tulip leaves had popped out of the ground overnight. The large planters in front of her house were full of the green leaves signaling that tulips would be blooming in a few short weeks.

She shook her head. It was too early. When the next frost came, the leaves were all going to freeze. Despite what the groundhog had predicted, that just wasn't right. Her tulips had never sprung out of the ground so early. *What is going on with the weather this year?*

Halfway to her coffeepot, she stopped, remembering her bet with Isaiah. First, the groundhog prediction for an early spring, then the tulips were behaving strangely. An odd tingle crept down her arms, and she shook her head. *It's just a coincidence.*

Sofia got the coffee brewing and sat down on the couch to review her orders before getting ready for work. She clicked to open her shop's sales tracker and was shocked for the second time that morning.

Her records indicated that she'd received fifty new orders since the previous day. That was a huge number for her in one day, and she suddenly wondered if she would be able to fill them. She flung her laptop to the side of the couch and stood quickly, ready to shovel down her coffee. She was going to have to make a few orders before work then do the rest at lunch.

She'd been spending every lunch break at the library with Isaiah. If she wasn't flipping through business-planning books, she was on her laptop, doing work for Emerald Hollow Artisanal. She wondered if she could create some jewelry at the library, or if Isaiah would wonder why she didn't just leave him there on his own.

Sofia paused. She was beginning to wonder that herself. There was no reason for her to stay with Isaiah in the library anymore. It wasn't like she was his supervisor, and he clearly knew his way around a computer, despite his memory loss.

So why am I still going with him every day? She rotated her shoulders and flexed her hands. *I don't need to explain myself to anyone. The library is a public place.* She carefully packed some of her jewelry-making supplies into her bag.

Fifteen minutes later, she was out the door, casting a quick, nervous look at her tulip leaves before driving to the Emerald House.

Chapter Twenty-Seven

ISAIAH

"Are we going or what?" Sofia's voice hit his ears like a perfectly plucked guitar string, reverberating just a little at the end. Her slightly exasperated tone had become so familiar to him. He jumped up from the comfortable seat in the Emerald House Café, where he'd been chatting with the barista, Allison, while waiting for her.

At first, he wondered if she would bring up the dinner invitation from Groundhog Day but could quickly tell that she was going to play it cool and not mention it. He grinned at her steely expression. He would let her think he'd forgotten about it then spring the dinner on her when she was least expecting it.

"It's preeetty nice outside," he said as he held the door open for her.

Sofia rolled her eyes, and he let out a laugh.

"I'm telling you—it'll freeze again. It always does."

"I'm already planning what song you'll be singing at karaoke. Allison's been educating me on pop music at the café. I'm thinking maybe... 'Party in the USA'?"

Sofia's jaw dropped, and he grinned.

He began to sing, and she quickly pressed the unlock button

on her keys to cause a loud beeping sound then slid smoothly into the driver's seat.

"No need for a preview," she said once he was inside the car. "I'll get to hear your voice when you're singing the song of *my* choice at karaoke."

Isaiah laughed. He couldn't help finding her ridiculously cute when she was in a spicy mood, which was often. "So, tell me more about Valentine's karaoke night. Does it happen every year?"

"Yep. One of Emerald Hollow's many traditions. It's open to anyone—singles, couples, et cetera. Just a time to belt out love songs whether you love or hate the holiday itself."

"And which camp do you fall into?"

"Hmm?" Sofia's eyes drifted over to him as she whipped her car onto Main Street. The woman drove like a police cadet during their defensive driving course, gliding around corners as if they didn't exist.

"Do you love or hate Valentine's Day?"

Her brow furrowed. "I'm in the craft business, so I'm not against a greeting card holiday. I usually make some decent sales off Valentine's earrings."

Isaiah rolled his eyes. "That's not what I meant."

"I usually spend the day at home with ice cream, watching a rom-com. I'm a romantic—don't get me wrong. But it's just kind of an..." She paused, and he thought she was searching for the right word. "Awkward holiday if you're single. I know a lot of people who aren't in relationships love going to the karaoke event, but as Ash mentioned, I don't sing."

"And why is that?" Isaiah studied her face as she pulled into the library's parking lot.

"I just don't."

"So there's no story there?"

He watched in interest as her lips pressed together in a tight line, but she shook her head. "Nope, no story." She parked, and they both climbed out of the car.

As Isaiah held open the library door, he leaned in and whispered, "Liar."

Sofia scowled, and he followed her inside. Isaiah took a seat at his usual computer in the sitting room and expected Sofia to sit at the window table she typically occupied, but instead, she disappeared into one of the other rooms of the renovated old house. He wondered if the 'liar' comment, which he'd meant in jest, had annoyed her.

He spent ten minutes on the internet, sending inquiries and doing searches, but his mind kept wandering to Sofia. He glanced over his shoulder to the window table, but it was still empty, so he stood and walked into the hallway, peeking into the other rooms.

After seeing no sign of her in the kitchen or dining room, he turned to the right, where a round hobbit-style door led to the children's section. He opened it and found her sitting in the empty room in a small, fluffy kids chair, jewelry parts strewn on the floor around her.

"Why are you doing that there?" he asked.

Sofia jerked, a piece of jewelry flying out of her hand.

He walked over to retrieve it from where it had slid under another seat then stood to see that Sofia was glaring at him.

"What? Am I not allowed to be sitting here?"

"That's a kids' chair." He couldn't keep the smile off his face. The wall behind her was painted with a bright rainbow, and a large arched window showed the forest outside. She looked like a human inside an elves' home in the room with furniture built for small children. *A very cute human,* he thought as she blew a curl out of her eye.

Sofia looked down to where her hips were spilling over the sides of the cushion as if it was perfectly normal. "And?"

"Why aren't you working at the table in the sitting room? Or the kitchen island? It seems like it would be easier."

Sofia let out a breath and threw her arms up in defeat. "Because I didn't want you to see me." It came out as a whisper.

Isaiah tried to suppress a grin. "What was that?"

"Because I didn't want you to see me!" Sofia said much louder that time, a jewelry piece flying off her lap again.

"Shhh!" someone called from the adjacent room.

Their eyes met, and they both burst into laughter.

"I haven't been shushed in a library since high school," Sofia said, gathering her jewelry supplies and placing them carefully in her organizer.

"Me either. Not that I can remember, anyway."

Sofia burst into laughter again and had to put a hand over her mouth to quiet herself. He watched as a stubborn curl fell over her face and her cheeks lit with color. When she wasn't trying to exasperate him, she was the most attractive woman he'd ever seen. *No, even when she is.*

A strange sensation was brewing in Isaiah's stomach. Even though he didn't have any memories of his time before Emerald Hollow, somehow, he knew that Sofia was special. It didn't matter that he couldn't remember anything. He knew, deep down, that he'd never met anyone like her.

Sofia finally got all her jewelry loaded and looked up to see him watching her. "Aren't you going to offer to help?" she asked in that icy voice that he knew was just a front.

"Aren't you going to ask?"

Sofia huffed and stood. The humor from their laughing session was still in her eyes. "Touché. So, did you have any luck today?"

He was confused for a moment then remembered why they were there in the first place. "Nope. Same old, same old. Leaving empty-handed."

"So either your family and friends think you're on some kind of extended vacation, or you are a complete hermit out there in the real world."

She had taken to calling his life before he'd lost his memories "the real world," which gave him the feeling that she didn't consider his time in Emerald Hollow real somehow. His stomach sank every time he heard the words, but he didn't let on.

"I'm going with option one. I'm probably a billionaire who was taking my yacht out on a private charter for a year."

"And somehow got lost on a hike in Oregon on the way to your yacht?" Sofia quirked an eyebrow at him as they left through the hobbit hole and returned to the sitting room. She carefully spread her jewelry supplies out on the window table, the sunlight making the caramel-colored highlights in her hair look like tinsel.

Isaiah laughed. "You got me there."

"Well, I have a little lunch break left. You want to lend me a hand?"

"Emerald Hollow Artisanal is going to trust an amnesiac with their designs?"

"Oooh no, you're not designing." Sofia pulled out a folder of small bags and labels. "You get to package."

"Oh, lucky me," Isaiah said, trying to match her constant sarcasm as he reached for the roll of stickers.

Sofia rolled her eyes, but Isaiah noticed she was trying to suppress a grin, and something inside his chest boiled like warm honey.

Chapter Twenty-Eight

SOFIA

On February fourteenth, Sofia woke up and said a quick prayer that was more like a plea. It hadn't dropped below fifty degrees in the last two weeks. It was Valentine's Day, and if Emerald Hollow didn't get a freezing spell at some point that day, she would have to sing at karaoke.

Maybe a cold front came in last night, she thought, heading straight for her front curtains.

Her jaw dropped again.

Not only was there no hint of frost, but all her tulips had burst into full bloom overnight. Her front planters were brilliant swaths of reds, pinks, and yellows.

For a few moments, Sofia forgot all about karaoke, and her heart soared. One of her favorite moments all year was the time when her tulips were in full bloom, greeting her every time she walked by.

She had gained a love for them during her brief time living in Germany in the military and visiting the tulip festival in Amsterdam. She'd jumped into gardening full steam when she'd been taking care of her mom, and the habit had stuck.

Looks like you win, Malingerer. She hadn't called him that to his face again, but she thought it in her head occasionally. Though she had to admit she'd long since dropped all thoughts of the amnesia being an act. *What would his motive be?*

He didn't seem to be gaining anything in Emerald Hollow other than free rent at the Emerald House. But Ash had said he was more than paying for it with the work he was doing around the property. And Ash didn't accept help easily, so it seemed like a win-win.

Sofia sipped her coffee and wandered to her closet. "What do I wear to humiliate myself in front of everyone in Emerald Hollow?" she mused, sifting through her dresses. She grabbed one that caught her eye then went to look for a matching pair of earrings. Just because she was single on Valentine's Day didn't mean she couldn't go all out on the holiday. She considered it advertising for her business. Once she'd found a pair of giant cherry-red broken-heart earrings, she laid them next to the dress. *Perfect.*

She spent the next few hours making jewelry and fulfilling orders, keeping the front door open wide to catch hints of the tulip scents floating on the breeze. Her Valentine's jewelry orders had gone out a few weeks ago, and she was back to mainly working on her WanderLost line. It was still booming, more than she'd ever expected.

Sofia took a break after another hour of work to go examine her tulips. They seemed to be bursting out of every planter, more plentiful than any year before. A smile subconsciously washed over her face, and she snapped a few photos to share on her business's social media. Since she was Emerald Hollow Artisanal, she might as well showcase some of the beauty of Emerald Hollow. *Even if these tulips are blooming freakishly early.*

Chapter Twenty-Nine

ISAIAH

Isaiah got started on some outside projects for Ash early in the morning on February fourteenth. He shook his head at the brilliant blue sky, the warm sun glancing over his skin. He'd mostly made the bet with Sofia for fun and never dreamed he would be right about it.

He contemplated how furious she was going to be that evening at karaoke, picturing a slight flush filling her freckle-covered cheeks, and blew out a breath.

After he finished raking the freshly mowed lawn, which was surprisingly green and healthy so early in the year, he was putting the equipment away when Ash poked his head into the shed.

"Hey, Isaiah. All good?"

"Yep. The flowers are insane this morning, right? They came out of nowhere."

Something that Isaiah couldn't read crossed Ash's face, and Ash shook his head. "I've never seen anything like it. I guess we're gonna get to see Sofia sing tonight."

Isaiah took his opening. "About that... How serious is Sofia about not liking to sing in public? Is it a real fear, or is she just jittery about it? She seems so confident in everything."

Ash scratched the back of his neck. "I've only seen her do it once, and she wasn't completely herself that night. I don't know the original story, but I think she had a bad experience with singing in public when she was a kid. It's been a long time, though."

Isaiah's stomach clenched. He felt a little bad about her losing the bet, but he didn't see a way out of it. "Huh. Do you think she'll actually show tonight?" As soon as he asked it, he knew the answer. She was way too proud to bow out of a bet.

"Oh, she'll be there. But we'll be nice. She can go on early, before the place is too crowded, or late, when people have had a few of our Love Potions. Just make her sing something simple like the Alphabet song."

"Love Potions?"

Ash grinned. "We like to lean into a theme here. They're one of our specialty cocktails. You'll have to try one. I've got to get back inside, but I'll see you tonight. Everything looks great out here."

Ash walked away, and Isaiah finished organizing the equipment in the shed. He got one of those weird sensations he'd been experiencing since he'd arrived, in which he knew something about himself while he didn't have any specific memories to tie it to.

The sensation had been triggered by the Love Potion description. He instinctively knew that he was more of a beer guy, but since he was a man with no memory and no last name, maybe a Love Potion cocktail didn't sound so bad.

Chapter Thirty

SOFIA

Sofia slipped into her hot-pink dress and secured the large earrings in her ears. She put on some low strappy heels and wore her curls loose and tousled. If they were going to make her sing, she might as well put on a show.

But her confidence started to wane when she pulled into the parking lot of the Emerald House. Part of the bet was that she had to sing a song of Isaiah's choosing. She groaned. *What is he going to make me sing?*

Her spirits lifted slightly when she spotted Holly as soon as she entered the Emerald House. It had been transformed for the holiday, paper hearts in every color hanging from the ceiling. Sofia ran and gave her a hug.

"Are the Love Potions out yet? I'm going to need one before this whole karaoke thing." Sofia peered around Holly, searching for the drink table.

Holly let out a soft laugh. "They're out, but be careful. Maybe they'll make your nerves worse."

"Nerves? What nerves?" Sofia asked, grabbing Holly's wrist and pulling her toward the drink table she'd just spotted. The

Love Potions were adorable: pink drinks served in large heart-shaped martini glasses, with bright raspberries floating in the center. Sofia picked one up and took a sip. "Mmm. Yes, this will ease the pain."

"I'm sure you can get out of it if you really want to. Why don't you talk to Isaiah about it? Maybe you can negotiate the terms of the bet."

Sofia shook her head. "Nope. A deal's a deal. I have to go through with it. Is he here yet?" She swiveled her head again, careful not to spill her drink as she pivoted on her heel.

"I haven't seen him yet. Maybe he's still in his room."

"Hmm," Sofia mused, narrowing her eyes. She took another sip of her Love Potion and scanned the room. It seemed to be the usual Valentine's karaoke crowd, some couples, some singles. All ages twenty-one and over were present. The room wasn't completely full yet, and she was debating the strategy of getting the singing over with early, when there were fewer people present, or later, when the ones who remained might have had a few drinks and therefore might be more forgiving.

"I'm just going to go find Isaiah. I need to know what song he selected." Adrenaline was buzzing in Sofia's veins.

"Good luck." Holly studied her face, her eyes full of concern.

Sofia lightly smacked her arm. "Don't worry. I'm fine."

Holly nodded, and Sofia watched as she headed toward where Ash was setting up the karaoke machine across the room.

Sofia passed through the lobby and into the hallway that connected the rooms on that side of the Emerald House, her heels clicking lightly against the floor. She hadn't been to Isaiah's room, but she knew which one he was staying in. Ash had placed him near his apartment. Sofia approached the door and knocked.

A few seconds later, it opened, and a grin pulled at the sides of Isaiah's mouth as he took her in. He scanned the pink dress, the sparkly heels, and the giant red broken-heart earrings. "You really embraced the holiday," he said, his eyes sparking.

Sofia held up her glass in a mock toast, her hot-pink nails wrapped around the rim. "Did you expect anything less?"

He laughed. "Not at all. But now I feel underdressed."

He looks pretty great in those jeans, and the short sleeves on that button-up are really showing off his muscles. Sofia shook herself at the thought and tried to refocus.

"But to be fair, I only have the outfit I arrived here in plus two others I picked up on Main Street my first week here. Ash lent me this shirt. It's a little small."

Sofia touched a finger to her lips. "You know, we're really going to have to do something about that. The weather's getting warmer..." A loaded pause followed as they both thought of the reason she had lost the bet. "And I could use a trip out of town."

Isaiah's eyebrows rose. "You want to take me on a shopping trip outside of Emerald Hollow, Wrecker?"

"If I have to sing, you have to humor me and be my personal Ken doll."

Isaiah gave a dramatic shiver and pretended to look down the hall for someone to save him.

She smacked him on the arm. "Oh, come on. I'll go easy on you. As long as you pick a song with a really shallow range tonight. Preferably a short one. Under sixty seconds would be great."

Isaiah leaned back and grinned. His voice came out even lower than normal as he asked, "Renegotiating, are we?"

Sofia's stomach did a little flip. "Not exactly. Just greasing the wheels. A girl can try, right?"

He studied her for several moments, so long that Sofia began to squirm.

Finally, she turned on her heel, holding her drink aloft. "Coming?"

She cast a glance over her shoulder and saw him flick off the light switch in his room and pull the door closed as he followed her, giving a grin that she begged herself to ignore.

Chapter Thirty-One
SOFIA

The first few hours of the party flew by, and Sofia had consumed three Love Potions by the time Ash announced it was final call for karaoke. A woman with short dark hair ran up delightedly and snagged the microphone. Within moments, she was belting out Shania Twain.

Sofia took the last gulp of her drink and rolled her shoulders back, straightening. Isaiah had mysteriously disappeared a while ago, and she knew it was time to take matters into her own hands to complete the bet. She leaned toward Holly. "This is it. I'm going on after Shania."

"Silver bells," Holly said calmly, and Sofia looked at her quizzically. "It's like 'Good luck.'"

Sofia shook her head, wondering why Canada had such strange expressions, then strode to the side of the small stage. She'd pestered Isaiah on his song choice all night, but he'd refused to reveal it. *If he hasn't decided by now, I'm choosing.* She scrolled through the list on the laptop screen.

Her mind was relaxed and slightly fuzzy after the drinks, and the crowd was enthused, singing along to the woman's messy version of the Shania Twain song. *This won't be so bad,* Sofia thought, queuing up her song choice. But a nervous shudder worked its way up her spine.

When the woman finished her song to a loud chorus of applause, she ran over and handed the microphone to Sofia, who took it with sweaty hands. She walked across the stage, putting a little strut into her step to appear confident. A few whistles reached her ears as she walked to the center of the stage, and the backing music came on. She locked her eyes on the screen where the lyrics were displayed, determined not to look out at the crowd.

Just as she was about to open her mouth to sing the first line, wanting to melt off the stage and her heart racing, the music stopped, a new song started playing, and Isaiah jumped out from somewhere to her side with a second microphone. He lifted it to his mouth and belted out the lyrics to Aretha Franklin's "Respect."

Sofia stared open-mouthed as he continued the raucous singing. He nodded toward her and nudged at her microphone. She raised it and began to sing along.

They continued to sing in tandem, Isaiah's confident voice much louder than hers. She couldn't believe it. He had an incredible voice and a bit of a stage presence. She found herself laughing and forgetting her nerves as they powered through the song together, the crowd cheering and singing with them.

By the end of the final verse, she was grinning so hard that she leaned over slightly and gripped her stomach, unable to contain her joy. As the crowd cheered, Isaiah laughed and took her hand, gently guiding her off stage. She collapsed into a fit of giggles and flung her arms around him.

"I didn't know you could sing." She laughed, pulling back just an inch.

"I wasn't sure if I could." He slipped a hand onto her waist as he effortlessly pulled her out of the way of a microphone cord.

"So you just went up there, not knowing if you were completely tone deaf, to sing in front of all those people? Why?"

"Why not?" Isaiah's hand was still on her waist, and goose bumps pricked her arms. In the near distance, Sofia could hear that people were beginning to file out of the party, but they were obscured by the café counter and tall stage lights.

Sofia locked eyes with him then, her gaze trailing from his eyes to his lips and back again. That grin that pulled at the sides of his mouth and drove her crazy was back, taunting her.

"Why'd you do it?"

"Because you didn't want to." He had moved his other hand to her hair, two fingers playing with a curl.

"That wasn't part of the deal." Her heart was racing, but she couldn't look away.

"You tried to change the rules once, if I recall."

She pursed her lips.

"Besides, we never agreed that whoever lost had to sing alone."

His hand being on her waist was distracting her, and electricity was zipping up and down her arms.

"That's true, but—" she said slowly, leaning forward ever so slightly. She was getting ready for another retort when he leaned down and closed the gap between them. She felt his lips on hers just as she tilted her face upward. His mouth was warm, and she slipped her arms around his neck, pulling him closer.

For a moment, Sofia forgot where they were. Nothing existed except for the places where his hands and lips connected with her body. Her entire body was warm and tingly.

Suddenly, singing came from behind them, and they broke apart as a man Sofia recognized as the owner of one of the stores downtown came around the corner.

"Oops, didn't mean to interrupt. Ash said there might be some to-go boxes back here." The man looked at them sheepishly.

Sofia quickly pulled away from Isaiah. Flustered, she tucked her hair behind her ear and squatted, grabbing a to-go box from the low shelves of the café counter. "Here you go, Mr. Harris."

"Happy Valentine's Day, you two," he said with a wink then walked away with the paper box.

Sofia turned back to Isaiah and bit her lower lip as she smiled at him. "Aaawkward," she said in a singsong voice.

He laughed. His eyes were still blazing, and her cheeks flushed.

"I blame that on the Grammy-worthy singing voice you've been hiding all this time," Sofia teased.

"Oh really? Not on the fact that I swooped in and saved you from having to sing on your own?"

"Hey, I was going to! You saw me up there." Sofia's temper flared, but there was no heat behind it. She *had* been extremely grateful when he'd jumped in.

"I have no doubt. Do you want to try again? The karaoke machine's still out. You can have your solo." He grinned mischievously.

Sofia shoved his chest. "You're impossible." She turned to walk away.

He slipped a hand around her wrist. "Where are you going?"

"Home. It's late."

"How many Love Potions have you had? Let me drive you."

"Holly already offered. She's obsessed with driving now that she has her license."

"Ah, got it. So, I'll see you...?"

She narrowed her eyes mischievously and poked his chest playfully. "You owe me a shopping trip, remember? And lucky for you, I have a free weekend trip I'm cashing in tomorrow."

"Weekend? You asking me on an overnight trip?"

Sofia rolled her eyes. "There's two bedrooms. Don't make it weird."

He shook his head but raised his hands in surrender.

"Aside from the shopping, we can each have our own little vacation. It's about time you saw something outside Emerald Hollow."

"I don't know. I like everything I've seen here." His eyes were still on her, that intense gaze that had been lit by their kiss still lingering.

Sofia shifted her weight on her feet. "Pick you up at ten," she said then thought better of it. He had to know she wasn't a morning person. "No, make it eleven."

"You got it, Wrecker."

She rolled her eyes, but a thrill went through her. The feel of his hands and his mouth were still fresh in her mind, and she turned away before he could see her flush.

Chapter Thirty-Two

ISAIAH

Sofia showed up at the Emerald House to collect him thirty minutes after their scheduled time the next morning, and Isaiah couldn't resist giving her a hard time.

"Feeling those Love Potions this morning?" he asked as he climbed into the passenger seat. He noticed her overnight bag sitting in the back and slipped a small backpack Ash had given him between his feet on the floor.

"Not at all," she said primly.

He glanced over and noticed that she looked fantastic, as always. If she'd gotten as little sleep as he had the previous night, she wasn't showing any signs of it.

"So, what do you have in store for me? I only need one or two more outfits."

Sofia raised her eyebrows. "I'll be the judge of that."

Isaiah waited a beat to see if she was going to rib him about the few outfits he'd been rotating since his first week there. But she left it at that, so he changed the subject.

"So, do I finally I get to hear the story of why you don't sing in public, or is that something only Ash can know about?" Isaiah hadn't believed her when she'd told him there was no story behind her phobia, and he didn't mind the potential side effect of sending both of their minds to the night before.

Sofia shifted a little in her seat. "Even Ash doesn't know the origin of that one."

Surprised, Isaiah turned to her. "Really? He was the one who mentioned it in the gazebo."

"He knows that I hate singing. But not why. I have told him three or four different stories, all fake. And he knows it."

"Dang. It must have been pretty bad to warrant fake stories in its place." Isaiah didn't think she would tell him if she hadn't even told Ash, but he wanted to know everything about her, and that story was no exception.

"You'll never know," she said, shooting him a sideways look.

They passed out of Emerald Hollow, and Isaiah noticed that the vibrant tulips that had been bursting along the roadways all throughout town became sparse then completely vanished as they headed away from the city limits. *That's odd,* he thought.

Sofia gave voice to his thoughts. "Huh, the tulips just disappeared. I wonder why Emerald Hollow is having such a powerful regional bloom."

"You mean it isn't typical for Emerald Hollow to have tulips bursting out of every ounce of soil like a Monet painting?" Isaiah was mildly interested in the tulips, but he was much more intrigued by the woman sitting next him. He had a chance to get to know her even better, and he didn't want to waste it.

Turning the subject back to her, he said, "Okay, karaoke is off limits—for now."

She shot him a skeptical look, and he grinned.

"So, what *can* you tell me about? Your time in the military? Your family?"

Sofia shook her head. "It's not fair. You can't tell me anything in return."

"That's exactly why it is fair. I don't have any memories, so you can help me fill my brain with some of yours."

Sofia turned her head slightly and seemed to study him for a moment before looking back at the road. "There's not much to say that you don't already know. Out of high school, I joined the military. Worked as a dog handler for most of the six years. My mom was diagnosed with cancer. I separated from the military and moved back here. I lived with her for a while then eventually got my own place, where I live now. I started working at the Emerald House and doing my jewelry on the side."

"What's next for your business? You've been putting in plenty of research at the library."

Sofia seemed startled by the question, but to his surprise, she didn't respond with a snarky retort. "I'm taking things one day at a time. I've started to create an actual business plan. I do pretty decent sales when we have local festivals, but my real goal is to scale my online presence. I can reach so many more people that way. Right now, I just do work within my themed lines, like Christmas or Valentine's Day or other themes. Eventually, I'd like to open up for custom orders as well."

"If you made a custom order for me, what would it be?" Isaiah loved the sound of her voice when she spoke about her business. All attitude faded away, and the underlying passion that he suspected fueled it all came through.

Sofia cast him a withering look. "You know I make jewelry, right?"

Attitude back, he thought with a grin.

"Maybe I want a custom belt buckle. If I had a belt, that is."

"We'll remedy the belt situation today. See? I told you you needed new things."

"You still didn't answer the question."

Sofia accelerated to pass a slow vehicle. "Usually, I try to make customs—gifts—that I feel fit the person. I've made custom earrings for Holly before. I don't think she's that into jewelry, but I always catch her wearing the earrings I've made her. Now that I think about it... I wonder why she's still wearing the Mrs. Claus hat earrings I made her at Christmas. Doesn't she know it's February?"

"You're sidetracking," Isaiah said, thoroughly enjoying listening to her talk.

Sofia huffed a deep breath. "Fiiine. Do you want morbid or fun?"

Isaiah raised his eyebrows, but she wasn't looking at him. "Morbid."

"Okay. I would make you a belt buckle displaying the woods and the trail where you were found."

Isaiah barked out a laugh. "You got me there."

She gave him a wicked grin, then a shadow passed over her face, and he wondered what she was thinking. He realized they'd driven for miles and managed to avoid any mention of the spectacular kiss they'd shared the night before. He wondered if it had been on her mind as much as it had been on his.

"Here we are," she said a minute later, pointing at the sign for Ashland, Oregon. "I told you it was a quick drive." She briskly navigated into the town and squeezed into the single open parking space in the central downtown area.

"Should I be scared?" Isaiah asked as they climbed out of the car and Sofia scanned the businesses for their first target. Her eyes seemed to glow as she surveyed the shops.

"Let's just say I've always wanted to have my own personal Ken doll to dress up." She winked.

He groaned, but his heart rate accelerated as he watched her walk, and he didn't think it was entirely because of the impending shopping spree.

Chapter Thirty-Three

SOFIA

"Okay, I think I'm stocked up for a year. Where to next?" Isaiah's words carried over the sound of cars and people in the bustling little city.

Sofia led him back to her car, where they deposited the two full bags of clothes, most of which had come from Sofia's favorite thrift stores downtown. Sofia had insisted on treating him to clothes in exchange for his promising to help her with order fulfillment. Her orders for her new WanderLost line still hadn't slowed down.

After closing the hatch, she glanced out at the sky. The sun was beginning to set, but they'd already agreed they weren't ready for dinner. "An afternoon snack, then I'll show you the park."

Isaiah raised an eyebrow. "Does it rival the one I've been walking the shelter dogs in?"

Sofia just smiled coyly and led him down the street to her favorite frozen yogurt shop. When they stepped inside and Isaiah looked around, he gave her an odd expression.

"Mystery Yogurt?" he asked, reading the name that was displayed in neon on the wall behind the counter.

125

"Just go with it," Sofia replied as they watched a trio of teenagers order at the shiny white counter. Directly behind it were rows of colorful yogurt dispensers. They reminded Sofia of the slushie dispensers on Bourbon Street in New Orleans.

"None of them have labels," Isaiah observed.

"That's the fun of it. It's a mystery. You pick what you want based on the color and go from there.

Isaiah eyed her skeptically but stepped up to the counter beside her. They hadn't stood that close all day, Sofia carefully keeping her distance as she critiqued the clothes he tried on. She was reminded just how tall he was, and his athletic physique was even more apparent, since he was wearing clothes that fit him.

Sofia cleared her throat and focused on the teenage boy behind the counter.

"One purple mystery please," she said with confidence.

"You sound like you've ordered that before," Isaiah said.

"I always order purple, but they swap out the flavors all the time, so it's still a mystery. Purple has never steered me wrong."

Isaiah gave her one last odd look then turned to the server. "I'll go with pink," he said, and the server turned around and started to prepare their orders.

Sofia cocked her head at him, surprised at the choice. "From all the neutral tones you picked out while shopping today, you didn't strike me as the pink type."

"Ah. So you brought me here as a personality test?"

"No, but that's not a bad idea." She leaned her hip against the low counter. "What would choosing pink say about you?"

"That I'm hoping for strawberry or watermelon."

Sofia laughed. "Good luck with that. That's not how it works, though. Usually, the colors don't match up with the flavors. It's all a fun way to trick your brain out of normal expectations."

Isaiah put on a faux-nervous expression, but a smile played at the corner of his lips. "What's wrong with normal expectations?"

"Oh, you know. They can just get a little bit boring," Sofia said.

The server returned with two cups of frozen yogurt swirled high in their small paper bowls, which were emblazoned with colorful question marks. He handed the purple to Sofia and the pink to Isaiah.

They grabbed their respective cups, and Sofia followed Isaiah to a booth. "Moment of truth," she said, holding up her frozen yogurt to cheers with his.

Together, they each took a first scoop of their frozen yogurt with a small spoon.

Isaiah made a face, and Sofia couldn't tell at first if he hated it or was simply surprised.

"What flavor did you get?" she asked.

"I can't tell. I swear that pink is throwing me off. My brain thinks strawberry, but instead, it's something sweet but not fruity. Caramel, maybe?"

"I could tell mine right away. Strawberry."

Isaiah's jaw dropped. "Are you serious?"

Sofia laughed. "Try it if you don't believe me." She held the cup out to Isaiah, and he scooped a large bite.

After tasting it, he shook his head. "Lucky."

"Lucky *you*," Sofia countered, pushing her cup over to him and taking his out of his hand. "Caramel is my favorite flavor."

Isaiah's eyes widened with delight, and he didn't try to protest. Instead, he took another giant bite of the purple strawberry-flavored dessert.

"So what do you think about this place?" Sofia was watching him closely, trying not to show her amusement.

Isaiah took another bite. "This is delicious. I still don't know about this whole tricking-your-brain thing. But I wouldn't expect anything less from you."

Sofia arched an eyebrow at him. "What does that mean?"

"Oh, you know. You're a little bit unconventional compared to the other people I've met in Emerald Hollow."

"Unconventional?"

"I mean, you did just take me shopping at vintage stores all day."

His voice was teasing, but Sofia was tempted to take her strawberry yogurt back and leave him with the caramel.

"Vintage is more sustainable and also more fun," she countered. "Most of them have been very lightly used and are way more stylish than the current trends. Besides, do men's trends really change that much?"

Isaiah shrugged. "I don't remember."

Sofia barked out a laugh. "Touché." She wanted to press more about what he thought was unconventional about her, but she forced herself to bite her tongue.

They sat in silence for a few moments, eating their yogurt. Isaiah's was disappearing at twice the speed of Sofia's.

Sofia was trying unsuccessfully not to think about how much she had enjoyed herself that day. Isaiah hadn't been a totally terrible sport when she was picking out clothes for him. And though he had vetoed one or two of her bolder choices, she felt he'd come away with a solid new wardrobe. She didn't think Ash would have tolerated it so well if she'd taken *him* shopping.

The yogurt shop was mostly empty, and Sofia was startled when a shout came from one of the teenagers at a booth across the room. She'd completely forgotten anyone else was there.

"Let's go!" one of the boys shouted, jumping from his seat. He looked to be about seventeen, and his face was bright red. The other boy jumped up as well, and soon they stood face-to-face. Sofia's heart rate kicked up. The girl who was with them was still sitting in the booth, but her eyes had widened.

"What's wrong?" she shouted, scooting toward the edge of the booth and reaching out toward the one who had shouted.

"Theo just texted me that you two kissed at River's party last night!"

The girl let out a shriek and put her hands to her mouth.

"It wasn't like that!" The other boy shouted defensively, putting his hands up.

"Oh really? Then what was it like?" the first boy asked in a low tone.

The girl jumped out of the booth, stepping between them. "Xander, please calm down. Let's talk about this."

Sofia's eyes shot over to the teenager behind the counter, who was looking at the trio nervously. She turned to Isaiah and noticed he was already on his feet, watching with his arms crossed.

She turned her eyes back to the teenagers just in time to see the first boy, Xander, sidestep the girl and shove the other boy.

Isaiah took a step forward. "Hey!" he called, his voice loud, deep, and reverberating throughout the room even though he hadn't shouted.

All three of the teenagers froze, and the employee behind the counter turned toward Isaiah as well. "You're not doing this here. Outside." He inclined his head toward the door.

The girl left out a muffled sob, and the boy, Xander, seemed to relax a little. He turned and walked out of the yogurt shop, and the girl ran after him. The other boy stood there by the booth, shaking slightly.

Isaiah walked over to him. "You good, man?"

The teenager nodded.

"Did you really kiss his girlfriend?" Isaiah asked, and Sofia gawked.

The boy nodded.

"And he's your friend?"

He nodded again.

"And you still want to be his friend?"

For a third time, the boy nodded.

"Then you'd better make it right."

"Yes, sir." Then he hurried out of the yogurt shop.

Isaiah watched him leave then slid back into the booth and began eating his yogurt again.

Sofia's jaw dropped.

"What?" he asked when he noticed her expression. He set down his spoon.

"Do you want to tell me what that was all about?"

"What do you mean?"

"It was like you knew exactly what to do and say. Your posture was even... different. And your voice..." A flush creeped over her skin.

Isaiah merely shrugged. "I was just doing what anyone would do."

Sofia shook her head, disagreeing but not wanting to go into more detail about it. "If you say so."

But she couldn't keep her mind off the way the boy had responded, meeting Isaiah's gaze, standing a little taller, and saying "Yes, sir." Something was bothering her, but she couldn't put her finger on what it was.

Chapter Thirty-Four

SOFIA

After they left the yogurt shop, Sofia and Isaiah strolled toward the large city park. Sofia decided she would show him a few of her favorite spots then they would go and check out the rental home she'd won for the weekend.

Before they entered the park, Sofia peeked in the window of one of the little shops that lined the path toward it. She could never resist keeping her eyes open for the gems she often found when she visited the town.

She inhaled sharply at the sight of a kite in the window. It was the classic shape and bright pink with streamers running down the ends.

Without warning, her mind flashed to a time on the beach as a child, flying a kite just like it through the air with her mom. It had been years since she'd thought of the scene, and it hit her like most unexpected memories with her mom did, magical and bittersweet all at once. She swallowed a lump in her throat.

"What is it?" Isaiah asked, and Sofia was surprisingly warmed by the feel of him standing next to her.

"That kite... It just reminded me of when my mom and I used to spend summers at the coast. There were perfect kite-flying conditions there." Her breath caught in her chest at the memory of how young, happy, and healthy her mom had been.

"Let's get it," Isaiah said.

Sofia turned to face him, her jaw dropping, before she shook her head. "No, that would be silly. I don't go to the coast anymore."

"So?"

"So? Should I just have a kite sitting in my house, never used?"

"If it reminds you of a happy memory, why not?"

Sofia frowned, but before she could process what she was doing, she found herself pushing open the door to the shop, which gave way with a little tinkle of a bell. She walked to the kite in the window and picked it up then stood holding it for a few moments. *Is Isaiah right? Is this a memento I should have?*

As she stood there, frozen in indecision, her thoughts were interrupted.

"Take it," someone with an ethereal voice said, and Sofia turned to see that a woman with silvery curls, which were dotted with tiny colorful gems and piled high on her head, had joined them. She was wearing a brooch with the shop's emblem. The woman had a second kite—a white one—in her hands and was passing it to Isaiah. "Take them both. Those kites have been sitting on my shelf for far too long."

Sofia reached toward her purse, but the woman shook her head. "It's my treat. I'm just glad to see them going to a good home after all this time."

"Are you sure? That's very generous." Sofia turned to thank the woman and was startled when she didn't have to look up. The shopkeeper was nearly the exact same height as Sofia. Then she briefly met the woman's eyes, and Sofia did a double take. *Are her irises...golden?*

But before she could look again, the woman with silver hair had turned away, off to greet another customer who had just entered the store. Isaiah opened the door for her, and Sofia left the shop, trying to shake the strange sensation that had come over her when she'd looked at the woman. She must have been wearing colored contact lenses.

"Why did you want me to get the kite?" Sofia asked, the question shooting from her lips automatically. She ran her hands over the edges of it, a warm sensation filling her fingers wherever she touched it. Isaiah hadn't known her mom. But he did seem to understand how much the sight of that kite had meant to her. The warmth moved from her hands and spread to her chest.

"I needed a souvenir from this trip other than thrift store clothes," Isaiah said, giving that grin she loved.

Sofia smiled and bumped her hip into his. "I hate to break it to you, but I think that *was* a secondhand store." But then she forced herself to stop the teasing that was so easy between them. She wanted to know the real reason why he had taken the leap that she couldn't and purchased the kite.

"I'm serious," she said. Their interactions were always filled with humor, but the moment in the shop had felt different, and her legs were slightly wobbly as they continued to walk toward the park.

Isaiah was quiet for a moment, and she wondered if he was coming up with another joke, but he surprised her when he spoke. "I don't have any memories, Sofia. I know the absence of your mom is with you every day, but her memories are there, too, right? If this kite helps you remember the good times, before she was sick..."

Sofia's stomach did a flip. It was like he had climbed inside her brain and seen exactly what she had been too scared to think. She didn't want memories of her mom to always be painful. Her mom had worked hard for Sofia's entire childhood to give her a whole collection of magic memories like the one on the beach. *Is it an affront to Mom's memory not to let myself relive those moments?*

Suddenly, she felt a surge of gratitude toward Isaiah. She didn't say anything but gave him a genuine smile and was surprised to see something that looked like delight flash across his face in return.

Sofia spotted an empty bench and took a seat, ready to lighten the mood. "What do you think? Beats the park in Emerald Hollow, right?"

Isaiah studied her face, making her squirm, then looked around. "I don't know. Emerald Hollow has it charms."

Sofia raised an eyebrow. "Really? You like it there? It tends to be a pass-through type of place for most people. They visit for the festivals then go home."

"Is that a bad thing? It keeps it... cozy for the locals."

"Cozy?" Sofia laughed.

Isaiah grinned.

"Have you ever thought about moving here?"

Sofia's head whipped back quickly, and she shook it. "Not really. One, I couldn't afford it. Two, I think it might lose its charms if I lived here. I like knowing it's so close, and it can be a little escape for me when I need it. And three, as much as I don't feel like a small-town girl at times, I really do love living in Emerald Hollow."

Sofia had never said it aloud before, but she knew it was true. As much as she sometimes complained about the lack of shopping or cultural life in Emerald Hollow, it was home, and she had no plans to leave.

A strong breeze grazed Sofia's arms, and her dress, which she was thankful she had paired with some opaque tights, suddenly blew up around her thighs. She gripped the kite firmly.

"Where did that wind come from?" Isaiah asked, looking perplexed. He stood and braced himself against the sudden gale.

Sofia stood as well, clutching the bottom of her dress in surprise. The weather had been completely calm all day.

Suddenly, a smile slid over Isaiah's face, his eyes brightening as he looked from Sofia to his kite.

"You can't be serious," she said, though a smile had appeared on her face as well.

He held up his kite. "I just got one of those feelings I've told you about, and I get the sense that I'm an excellent kite flyer." He turned so that his back was to the wind and began to spread out the kite.

"Is that a challenge?" Sofia asked, cocking her hip and placing her hand there.

"Of course."

Sofia laughed in delight and indignation when he effortlessly got the kite off the ground. She quickly grabbed hers and followed him to the open grassy field.

Together, they ran back and forth across the spacious green lawn, their kites flying high above them, bending and whooping in perfect unison. A few other park-goers gathered around to watch, and Sofia was reminded of the days when she put on a show for her mom at the beach.

After about fifteen minutes of running, laughing, and trying to avoid tangling her kite with Isaiah's, the wind suddenly changed, and the kites began to dive as if of their own free will. The kites came swooping down around them, and before either of them knew what was happening, the kite strings had tied them together, the kites somehow still flying a few feet above them.

Sofia let out a sharp laugh, in disbelief at their situation. She gripped Isaiah's arms so that she wouldn't fall over from the tight string around her ankles. Then she held her breath as she realized what she was doing—how close they were—but Isaiah merely slipped a hand around her waist to steady her, as if it was the most natural thing in the world.

She was surprised that he didn't immediately try to untangle himself, and they stood there for a few seconds, staring at each other. A whistle came from the small crowd, and they both began to laugh, the strange energy of the moment breaking. Then the wind died completely, and as the kites fluttered to the ground, they carefully pulled apart. It took a minute to untangle themselves from the kite strings.

"I'd say I won that competition," Isaiah said as they finally broke free of their strings and the crowd around them dispersed.

"No way. Mine got way more altitude."

"I wonder where that wind came from," Isaiah said, still a little breathless from their laughter as he carefully rolled the string onto the spool of his kite.

"I don't know. It appeared as if by magic." A little spark ran up and down her arms then evaporated. She glanced around, wondering where the feeling had come from, then shook it off and began to spool her string as well.

Isaiah tucked both of their kites under his arm, and Sofia led him to a little bridge where they paused to watch the water flow underneath them.

"This is the last thing I wanted to show you before we go check out the rental," she said. Though the little bridge usually brought her a sense of peace, her heart rate was still erratic from the few moments they'd been tangled in the kite strings.

The moment with the kites had sent her mind straight to the kiss they'd shared after karaoke. Both moments had seemed to be fueled by an inexplicable driving force that Sofia had never experienced before.

"So, about last night..." Isaiah began, and Sofia knew that his mind was exactly where hers was. She wondered if his pulse was anywhere near the same range as hers.

When he turned to look at her, his eyes were blazing, and Sofia thought she had her answer. With a cough, she averted her eyes and looked across the park in the last remaining sunlight, where two people were setting up instruments.

She'd been wondering when the kiss was going to come up.

It had been lingering between them all day, and she'd contemplated letting it remain unspoken forever. She certainly wasn't going to be the one to bring it up. Since he had, though, her chest tightened. The kite strings had wrapped them up like a Christmas present and literally forced them together, and they couldn't avoid the subject any longer.

"What about it? We'd had too many Love Potions, right? Those drinks were well named." A nervous flutter formed in her chest. The kiss had meant something to her, but maybe it had just been a Love Potion-induced accident for him.

"I only had one Love Potion early in the night. Turns out I'm more of a beer guy," Isaiah said. His gaze was on her, and her cheeks warmed. "But I may have been a little high on the post-karaoke buzz. Is that what rock stars feel like after every show?"

Sofia laughed, grateful for the break in the tension that was boiling between them. "Rock star, huh? Someone is mighty confident in their performance."

"Maybe that's my real identity. I'm a rock star who was sent off to rehab and somehow escaped but bumped my head in the woods. That's why no one's looking for me. They think I'm still at the ranch."

"The ranch?"

"You know. The rich-people code word for rehab."

Sofia nodded solemnly. "Ah. That must be it. I think you've solved the mystery." She paused then voiced what had been bothering her. "You really only had one Love Potion and no other drinks?"

"Just the one, hours before we kissed." He was standing close to her—a heartbeat away—and his presence was like dew in the air early in the morning, effortlessly clinging to everything.

Tension was sizzling between them. Unexplainable tingles stretched over every inch of her skin. She wanted to put her hands on his chest, grab his shirt, and pull his lips to hers again.

But all her internal protestations were still there, even

though they'd softened over time. They still didn't know who Isaiah was, where he had come from, or why he had ended up in Emerald Hollow.

On the other hand, her affection for and attraction to him were getting beyond her ability to deny. The few minutes of flying the kites with him and what had happened after had filled her with a sense of real-life magic that she'd long since thought she could never experience again. For that brief slice of time, she'd been the main character in a fairy tale.

She could let herself give in, just for a fraction of a second, just to see if it was as magical the second time, when she didn't have a few love potions in her system.

"So, if you weren't just having a rock-star moment…" She met his eyes, which were smoldering.

"I must have really wanted to—"

Before he could finish his sentence, she grabbed the front of his shirt and pulled his lips to hers.

Chapter Thirty-Five

SOFIA

When they checked into the vacation rental Sofia had won at the auction on New Year's Eve, she quickly claimed the largest room then said good night and shut the door.

After their kiss, she had taken a step back, trying to force the electricity between them to dissipate as she stepped out of his orbit. It hadn't worked. She hadn't stepped back because their second kiss wasn't as good as their first—it was the opposite. She never wanted the kiss to end. And that was a problem.

Isaiah had allowed her to step away, and they hadn't said anything as they'd driven to the rental home.

She paced her room restlessly, wondering what Isaiah was doing at the moment.

And what am I doing? she asked herself, finally deciding to quit pacing and take a hot shower. The bathroom in the rental was much more luxurious than the one she had at home, with a massive clawfoot tub with dozens of real plants surrounding it. In other circumstances, Sofia would enjoy the escapism of being inside a plant jungle, but she barely noticed her surroundings.

Her mind kept showing her pictures of Isaiah's face just

before she had kissed him. She had an entire conversation with herself as the steam fogged up the mirror in the bathroom.

This is a man who doesn't even know who he is. Am I taking advantage of him? And where could this... thing... between us be going anyway? What's going to happen when he eventually finds out who he is?

And besides the instinctive feeling she had that he would know if he was in a relationship in his real life, she still didn't know for sure that he didn't have a girlfriend somewhere out there.

Out of all the guys in the world, why did I have to fall for someone with amnesia? It's like the plot of a movie. She let out a mirthless laugh and shook her head as she gently towel-dried her curls and lathered on her favorite body lotion.

Her mind went to her mom for the second time that day. She could practically hear her mom speaking to her, teasing her about wanting a love story that was worthy of a Hallmark movie. That had been Sofia's dream as a preteen as she scribbled designs in her heart-stickered notebooks. Her hopeless romantic spirit had started at a young age and carried on for years, until it had been crushed by Noah.

And there she was, living a romance movie, and she was more unsure than ever. She'd given up her dream of romance years ago, choosing to make her life into the dream she'd imagined on her own—long baths on the weekend, candles in her kitchen while she cooked, rom-coms on the TV. But none of them had involved another person. She knew from experience that it wasn't safe to let one person have that much control over her happiness.

She'd lost Noah, then she'd lost her mom, then it had just been her. And aside from a couple of amazing friendships, mainly with Ash and Holly, that had suited her.

Sofia scrunched some oil into her wet curls with extra ferocity.

By the time she'd slipped into her pajama top and shorts, she'd made up her mind.

She would make it clear that she couldn't continue the relationship until he had his memories back and they knew for sure that there was no one else in the picture. While their kisses had been nothing short of magical, she couldn't let it happen a third time, at least not yet. They needed to double down on figuring out his identity. If she couldn't commit to him, she could at least commit to that. And she hoped it would be enough for him.

Chapter Thirty-Six

ISAIAH

It felt like Sofia had been in the shower for an eternity. Isaiah had been so restless that he'd walked down the street and grabbed some take-out dinner for them. He sat on the couch while picking at it, mindlessly flicking through TV channels. He hadn't even checked out his room other than to drop off his backpack.

Isaiah could tell that their second kiss had spooked her. He wasn't sure why, but he sensed something in her past was holding her back from trusting that things were real between them. He wished he could assure her that everything he felt for her was genuine and that he would never hurt her. *But can I really promise that?*

After all, he was a man with no memories of who he'd been. One thing he could never do to Sofia was make promises he couldn't be certain to deliver on. *But where does that leave us?*

When Sofia's door opened, Isaiah looked up, and she stepped out in a cloud of spicy floral aroma and a set of silky pink pajamas. Her damp curls were beautifully framing her face.

She jumped when she noticed him. "I thought you'd be in bed," she said, her tone accusatory.

He pushed the boxes of food across the coffee table toward her. "Hungry?"

Sofia seemed like she was going to decline, but after a few moments, she plopped into the armchair across from him and reached for the container and some chopsticks.

"How was your spa date?"

"Huh?" Sofia asked, slurping a noodle. She arched an eyebrow at him.

He grinned. "Well, you were in the shower for hours and came out smelling like a candy shop, so I figured you must have been having a full-on spa experience in there." He didn't mention that the smell had been driving him crazy since he'd first met her. *Is it her shampoo? Lotion?*

Sofia rolled her eyes. "It wasn't *hours*. Forty-five minutes, tops." She took another bite then narrowed her eyes as the rest of his words hit her. "*A candy shop?*"

"I don't know. It's like floral and spicy." Isaiah couldn't help teasing her. That kind of interaction was so much easier than facing what was going on between them, and he wanted to hold on to those feelings as long as possible.

Sofia's cheeks reddened slightly, but she ignored him and resumed eating, letting her eyes wander to the television. He had the feeling she was purposefully ignoring his gaze. Something had changed while she took that marathon shower, but he didn't push her to find out what it was. He wasn't sure he was going to like whatever she had decided.

"Hey, turn that up," Sofia said suddenly, putting the take-out box back on the coffee table. Isaiah picked up the remote and increased the volume.

"Tulips in Emerald Hollow have been blooming out of control early in the season. Tonight, we interview local Oregon master gardener Tom Maryland, who tries to explain the phenomenon."

"Wow, Emerald Hollow made the news," Isaiah said,

watching as images of the brilliant tulip blooms were spread across the screen.

"There's my house!" Sofia squeaked when a tiny, quaint home bursting with tulips all around the front yard appeared on the screen.

Isaiah's chest squeezed when he saw it. They'd spent so much time together the past few months, but he had never been to her house. He couldn't imagine anything that suited her more perfectly.

She pulled out her phone—he assumed to take a picture—but the image changed before she could capture it.

"Holy smokes! I didn't realize we were making regional news."

"So, this really is that unusual?" Isaiah asked.

"I've never witnessed anything like it. Maybe that master gardener will be able to explain it. The snow melting so suddenly then the tulips popping up and blooming *everywhere*. I have never seen so many. It's like someone planted a bunch of extra bulbs last year without telling anyone."

"Weird," Isaiah said, but his mind wandered from the tulips to whatever was going on in her head. *Is her mind fully made up, or do I still have the opportunity to sway her?* No matter what she had decided, and despite that he couldn't make any guarantees about who he'd been before arriving in Emerald Hollow, he was going to make his intentions about who he was and what he wanted perfectly clear.

"So, I was thinking I should take you on an official first date. Tomorrow? Before we head back to Emerald Hollow?"

He watched her expression carefully, and a shadow passed across her face. His stomach sank. Even though he'd been prepared for it, he was hoping for a different outcome.

She pushed a wet curl behind her ear. "About that... I was thinking we should set some ground rules."

"Ground rules?" Isaiah asked, keeping his voice even. "Like

we're baseball players?" He tried to joke, but he didn't think he'd pulled it off. *Where is she going with this?*

"It's just that we still don't know who you are, where you're from, or who you might have... waiting back home."

Isaiah sat forward. "We've been through this. I'm not in a relationship. I would feel it if I were, just like with all the other things I instinctively know."

"But we can't know for sure. Maybe in your real life, you don't even like women like me."

"Women like you?" His heart melted, and he scooted closer so that their knees were touching. Again, he sensed that her insecurity went deeper than what was going on between them. Someone had hurt her. Something flared in him then, and he had to take a deep breath to ensure he didn't sound angry when he spoke. He wasn't angry with her. But he did want to tackle whoever had made her feel she wasn't good enough. He was angry at *them*. "What do you mean by that?"

Sofia pulled back, breaking their contact. "I just mean that none of this can be real until we know who you are."

Isaiah could tell there was more that she wasn't saying, but he didn't push. "So where does that leave us?"

"We're just going to keep things friendly. Like we have been."

"Sooo, friendly includes what? Hand holding? Kissing? Dates?" He didn't know how far to push it, but he didn't want to completely let her off the hook. He had a feeling fear was operating more than logic.

"Just friend dates and no kissing, just in case..."

Isaiah knew he could never fully convince her of his sincerity until he got his memories back. If she'd been hurt, he could understand why she didn't want to commit.

But what if I never get my memories back? As far as I'm concerned, this is my life now. And Sofia was an integral part of it.

He studied her face, sensing all the conflicting emotions that were warring there. Something stirred in his chest.

Isaiah made his own decision then. He couldn't give her the assurance of a complete history of his old life. But he could show her who he was currently. He could prove that he wasn't the kind of guy who would ever hurt her. And he wanted her to know that she had power in the situation, and he wasn't going to take it from her, no matter what she had experienced before.

"Okay, then. We remain..." He seized on the word she had used. "Friendly. But I want you to know that when you're ready, it's all or nothing for me. I'm not a half-in, casual kind of guy. The next move is on you, Wrecker."

Her jaw dropped, and he stood up and said simply, "See you in the morning."

As he walked away, he could faintly hear the Oregon master gardener talking about the unprecedented tulip bloom in Emerald Hollow, but the words barely registered.

Chapter Thirty-Seven

SOFIA

Sofia screamed into her pillow. She barely noticed the sunlight that streamed through the thin blinds the next morning. *What have I done?* She'd basically told Isaiah to back off, and he'd given her exactly what she'd asked for. *But it wasn't what I actually wanted.* She questioned that thought as soon as it went through her head, and she let out another small, smothered scream.

She emerged from her room uncharacteristically early, having been unable to go back to sleep. She'd dressed and done her makeup with extra care, preparing to slip out to a coffee shop alone, when she spotted Isaiah at the dining room table, a coffee in his hand and another on the table.

She let out a laugh. "Should have known you were an early riser. I'm surrounded by them."

"How'd you sleep?" he asked, his teasing tone telling her he suspected the answer.

"Like an angel," she said primly, taking the second cup from the table and giving the coffee a sip. Her eyes widened when she realized he'd ordered her favorite drink. *Did he pick up on it at the*

Emerald House? "Thanks for this. I'm a zombie in the morning without coffee."

"What are friends for?" Isaiah asked.

She thought he'd put a little too much emphasis on the word *friends* and was torn between wanting to wipe the smirk off his face with a retort and pulling him up into a kiss. *Why is being around him suddenly irresistible?*

Sofia decided on neither, letting out a quick breath and turning away from where he sat looking far too attractive in a new athletic shirt and jeans. Sofia had long suspected he worked out regularly in his real life.

She caught herself as she thought the words. *Does it bother him when I refer to his life outside of Emerald Hollow as his "real life"? But if that isn't what it is, what is it?* Her head began to ache. She'd been through someone living a double life before, and it had nearly destroyed her.

She took a big drink of her coffee and closed her eyes as she took in the familiar taste. *Perfect. That's enough of that.* It was too early in the morning, and she hadn't had enough caffeine to be having those kinds of philosophical conversations with herself.

"So, are we ready to head back to Emerald Hollow?"

"You're the boss," he said, his voice low and exaggeratedly sweet.

Her stomach did a little flip in response as a tiny but vocal part of her wondered if maybe, just maybe, things could be different with Isaiah. If only they could get his memories back.

Chapter Thirty-Eight

ASH

Ash hadn't been surprised when Holly told him she was heading to Finland for a few days to see her friend and the oldest elf, Lumi Kringle. She hadn't said why she was going, but she was still getting used to the new routine of living in Emerald Hollow and not traveling around the world all the time. If going to visit a friend in Finland now and then helped with that adjustment, then he was all for it.

He paused in his living room near the small framed photo he had of himself, his dad, and his mom when he was a child. His parents were each holding one of his hands as he jumped in the air, and the smile on his mom's face was radiant. There was no indication from the photo that she would leave her family in the not-too-distant future.

Ash thought he had resolved his issues with his mom leaving, but since Holly had been in his life, he experienced an ache that the two would never know each other. He had found a truly magical woman he knew his mom would adore, and it was another aspect of his life that she would miss out on entirely.

He extricated himself from his wandering thoughts and left the apartment. His best friend also had a mom missing from her life, though in an entirely different way, and he wanted to see how she was doing. He didn't want her to feel like he was abandoning her since he had Holly, though it hadn't escaped his notice that she'd been spending a lot of time with Isaiah lately.

He pulled Sofia aside toward the end of her shift, just as they were getting ready to close the restaurant for the night. He hadn't seen her since Valentine's Day a few days ago, and he wanted to ask her about her weekend trip.

"Hey, Sof. That was some impressive singing at karaoke. I think you and Isaiah might have a shot at Broadway."

Sofia punched him lightly in the chest. "Ha ha. Where's Holly? I didn't see her today."

"She's traveling again," Ash said, following Holly's philosophy of keeping things close to the truth. The North Pole tradition was that Clauses could tell their partners who they really were, but beyond that, it had to be kept secret. They both hated keeping something from Sofia, but they didn't have another choice. Some secrets were too sacred to share, no matter who it meant keeping in the dark.

"She's such a boss." Sofia waved at the last customer on their way out then began to close out the till.

"How was Ashland?" he asked, wondering why she hadn't already filled him in on every detail, as she normally would have.

Sofia's face twisted into a weird expression, and she let out a heavy sigh. "It was fine."

Ash studied her more closely. Sofia never answered a chance to talk about a trip out of town with only three words. "Did you get Isaiah some new clothes?" he prodded.

"Yep."

"Talkative today, aren't you?"

Sofia's faced relaxed, and she gave him her usual playful smile. "Okay, you got me. It was great until the end. Then things got a little awkward between Isaiah and me."

Ash tensed, and Sofia quickly read the look on his face,

shaking her head. "Not like that. He just kind of... wants to date me, I think."

"Would that be so bad?" Ash had grown to like Isaiah very much, but he could tell that Sofia was holding back with him. He understood that his past was a mystery, so she would hesitate, but everything he had seen from Isaiah so far had been nothing but upstanding character, and Ash thought Isaiah would make a fun friend.

Sofia let out a huff. "Ash, we still don't know who he is. Wouldn't jumping into a relationship with him be a little reckless?"

"I didn't know that much about Holly when I fell for her. Sometimes fate just works these things out." Ash couldn't tell her that magic had had a hand in his and Holly's relationship.

Sofia shook her head. "New topic, please."

Ash grinned and obliged. He knew he couldn't convince Sofia of anything. She would have to convince herself in time. "So, I was thinking..."

"Go ahead. What harebrained idea do you have now?" Sofia didn't even look up from her counting.

"Our last couple of festivals have been really successful. I'd like to keep the momentum going. You know, make Emerald Hollow a festival destination."

"Okay, so what's the next holiday? Fourth of July?"

"I'd like to do something sooner. With these insane tulip blooms we're having right now, I was thinking we could host a tulip festival."

Sofia paused and looked up at him. "A tulip festival? Like they have in Europe?"

Ash hoped he had her. She'd told him about a tulip festival she'd attended when she briefly lived in Germany, and she'd always spoken fondly of it. "Exactly. Not quite as big, but I think we can attract a crowd. There's never been a tulip bloom like this before. If we get the word out on social media and set up some photo ops, I really think it could be something."

Sofia seemed to think about it for a moment, then she nodded. "It's not your worst idea ever. But when do we have it? Tulips only bloom for a couple of weeks at most. We'd have to throw this together really fast."

Ash's mind raced. He couldn't tell her that Holly thought it was the North Pole magic affecting the tulips and that they were likely to bloom much longer than normal.

He averted his eyes, pretending to wipe the counter. "There's a weird soil effect in place this year. The bloom is expected to be longer than normal. But you're right. We'd have to move fast. I'm thinking we host it on the first of March."

Sofia completely stopped what she was doing, and Ash tried not to let her see him sweat.

She looked at him skeptically. "A soil event? Where did you hear about that?"

Ash continued to avoid meeting her eyes. He'd forgotten Sofia was a fairly avid gardener and she knew a thing or two about soil. He racked his brain, and it snagged on something from the previous night. "I think I saw it on the news. Just trust me. Are you in?"

Sofia huffed out a sigh but smiled. "I'm in."

When life gives you magic tulips... Ash thought with a grin as he reached for the mop.

Chapter Thirty-Nine

HOLLY

Holly arrived in Finland and was greeted by much colder air than Emerald Hollow had been experiencing. She made her way to the café that her friend and the oldest elf, Lumi Kringle, owned and operated.

She hadn't been back to Helsinki since she'd discovered that her Finnish friend Lia was in fact an elf from their very own North Pole. Even though Holly had had a few months to digest the information, it was still startling. Up until that revelation, she'd had no idea any of the elves left the North Pole at all. It had been just one of many things about North Pole magic she'd discovered she'd been completely ignorant of.

She had come back to Lumi with a question. The oldest elf knew more than anyone alive about the North Pole and its magic. If anyone would know the answer to what Holly needed to ask, it was her.

The café bells tinkled as Holly stepped inside. She spotted Lumi immediately, sitting at a corner table with a mug in front of her. She smiled when she saw Holly and beckoned her over.

"Holly, dear, how are you?" Lumi signaled to someone behind the counter, and they brought over a pastry and placed it on the table in front of Holly. It was one of her favorites, but she resisted taking a bite for the moment. She wanted to get the conversation out of the way.

Holly studied Lumi. Her golden eyes were hidden behind her glasses, and her elvish ears were suspiciously missing. "It's a little strange being back here now that I know..." They weren't the only ones in the café.

"I'm still me, Holly. I'm glad you came. But what brings you to Finland? I wasn't sure if you'd be back here now that you don't need to travel to collect Cheer."

Holly's brow furrowed. "It's about something you said last year when you were teaching me how to snow tunnel."

Lumi leaned forward slightly. Her expression was serene, but Holly could sense that the question had surprised her.

"What about it? You haven't had the need to snow tunnel again, I hope? The reindeer can still fly?"

"They can. Everything's fine with my magic and the North Pole, as far as I know. I remember you said something about making sure that no humans were nearby when I snow tunneled. That there could be unwanted effects if there were. What did you mean by that?"

Lumi's expression tensed slightly. "Has something happened?"

"I'm not sure." Holly took a deep breath and decided to share everything she knew so far. "On New Year's Eve, my friend Sofia found a man in the woods, lying in the snow. He didn't have anything with him, and he didn't remember where he came from. We've been searching but haven't come across any missing persons reports. It's like he just fell out of the sky. I went to the spot in the woods where he was found, and the strangest sensation came over me." Holly shivered, the memory of the feeling creeping up her spine. "It felt like magic, but something was off about it."

"Mother of bells," Lumi said quietly.

Holly was instantly alert. "What is it?"

Lumi sighed. "I think some of the elves must have started snow tunneling again."

Holly nearly jumped. "But how? You said only the oldest elves knew how to do it. I assume you all know how to do it responsibly."

"Of course we do. But last year, when I taught you how, maybe..." She let Holly fill in the gaps.

"You think someone overheard?"

Lumi nodded. "It's possible. There could be another explanation for the man losing his memory in the woods. But the way you described the magic feeling off in that area... That's what used to happen before, when elves were snow tunneling irresponsibly and humans were affected. It's the reason we stopped passing on the method to the younger elves."

Holly's heart raced, her mind on Isaiah and Sofia. She remembered her first and only time snow tunneling at Christmas the previous year, the feeling of the snow swirling around her and passing through the tunnel, her reindeer at her sides. There had been no humans around then. She'd made sure of that. But maybe a young elf was snow tunneling and didn't know about the side effects to humans.

Her stomach sank. It was all her fault.

There hadn't been a snow tunneling incident in decades. But then she'd asked Lumi to teach her how a few months ago, and this had happened. It couldn't be a coincidence.

"Is there a way to undo it?" she asked, hoping Lumi couldn't hear the degree of desperation in her voice.

Lumi nodded, and Holly relaxed slightly. "We need the elf who cast the snow tunnel the young man experienced the lingering effects of. They can create another tunnel for him to pass through, and that will essentially reverse the process."

"But how? We don't know who did it. Do we put out an announcement at the North Pole and ask whoever did it to come forward? The elves who still don't know about the snow tunneling might be angry that it was kept from them."

"You've been spending too much time with humans, Holly. Do you really think the elves would be angry if we explained why we haven't passed on the snow tunneling secrets? You have a prime example of the consequences there in Emerald Hollow."

Holly took a deep breath, forcing herself to trust Lumi. She knew Lumi was right. The elves' temperament was much different from humans'. And they had no other choice. If Isaiah was ever going to have his memories restored, that was the only way. "Okay, so what next?"

"You go to the North Pole and find out who's been snow tunneling." Lumi stood. "And I'm coming with you."

Chapter Forty

ISAIAH

Isaiah had fallen into a routine in Emerald Hollow before the overnight trip to Ashland with Sofia. He woke up and went for a run then did some push-ups and pull-ups in a usually empty park playground. He wouldn't have been surprised if he'd had a gym membership before, because his desire to work out daily was as natural as the sun rising in the morning. After he'd showered, he did some work around the Emerald House, whatever Ash assigned or something he saw needed to be done.

On days Sofia worked, he grabbed some food at the restaurant during her shift, then they went to the library together. He wasn't sure if Sofia was going to continue joining him on his daily library trips, since he'd thrown the ball of whatever was between them into her court. He hadn't seen her since they'd arrived back in Emerald Hollow the previous day, and he decided maybe he should skip his usual lunch at the café during her shift.

He couldn't decide whether he was skipping seeing her that day because he wanted to playfully keep her on her toes, or if it was something deeper. Sofia had said the real him wouldn't like someone like her. Isaiah had sensed it came from a previous experience of hurt. But her musing had cracked open something that hadn't occurred to him.

What if she *wouldn't like the real* me? For all he knew, he wasn't a good guy, even though his instincts since he'd arrived in Emerald Hollow seemed good. *If I was a good person, with people who cared about me, someone should have come looking for me.*

Being idle with his thoughts was making him restless. He decided to head downtown, hoping to run across something that would distract him. After ten minutes of walking, he passed by the town's museum and spotted some old maps on display in the window. On impulse, he pulled open the door and stepped inside.

"Hello there" came a voice from somewhere to his side.

Isaiah looked to his left to see a man sitting behind a counter with a boy of about ten. The boy was doing something on a cell phone, and the man was peering at a computer screen as if it were a complex puzzle. "Are you here for a tour?"

"I saw the maps in the window and was curious about them."

The man grinned and stuck out a hand. "Ben Hadley. I'm a volunteer here at the museum. This is my son, Henry."

Henry looked up from the phone and gave Isaiah a wave and a smile.

"I'm working on a new map digitization project for the town right now." Ben turned the computer screen so that Isaiah could see it. "We're using some free software, but for the life of me, I can't figure out how it works."

Isaiah leaned in and studied the screen. Automatically, he reached for the mouse and said, "Do you mind?"

"Be my guest," Ben said with surprise.

Isaiah made a few movements with the mouse and typed in some codes he seemed to know naturally, and the scanned map rapidly adjusted to fit the screen.

"Whoa! How'd you do that?"

"Must be something I know how to do," Isaiah said, unexpectedly excited by the skill he'd uncovered.

"Oh right, you're the one Ash and Sofia found out in the woods. You still haven't got any of your memories back?"

Henry looked up in interest.

"Afraid not. But skills and likes or dislikes seem to come back when needed, like in this case."

"I wonder if you used to volunteer at a museum," Ben said with a laugh. "Hey, what are you up to today? I'm closing up here soon, and Henry and I were about to go out and do some geocaching. He's homeschooled, and we give his mom a break every now and then. He's choosing our next spot right now."

Henry held up the phone to show Isaiah the screen. "There's one on a hill in the woods behind the Emerald House that we haven't found yet."

Isaiah stared at the screen, where there was a map and a colorful dot on a location in the woods. "What is geocaching?"

Henry jumped in, talking animatedly. "There are these containers hidden around in the wild. They're all listed on the map here. You navigate to them and look for the container. Usually, they're pretty small. There's a notebook and pencil inside, and you sign your name, showing that you found it. Sometimes, there's trinkets in there, and you can trade one out. We always bring gems to trade out for something."

"Fake gems, obviously," Ben added, smiling at his son. "There are digital geocaches these days, too, but we stick to the traditional physical ones. Emerald Hollow's not that tech savvy yet. What do you say? Do you want to join us?"

Isaiah thought it sounded like as good of a thing to do as any, and the lingering excitement over discovering his skill with the mapping software had him wanting to spend more time on a related project. "Sure. Why not?"

Henry's face broke into a grin.

~

Forty-five minutes later, Henry let out a shout. "I see it!"

Ben and Isaiah had been walking a few yards behind him, searching the ground and the trees for a container. Isaiah looked where Henry was pointing and saw what appeared to be a tiny birdhouse nestled on a tree branch. Henry jumped, but he couldn't reach it.

Ben walked over and retrieved the birdhouse then opened it carefully from the back. "Nice work, Hen."

He pulled out a miniature pencil and notebook and passed it to Isaiah, who wrote his first name and passed it back.

Henry was already sifting through the tiny trinkets. "There's an army guy in here!" He slipped the green figurine into his pocket and replaced it with a bright topaz gem. "Do you want to take something?" he asked Isaiah.

"I don't have anything to swap it with."

"That's all right," Ben said, pulling a gem out of his pocket. "We'll throw in an extra one."

Isaiah took the tiny birdhouse from Henry's outstretched hand and felt inside. He touched a smooth, round surface, and he pulled the object out. It was a silver coin slightly larger than a quarter, and the words "Not all who wander are lost" were engraved on it. His palm seemed to warm as the coin sat in it, like it was giving off energy. Isaiah blinked, and the warmth was gone. He wondered if he had imagined it.

Isaiah stared at the coin, unable to explain the effect the words were having on him. His chest tightened as he read the words a second time. It was like the coin had been placed there exactly for him.

His thoughts were interrupted when Henry asked, "Is it a coin?"

Isaiah showed it to the boy, who read the inscription then said, "Cool."

"Well, I guess we're all set here. We can mark this one off our list. Good job, Hen."

Ben Hadley and his son high-fived, and Isaiah grinned. The outing had been funner than he'd expected, and the words on the coin had lifted his spirits.

Sofia had never explicitly told him the details of the new jewelry line she'd launched after he arrived, but he'd searched for her website out of curiosity one day at the library and had seen the popular collection titled WanderLost. It was so similar to the quote on the coin he'd just found that he didn't feel it could be a coincidence.

Maybe his being in Emerald Hollow wasn't just random. Maybe he had a purpose. *If only I can get Sofia to see it that way too.*

"You've got a knack for navigation," Ben observed as they made their way out of the woods toward the Emerald House. Isaiah had helped the father and son reorient themselves on a few occasions as they'd sought out the birdhouse. "Might be connected to your skills with that mapping software."

"Might be," Isaiah said, experiencing a lightness that had been gone since Sofia had broken away from their kiss. As the Emerald House came into sight, he found himself smiling, thinking that maybe his situation wasn't impossible after all.

Chapter Forty-One

HOLLY

Lumi rode in the sleigh with Holly from Helsinki, and as soon as the North Pole was in sight, they both knew something was amiss.

"The buttercups!" Holly exclaimed.

Lumi pursed her lips.

The North Pole, which was normally covered in snow year-round, was bursting with brilliant yellow buttercups. The fields stretched as far as the eye could see, the land a swath of bright yellow.

"Have you ever seen this so early before?" Holly asked as the sleigh landed at the reindeer stables.

"We always get buttercups bursting through the snow in the spring, but to this extent, and this early... I have seen it before, but it's been a long time."

Holly was about to say something when she noticed Clementine, the elf mayor, approaching the sleigh through the light-covered walkway. "Clementine, is everything okay?"

The mayor inclined her head and raised an eyebrow as if to point out the obvious. "We're having a bit of a super bloom here."

Holly's mind flashed to Emerald Hollow. Ash had described the tulips as a super bloom too. She'd told him that she thought her magic might have something to do with the early and extreme blooming of the flowers in Emerald Hollow, but she'd never imagined that it might be happening at the North Pole as well.

"We're having one in Emerald Hollow too."

"Do you think it's a side effect of your living there mostly full time now?" Clementine asked, her posture rigid. "Is it an overabundance of magic?"

"I thought that might be the case for Emerald Hollow, but why would that change things here?"

Simultaneously, Holly and Clementine turned to Lumi Kringle. The oldest elf let out a little sigh and looked around. They could see some of the Keyblar elves tending to the reindeer near the stables.

"Not here," she said under her breath, and they turned to walk toward Merriment Square.

~

A FEW MINUTES LATER, LUMI, CLEMENTINE, AND Holly were all settled in Holly's home. The large fire was roaring despite the springlike weather, but the temperature was always comfortable in the North Pole. The fireplace was more for ambiance than for heat, as tied to the North Pole magic as anything else.

"Okay, Lumi, what are you thinking? You said you'd seen this before?"

Lumi nodded and took a sip of her spiced cider before setting it down to look at them both. "Remember how I told you that snow tunneling got out of hand in the past and that was the reason the elder elves shut it down for the younger generation?"

Holly nodded. Clementine looked confused, her golden eyes thoughtful, but she didn't say anything.

"Back in those days, too much snow tunneling could have effects both at the North Pole and where the snow tunnel was connected. Usually, the impacts on the human side were not noticeable, unless a human was too close to the tunnel." She looked directly at Holly then. "That's what I warned you about when you had to use the snow tunnel to come back last Christmas."

Holly nodded, her face solemn. "No one was around, Lumi."

"I know. I don't think this is from that." Lumi filled Clementine in on what they had discussed in Finland, that they thought some of the younger elves had learned how to snow tunnel.

Shocked, Clementine asked, "You think elves have been snow tunneling out of the North Pole without my knowing about it?"

Lumi's face was impassive as she said, "I've been doing it for decades along with a few other elder elves. And as you know, there haven't been any side effects at the North Pole. I'm very skilled and very careful. If some younger elves learned how, though, without any proper training or guidance, it would explain what we're seeing here. So now we need to figure out who's been snow tunneling. We think it may also be connected to a problem someone in Emerald Hollow is having."

Holly explained the sudden appearance of Isaiah in the woods of Emerald Hollow and that he had no memories of where he came from or who he was.

Clementine's face creased with worry. "If that's true, this is very serious. I'm going to investigate this immediately."

"Is there anything you want me to do?" Holly asked. She liked to leave the elf mayor to her purview over the North Pole, and she had always trusted Clementine to run things in her stead. She didn't want to step on any slippers.

"I don't want to draw too much attention to this just yet," Clementine decided then turned to Lumi. "But I could use your help. I think you'll have a better idea of where to search for who is doing this."

Lumi nodded. "I can get started immediately."

The two firmed up their plans while Holly listened, and they all agreed it was best if she returned to Emerald Hollow while they carried out their investigation to try to keep things as normal as possible.

Holly stopped by the North Post in Merriment Square on her way out and pressed her palm against the snowflake on the post. Her hand tingled as the Cheer she'd collected in Emerald Hollow discharged into the post. The North Pole had nearly met disaster the previous year when she had failed to collect Cheer that could charge the post and power the whole of the North Pole and its dream-making operations.

Holly breathed a sigh of relief as the post continued to glow at full brightness. At least the side effects of the snow tunneling had not affected her Cheer. The buttercup blooms themselves might not even be a huge concern on their own, but the issue with Isaiah was another matter.

Holly knew her best friend was falling for him, and he for her. For both their sakes, she needed to get Isaiah's memories restored. If their relationship—or whatever was going on between them—was going to continue in earnest, Isaiah needed to remember his past, and the two needed to figure out what their life was going to look like going forward. None of that could happen while he had no memories of who he was before he'd arrived in Emerald Hollow.

Holly waved to the elves in Merriment Square as she headed back up the path to the stables. She could trust Clementine and

Lumi to sort things out at the North Pole. But the side effects in Emerald Hollow were another story. She suddenly longed to be back there, taking a stroll through the woods with Comet and discussing everything with Ash.

Chapter Forty-Two

SOFIA

A week had passed since Sofia and Isaiah returned from their overnight shopping trip to Ashland, and Isaiah had gone dark. He was no longer having lunch in her booth during her shift, and he hadn't once asked her to accompany him to the library.

She'd only seen him twice that week, and both times, he'd been talking to the attractive female barista on the coffee shop side of the Emerald House. Sofia had thought that steam might be coming out of her ears, but she walked by quickly, hoping he hadn't seen her.

Sofia had worked a rare morning shift, and she took off her apron with relief, ready to call it a day. She filled a paper cup with drip coffee to take with her. "Two o'clock's not too late for coffee, right?" she asked her coworker Marissa, who was just coming in to replace her.

"Never," Marissa said with a wink.

Sofia took a large drink. She was preparing to head out when she stopped short at the sight of Isaiah leaning against the counter, looking far too good in an athleisure outfit she'd picked out for him.

"Wrecker," Isaiah said in greeting, his eyes crinkling in amusement.

Sofia tried to ignore how the sight of those eye crinkles made her want to see that expression again and again. "What are you doing here?"

"Am I not allowed to stop in for a cup of coffee?"

"I thought you got that from the *coffee shop* these days." She looked him straight in the eye.

A grin spread over his face, and he took a step back to look her up and down. "Is someone jealous?"

She pursed her lips and took a sip of her drink, deciding to change the subject. If he'd intended to make her jealous, it had worked. But he didn't need to know that. "So, is the impasse over?"

"No. But I didn't say no contact. Just that we're only friends unless you decide otherwise. There's something I'd like to do today as *friends*."

"Okaaay," she said, her curiosity defeating her stubbornness in the battle of two of her stronger emotions.

Isaiah looked down at her feet. "Good, you're not wearing heels."

Sofia raised an eyebrow. "Hey, you know you like me in heels."

Isaiah's eyes flashed with delight, and the side of his mouth twitched. Her stomach did a flip. "I certainly do. But it's not the appropriate footwear for today."

"Oh no. Please tell me we're not going hiking." Sofia had already warned him that when she'd found him that day in the woods, that was a once-a-year outing for her.

"Not exactly," he said evasively.

Sofia narrowed her eyes at him, though anticipation trickled through her. She hadn't admitted it to herself, but she'd missed him all week, and she was glad he had finally turned up again—and that she hadn't had to go groveling to him.

She didn't regret the decision she'd made to remain friends, but the reality of it was becoming more and more impossible with each minute she spent with him. She was drawn to him like a hummingbird to nectar.

"Fine. I'm trusting you. I take it we're going in my car?" she asked, turning back toward the door.

"You got it." He followed her out, and they settled in her Subaru. Sofia took a moment to enjoy a few sips of her coffee before she put the car in drive.

"All right, Mr. Mysterious. Where to?"

"I'm going to need your phone."

Sofia eyed him warily but pulled her phone out of her purse, unlocked it, and handed it to him. She looked over and saw he was downloading an app. She put the car back in park.

"Geocaching?"

"You know what it is?"

"I've heard of it, but no, not really."

Isaiah launched into a tale of meeting Ben and Henry Hadley at the museum and finding a birdhouse geocache in the woods behind the Emerald House. He talked animatedly, and Sofia was glad he'd seemed to find something he enjoyed doing that week, even if it was without her. If he was ever going to get his memories back, it wasn't going to happen through sitting around at the Emerald House all day.

Then Isaiah mentioned that he'd been skilled with the mapping software Ben Hadley had been using at the museum.

Sofia's eyes widened with surprise. "Really? That sounds like one of the strongest intuitions you've had yet. That has to be a good sign that your memories are coming back, right?" She tried not to sound too hopeful, but the news excited her.

She'd put them back in the friend zone but only because she wanted to focus on finding out who he was and getting his memories back. The news felt like the first solid step toward that, and hope bloomed in her chest as instantaneously as the tulips had in her yard.

"I have to admit it felt really good. Like a piece of me clicked into place."

"That's amazing, Isaiah," Sofia said, warmth infused in her voice.

They locked eyes for a moment, then Isaiah cleared his throat and spoke.

"Back to the geocaching."

Sofia nodded, the sizzle of the moment dying down but not completely. "So, we're going to... go traipsing through the woods, looking for a birdhouse?"

"Give me a little credit," Isaiah said. The app finished downloading, and he began studying a map on the screen. "According to this, there are five hidden on or around Main Street. We can eat, find them, do a little shopping, see if anything triggers my memory..."

Sofia immediately put the car in drive and whipped it out of the parking lot.

"What was that for?" Isaiah asked, grinning.

"For not making me tromp around in the woods."

Sofia kept her back straight and didn't even crack a grin as she sped toward Main Street. She cheered herself on her restraint because she could see that devilish smile of his out of the corner of her eye, and her stomach flipped at the sight.

THEY FOUND THE FIRST FOUR GEOCACHES QUICKLY, with Isaiah navigating, but he'd passed the baton to her for the last one, insisting she give it a try.

"What? Don't think you can handle it?" he'd asked, and that was all it had taken for her to pluck her phone from his hand and begin walking north.

After circling around a block of four buildings for ten minutes, Sofia sank onto a bench and let out a huff. "They must have removed it," she said, closing the app.

"Giving up so easily?" Isaiah asked, one arm resting against the building as he stood beside her, his biceps looking like those of a Greek god.

Sofia quickly averted her eyes. "It's not giving up if it doesn't exist. It's just good sense."

"Willing to make another bet on it?" Isaiah's eyes crinkled at the corners, a mischievous smile on his lips.

Sofia sighed in exasperation. "There are no more karaoke nights scheduled in Emerald Hollow for a while, you know."

"How about we lower the stakes? Winner gets to choose the movie we watch after we find all of these. I have no memories of any specific movie, but I have a feeling I don't like rom-coms."

Sofia jumped to her feet, thinking of the new, sappy romantic comedy she'd been wanting to see for months. Isaiah would hate it. *Perfect.* She stuck out her hand. "You're on."

They shook, and Isaiah held on a second too long, locking his eyes onto hers, that mischievous expression still there. Then he took the phone from her other hand and began to navigate.

He walked around for a minute then stopped in front of a lamppost. Sofia inched closer, wondering why he had paused. He reached for a combination lock on a small silver box attached to the post and opened it.

"No way!" she shouted, moving closer to look inside. The box was tiny, but a few trinkets were crammed inside. "I didn't think they could just be attached to a pole like that."

Isaiah grinned at her. "I saw a poster for a thriller when we walked by the movie theater," he said as he relocked the box. "Hope you like jump scares."

Chapter Forty-Three

SOFIA

Sofia sat on her couch late that evening, preparing a special jewelry line for the tulip festival. Her mind was on Isaiah as she feverishly beaded and assembled wires.

She hadn't admitted it to him, but she'd had fun geocaching, a hobby she'd never thought she would enjoy. Then she had jumped, screamed, and covered her eyes in the movie more times than she cared to admit, but she'd liked the excuse to snuggle her face into Isaiah's shoulder a few times and even grabbed his hand at one point.

Maybe scary movies aren't so bad, she thought, though she'd turned on something decidedly not scary to wash away the thriller's plot while she worked. Reality TV could drown out any lingering fictional fear.

She'd dropped him off at the Emerald House after he'd made sure she wasn't too scared to drive home alone. She insisted she was fine, and they said good night. Sofia had tried to swallow her disappointment as she drove home that they didn't currently have any plans to hang out again.

And whose fault is that? she thought with exasperation. *Is it really worth it to fight the pull we seem to have toward each other?*

What if Isaiah's instincts are right, and he really doesn't have a significant other out there somewhere?

Noah's face flashed across her mind then, and she shuddered. *No, it's better to be safe than sorry.*

Sofia finished a pair of red tulip earrings and carefully packaged them for sale. Ash had been working at his usual rapid pace to spread word about the tulip festival and get things into place, and they were expecting a great turnout. Ever since Holly had worked her decorating magic at the fall festival and again at the Christmas Faire, people were clamoring for a chance to attend an Emerald Hollow event.

The Emerald House was already booked up for the event days, and online ticket sales gave them a rough head count. Still, they were going to allow same-day sales for a few dollars more, so they couldn't be certain of the exact number to expect.

Sofia put aside the earrings and looked at the sketch of a belt buckle she'd been toying with. She'd never made a belt buckle before, and if she was going to add them to her line, she needed to do it right. She'd been doing research and had started creating one, but she'd ended up taking it apart in a fit of frustration. She flicked off the TV, allowing herself to be silent with her thoughts for once.

The belt buckle brought her mind right back to Isaiah. She wished she had a crystal ball and could see what would happen when they eventually figured out who he was. Another thought crept in then and filled her with icy sadness. *What if we never figure it out?* It had been nearly two months, and they hadn't had any leads beyond Isaiah's flashes of instinct.

Sofia's ruminations were interrupted by the sound of a soft tinkling at her window. She pulled back the curtain and was shocked to see, under the illumination of her porch light, a pair of hummingbirds hovering around her birdfeeder. Brilliant flecks of green and blue feathers reflected the light, making them look magical against the night sky behind them.

She put a hand to her chest. Sofia had kept the feeder full since she'd moved in and installed it, but in all the years she'd had it hanging there, she'd never once attracted a hummingbird. Suddenly, there were two—and late at night, at the one time when the house was utterly quiet and she was still awake to hear them. *What are the chances?*

A shiver went up her arms, and she swallowed the lump that was forming in her throat. The hummingbird was her mom's favorite animal, and she'd always claimed that it symbolized love and luck. *Seeing one is a sign to take a risk, because it means blessing will be on you.* Her mom's frequent phrase came to her, and for the first time since she had passed, not one but *two* hummingbirds had found their way to her.

Sofia wiped her eyes and swallowed hard. Something shifted in her then, and she continued to watch the hummingbirds. If her mom were there, she would tell her to give love a chance and to not compare every man to Noah. The hummingbirds were the closest sign of her mom's presence she had ever experienced since her passing. She couldn't let her mom down, not when she had so clear of an opportunity to take her wisdom and do something with it.

The birds flitted around for a few more seconds then darted away into the darkness.

"Okay, Mom, have it your way," she whispered and prayed that wouldn't be the last time she would see those birds.

Sofia's phone rang, and she lunged to answer it, nearly jumping out of her skin at the loud noise after the otherworldly few moments that had just occurred. "Hey, Ash," she said, struggling to keep her voice calm. She'd just had something akin to an out-of-body experience, and it took her a few moments to recover.

"Hey, Sof. Holly's back from her trip. She wants to get together. Can you do dinner this week?"

Sofia had calmed down a little while he spoke, and her mind

was sparking. Despite her fighting against it, it was time to take a chance. If the hummingbirds weren't enough to convince her, nothing would be.

She thought over the past few weeks with Isaiah—of sitting in the library, near enough to sense each other's presence but doing their own thing; of the karaoke night, when the music had suddenly changed and he'd appeared on stage with a microphone; of shopping and laughing together; of that moment at the park when the kites had tied them together as if they'd had a will of their own; and finally, of a simple, sweet day geocaching with him that had been as fun and natural as spending time with a childhood friend.

She remembered all the times and ways he had teased her and how he seemed to love when she teased him back. He'd been driving her crazy the past few days, giving her space but also making himself known in not-so-obvious ways that had plagued her, like talking to the barista when she was around. Everything about him seemed to infuriate and delight her all at once.

Maybe it's my turn to drive him *crazy. Perhaps that's not such a bad thing after all.*

And hanging out as a group of friends would be a good excuse to get together again.

"I have a better idea," Sofia said to Ash, doing a quick search on her phone for show times.

"I'm all ears."

Chapter Forty-Four

SOFIA

The next day, Sofia, Isaiah, Holly, and Ash met at the Emerald House to drive to the cabaret. Before they climbed into Ash's truck, Sofia pulled Isaiah aside for a whispered conversation.

Ever since her encounter with the hummingbirds the previous night, she'd committed to going with her old instinct of acting with her heart rather than her brain. That instinct had been crushed by Noah, but she was determined to try to mend it, for her mom's sake and for her own.

The plan she'd come up with was a little juvenile, but at that moment, with Isaiah looking at her like he was, she couldn't find it in herself to care. She took a deep breath and plowed ahead.

"I have an idea," she said when Isaiah had followed her a few steps away from the vehicle, out of earshot of Holly and Ash. Her heart was hammering, and she didn't know if it was more from nerves or exhilaration. Either way, she was pretty sure Isaiah wasn't going to be expecting what she was about to say. "We're going to make tonight into a trial run."

"A trial run? Of what?" Isaiah kept his face neutral but curious.

"We're going to act like we're a couple and see what happens."

"So... we're pretending?" Isaiah asked, raising an eyebrow at her though smiling. "You're okay with pranking your friends like that?"

"It's a *trial*, not a prank. Just to see how things go when we escape Emerald Hollow for a night with more than just the two of us. It might be a total disaster, and we can cut our losses. Besides, Ash is owed a little mischief after he told you about my karaoke phobia and let you use it against me."

"I didn't—" Isaiah began, but Sofia waved him off.

"You rescued me like a white knight. Yes, I remember. So are we doing this?"

"What exactly does 'this'"—Isaiah put air quotes around the word—"entail?"

Sofia thought for a moment. "We just start... acting like a couple. I'm sure you've been in a relationship before, on the other side." She'd decided to stop referring to the time before he'd lost his memories as his real life. It didn't feel right anymore. "The other side" was the only thing that seemed to fit. And Sofia was trying to allow herself to focus on *this side*, for once. Because maybe, for the rest of Isaiah's life, that was the only side there was.

Sofia was waiting for an answer, her heart sinking as she began to think he was going to say no, when Isaiah slipped his arms around her waist and dipped her within the span of what felt like a nanosecond. Her breath caught.

He brought his face close to hers, until their lips were centimeters from each other. Sofia thought her heart was going to hammer out of her chest. But then he grinned and pulled up, carefully drawing her back to both feet and taking a step back.

Sofia could hardly breathe, much less speak.

"What's the matter?" Isaiah asked, shoving his hands into

the pockets of his long-sleeved flannel shirt, his eyes sparking. "Was the show not supposed to start until we left town?"

Heat flushed Sofia's cheeks, but she raised her head and looked him squarely in the eye. She was still flustered, so she couldn't manage to say much, but her brain formed three words, and she delivered them as crisply and clearly as the spring day: "Game on, *Lover*."

Chapter Forty-Five
SOFIA

"Are you finally going to tell us what show we're seeing?" Ash asked after they had merged onto the freeway. Holly was driving, as usual.

Sofia was distracted by the glances Isaiah kept throwing in her direction in the back seat, but she managed to formulate a response. "I'll give you a clue. We've watched the movie together."

Ash threw up his hands. "What movie *haven't* we seen together?"

"No fair," Holly piped up. "You know I haven't seen a lot of movies. And neither has Isaiah."

"Another hint?" Ash probed.

"I already gave it to you."

"What?" Ash asked, confused.

"I already gave you the other hint," Sofia insisted.

"You're impossible."

"I guess you'll find out when we get there, then," Sofia said, a mischievous thrill coursing through her. For better or for worse, she and Isaiah were going to give what they'd been feeling a chance that evening.

From the other side of the back seat, Isaiah took her hand, threading her fingers between his. Sofia thought she saw Holly notice it from the rearview mirror.

"All right, let's get the elephant in the room out of the way before we get to the show," she announced.

"What elephant?" Holly asked, her voice sweet as ever.

"The one where I respond to the question both of you are too polite to ask. Yes, Isaiah and I are giving things a shot. It was clear that I'm irresistible, and I got tired of saying no."

Isaiah barked a laugh. Holly covered her grin with a hand.

Ash shook his head. "You always tell it like it is, Sof. Isaiah, anything you want to add? You all right, man? She's a handful."

Sofia gently smacked Ash's arm.

Isaiah laughed. "I like a handful," he said, turning his eyes to Sofia.

Sofia thought her insides might be melting. As much as she talked big and teased about being irresistible, she still couldn't understand why Isaiah was so interested in her. He was confident, kind, hilarious... but those were things she'd thought Noah was, too, at least until she discovered what he was really like.

She tried to halt her thoughts, not wanting to let her insecurities about the situation arise. If they were going to give it a shot, she couldn't let Noah continue to creep into the way she thought about Isaiah.

It's just a trial run, she reminded herself. *You can do this.* She flicked her eyes up to Isaiah and found him looking at her.

"Okay, okay. No need to steam up the back windows with your eyes," Ash said.

Sofia bit her bottom lip playfully before tearing her gaze from Isaiah's face. *It doesn't help that he's gorgeous,* she thought as she tried to steady the flips in her stomach.

They found a parking spot in the busy little city by sheer luck again and began the short walk through the downtown streets to the cabaret. Sofia handed her phone to the usher to scan their tickets, and they made their way inside.

A large *Clue* poster was hanging in the lobby, and some of the other guests were dressed up as Miss Scarlet, Professor Plum, and other characters from the board game and movie.

Ash grinned and turned to her. "We're seeing *Clue*," he said, clearly delighted. It was one of their favorites. They rewatched it every October.

"Do you have any idea what this is?" Isaiah faux whispered to Holly.

She smiled and shook her head. "Not a clue."

"Ha ha." Sofia grabbed Isaiah's hand. It felt so natural to fit her hand in his. She tugged him forward. "Come on. Let's go find our seats."

"MAYBE WE NEED TO BE MORE LIKE THEM TO HELP discover your identity," Sofia suggested as they walked out of the theater a few hours later. The sky had darkened while they were inside, and the faint light of stars glittered overhead.

"What?" Isaiah asked, aghast. "Running around in the dark, speaking at a hundred miles per hour?"

Sofia rolled her eyes. "Well, I wouldn't mind splitting into teams and exploring a dark abandoned house with you," she teased.

"You two are terrible," Ash said, coming up behind Holly and wrapping his arms around her shoulders. He nuzzled his face against her ear.

"Oh, *we're* terrible? Look at you two canoodling like a Hallmark card."

Holly reddened a little but smiled, her cherry-red lips forming the perfect bow. Sofia grinned as well, and Isaiah reached out and took her hand. She felt secure with the warmth of his hand encircling hers. As far as trial runs were concerned, they were off to a good start.

"Where to next? The night is still young." She broke free from Isaiah and did a little twirl.

"Young for those who sleep in until ten every day. I've got to be up early tomorrow. We have a shipment coming in with decor for the tulip festival," Ash said.

"You're such a buzzkill." Sofia sighed, but there was no heat behind it. She inclined her head toward Isaiah. "Romeo, take me to my carriage."

Isaiah laughed and put his arm around her shoulders. He leaned close and whispered into her ear, "As you wish, my lady."

Sofia's stomach clenched, butterflies she hadn't experienced in years filling her entire midsection. She couldn't help but be cautiously optimistic at how the night had gone. Going on a double date with her best friends was a dream come true. Everything about the evening had felt entirely natural.

And he's not Noah, she told herself. The part that warned her, *You don't know who he is,* was quickly getting quieter.

Like Holly had for Ash, Isaiah seemed to have fallen out of the sky into Emerald Hollow, tailor-made for her. *Maybe there doesn't have to be a catch.* She leaned into him a little closer as they walked side by side, praying that it wasn't all too good to be true.

WHEN THEY GOT BACK TO THE EMERALD HOUSE later, Ash and Holly went ahead, prepared to let Comet out and take him for a quick walk. Sofia and Isaiah lingered by her car. She wasn't ready for the night to end.

The evening had been so perfect, and that scared her as much as thrilled her. She didn't want to overthink the situation, but she couldn't help it. If she forced herself to be cautious with her heart, as she had been for so many years, she would miss out on all the fun that, deep in her bones, she knew was something unique to them. But if she wasn't cautious, they could both get in too deep and be unable to get out when he got his memories back.

Neither route was easy, and she still wasn't sure that what she was doing was right. But between the hummingbird sign and the night they'd just had, the scales had clearly tipped to one side.

Being with Isaiah was like being at a concert you didn't want to end. Every new song seemed to be better than the last, to the point that you thought the next moment could never top what you'd just experienced, yet somehow, it did. Maybe their concert didn't have to end.

"What's going through your mind? Another plan to keep everyone guessing?" Isaiah interrupted her thoughts, taking her hand and drawing her close.

"Not everyone."

"Just me?"

"I'm not the one keeping you guessing."

"Was there anything about my actions tonight that required guessing?" He tucked one of her constantly loose curls behind her ear.

"Oh no, your actions were crystal clear. But maybe you're an actor on the other side," she said playfully. She had to press the issue one more time, then she knew she was ready to let it go.

Isaiah let out a sharp laugh. "You're unbelievable."

"What I'm saying is... are we really doing this?"

"What's 'this'?"

Sofia rolled her eyes, but she didn't give a teasing retort that time. She wanted a serious answer. "I don't want to get off the ride yet."

He gently lifted both hands to the sides of her face, seeming to study every freckle as his gaze worked his way to her eyes. "Then don't."

Chapter Forty-Six

HOLLY

"Isaiah and Sof sure seem to be going full steam ahead," Holly observed as they took Comet for a late-evening walk and stopped to give her reindeer a treat.

"I wouldn't expect anything less from her in other aspects of her life but..."

Holly waited, wondering where his line of thought was heading.

"She's been very reserved in her relationships since she moved back here. She hasn't really done any serious dating. At first, I thought it had to do with her mom being sick then passing away, but as the years went on..."

Holly watched his face, seeing his unease in the tightness of his brow.

"I've kind of wondered if something happened while she was in the military. I've never asked her directly, and she hasn't brought it up. She just tends to joke around when anyone asks her about her relationship status."

Holly's heart sank. In her adult life, as she'd traveled around the world, collecting Cheer to power the North Pole and all its magic, she focused on happy emotions and ran away at the first inkling of anything negative. It was the way her magic functioned. She had a hard time processing all the hurt that humans could do to one another. And the idea of anyone hurting Sofia, her fun, vibrant best friend, was heartbreaking.

"Then there's the fact that she was so suspicious of him at first," Ash said, bringing Holly back to the moment.

Holly wondered if it was the right time to share what she'd really been doing in Finland, and she readied herself to speak, but Ash continued his thought.

"It might stem from the hospital visit when Isaiah first arrived. We have really limited resources here in Emerald Hollow, and Sofia was often worried about getting the right level of care when her mom was sick. I think the idea of someone faking an illness or injury and taking those resources from someone who needed them really got to her."

"But she doesn't think he's faking it anymore."

"She's spent too much time with him now to think that anyone could be that good of an actor."

"And there's some kind of pull between them, like there was between us," Holly noted, warmth spreading through her body.

Ash stopped walking and pulled her in close. "Nobody has a pull between them like us."

Holly grinned as she leaned into his chest.

"But there's definitely a spark there," he admitted. "I've never seen Sofia like this. I really hope Isaiah's intuitions are right, and that there isn't someone else in his life. I just wish I could do something more to help get his memories back."

"About that," Holly said, pulling back to study his face. "There's something I need to tell you."

Then she shared everything she knew.

Chapter Forty-Seven

SOFIA

The week leading up to the tulip festival flew by. Before Sofia knew it, she was loading the back of her car with folding tables and bins for her stall. She'd created mounds of earrings plus some bracelets, necklaces, and rings and designed some new display pieces to lean into the tulip and floral theme.

She finished loading the car and began the drive to the Emerald House, where she was picking up Isaiah, who was going to help her set up her booth. She caught herself grinning as she thought of spending a whole day with him, and she tried to settle her expression as she pulled up. He was waiting outside, leaning casually against the wall, looking like a male model.

She rolled down the window and shouted, "'Get in, loser! We're going shopping!'"

Isaiah gave her a bewildered expression but smiled as he walked toward the car. The look made her insides feel like freshly warmed butter.

"I have no idea what that meant, but I'm sure it's a quote from a movie," Isaiah said as he slid into the passenger side. The seat was already scooted back all the way from his sitting there on their trips to the library and all the time they'd had together since then. His long legs took up most of the space in front of his seat.

Sofia sighed. "I always forget that your pop culture memory only includes what I've shown you so far. That one is a *Mean Girls* reference."

"*Mean Girls?*" Isaiah raised an eyebrow.

Sofia navigated out of the parking lot. "I'm not even going to try to explain it. So, how did Ash seem this morning? Did you see him? Is he losing it?"

"I did see him. He was moving fast, as usual, but Holly was with him, and together, they seemed to have things under control."

"She's really helped to calm down some of his overanxiousness. He actually lets her help him with things. It doesn't hurt that she's a whizz with decorating either. I can't wait to see the clearing."

Sofia parked her car along the path that led to the meadow and opened the trunk, revealing the boxes and bins that were crammed inside.

Isaiah whistled. "Think you brought enough stuff?"

"You won't be laughing when I sell it all and buy you dinner with the profits." She reached for a fold-up wagon from the top of the stack and started to assemble it on the ground, ready for loading.

"Can't argue with that one," Isaiah admitted. He grabbed a folding table and looked toward the clearing. "That way?"

Sofia nodded. She finished loading her rolling wagon then followed him. A smile spread from ear to ear as she stepped into the clearing. Her memory flashed to the previous fall, when Holly had created a gorgeous harvest arch to welcome people into the clearing for the fall festival.

For the tulip festival, there were giant barrels filled with flowers surrounding the entrance on either side. Connecting them was a massive arched trellis that had been laced through with brilliant bright flowers. Straight through it, on the far side of the field of tulips that covered the clearing, was a miniature version of a Dutch windmill.

The whole scene was straight out of a magazine. Sofia could already picture the line that would form to get a picture with that view as the backdrop. She made a mental note to get a picture there for her business social media accounts before the festival started.

Isaiah already had the table in place in one of the empty vendor stalls, and Sofia paused to watch him as he took in the massive field of flowers. Her heart leaped when he turned and caught sight of her.

"Is this stall okay? I grabbed the first open one I saw."

"Yep," she said, dragging the wagon the rest of the way. They unloaded it together, then Isaiah went to get another load while Sofia began to set up her stall. She tuned out everything, barely stopping to say hi as another vendor began to fill the stall next to hers. She was meticulous about setting up her display.

It took nearly an hour before she'd placed it all exactly as she wanted. Isaiah had brought over the last few loads, then he'd seemingly disappeared, probably noticing that she preferred to get in the zone and set everything up herself. Once it was ready, she snapped out of her near trance and looked around for him.

She caught sight of his tall frame near the arched trellis entrance as he talked to Holly and Ash. Holly cast a glance her way and smiled when she noticed Sofia looking at her.

Is this how it could be? Sofia thought as she watched the three of them. *The four of us, like this?* She smiled at the thought and began to walk their way but was interrupted by Matilda, a local woman who sold handcrafted soy candles.

"He's sure a handsome one," Matilda said, eying Isaiah.

Sofia grinned. "You think?" She couldn't help fishing.

"First that beautiful Holly shows up last year, and now we

have this young man. Emerald Hollow doesn't usually attract folks their age, but I'm glad it has. They've both brought a lot to the town."

Sofia turned to Matilda, confused. "What do you mean?" She knew what Holly had brought to the town, with her miraculous decorations and constantly helping with town events, but the tulip festival was the first time Isaiah had helped at a town event.

"Ben says he's been a huge help at the museum, digitizing all the town's old maps, and claims he has quite a knack for it. And Henry's fond of him. Apparently, his navigation skills are better than my husband's." Matilda laughed.

Sofia's eyes widened. Isaiah had told her about his first time going to the museum and how he'd ended up geocaching with Ben and Henry, but she hadn't known he'd been back and was helping with a project there.

Isaiah looked over and must have noticed she was done setting up, because he said something to Holly and Ash then began to walk toward her. Matilda gave Sofia a wink and went back to her stall.

"What were you and Matilda talking about?" Isaiah asked when he reached her.

"Oh, so you admit you know her?"

Isaiah raised his eyebrows. "Am I not supposed to?"

"I was just curious *how* you knew her."

"Oh, uh—" Isaiah ran a hand through his hair and looked away for a second. "That day I went geocaching with Ben Hadley and his son, you remember how I told you that I was familiar with the mapping software he was using? It was the closest hint I'd had to my identity, and I really enjoyed doing it, so I offered to continue helping Ben with the project of digitizing their old maps. He showed me their process, and now I drop in a couple of times a week to help while you're working. I've been able to make their system much more sophisticated than it was. It hasn't sparked any new memories yet, but I'm hopeful."

Impressed, Sofia said, "I'm sure Ben appreciates the help. Do you think you used that software in your job?"

"It's possible. Or maybe in school? I obviously learned it somewhere." He shrugged and turned to look at her display. "Wow, this is incredible."

"Thanks. I really leaned into the tulip theme. I hope people will love it."

"They will," Isaiah said so confidently that Sofia grabbed his hands and planted a kiss on his cheek.

"So, what were you, Ash, and Holly talking about while I was setting up?"

"Oh, that. They want me to meet a friend of theirs tomorrow. Something about helping me get my identity back. He's a specialist in that sort of thing or something. I didn't totally understand, but I figured I should meet the guy."

Sofia's eyes narrowed, and she turned to where Ash and Holly were greeting the visitors who were starting to pour in. Holly was wearing a stunning tulip-red dress and had flowers weaved into a crown in her hair. Sofia softened slightly, but a sense of wariness passed over her. *Why didn't they mention this to me?*

"Sof, are you okay?" Isaiah asked, and she realized she'd been staring at nothing for too long.

"Yeah, I just... Did they say where this guy came from? It seems kind of out of nowhere."

"I was surprised, too, but you and I have kind of hit a dead end with our research. Aside from the mapping software, I haven't had any another real leads. Maybe a specialist will help us figure out what to do next."

Us. The tightness in her chest loosened a bit.

"You're right. Well, I hope he can help. When are you meeting him tomorrow?"

"I think around lunchtime. You'll be okay if I slip away from your booth?"

Sofia laughed. "I've been doing this by myself for a long time. I think I can manage to cover your lunch break."

Just as she said it, two women approached the booth and began to look through the tulip earrings. Business—and the festival—had officially begun.

Chapter Forty-Eight
HOLLY

"I still think we should have told Sofia about what we're going to try tomorrow."

When Ash looked at Holly in alarm, she quickly added, "Not the elves and snow tunneling and magic part, but just that we were planning to have him meet with someone to try a new method of restoring his memories."

Ash shook his head. "I know it was hard not to approach her first, but it's Isaiah's mind and his memories. He had the right to consent before anyone else."

Holly knew he was right. But she hoped Sofia wasn't upset with them.

"Besides, Isaiah said he was going to tell her right after he spoke to us. It wasn't a secret."

Holly nodded thoughtfully. Ever since she'd called the North Pole through her watch and Clementine had confirmed that she and Lumi had discovered who had been snow tunneling out of the North Pole, Holly had been experiencing a strange fluctuation of emotions somewhere between guilt and anxiety. She couldn't believe her elf assistant, Auryn, had opened the snow tunnel they believed Isaiah had inadvertently passed through.

But once she'd gotten over the initial shock, it all made perfect sense. Auryn had explained to Clementine that he was in the house when Holly called to ask Lumi how to snow tunnel the previous year. He'd overheard the explanation, been overtaken with curiosity, and tried it out for himself. Since Emerald Hollow was where Holly was currently residing, his first snow tunnel had opened there with relative ease.

Holly looked up at the sound of a megaphone.

"It's time for the first annual tulip festival floral design competition! If you've entered, please make your way to the tables at the east side of the clearing."

Ash touched a hand to her waist and led her toward the tables. "You ready for this?" he whispered into her ear.

Holly grinned, her fear of the next day's events dissolving at the sound of Ash's voice and the hint of a challenge in it. "The question is 'Are *you* ready?'"

"Well, now that I know about your magic, one might say you were cheat—"

Holly pushed Ash playfully in the chest, and he grabbed her hand and folded it into his.

"Just kidding. Remember, your magic is the whole reason this festival is even happening."

"So we think," Holly said, her smile relaxing a little. The idea that her magic was constantly impacting Emerald Hollow was still a little unsettling. Aside from Isaiah's memory loss, which they were pretty sure could be attributed to the elves' unsanctioned snow tunneling, not her magic, the magical goings-on in Emerald Hollow all seemed to be positive or at least neutral. It was hard to argue that the tulip super bloom was doing any real damage to the town.

Still, she wasn't sure how their new arrangement was supposed to work. Her parents had spent most of their time at the North Pole, but she and Ash were trying to make their home in Emerald Hollow. If her presence was somehow causing epic floral displays in early spring, she wasn't sure what to expect for the rest of the year.

As they walked toward the tables Luis had indicated, she glanced sideways at Ash. She had filled the boxes on top of them with supplies earlier that morning.

Her heart squeezed as she looked at him. If her magic got too out of control, and the impacts on the town became too noticeable, she might have to make a decision to leave and make a permanent home at the North Pole with him as her parents had. *And what would that do to Ash?* Emerald Hollow was his home. As she scanned the people around the clearing, she knew it had become her home too.

Luis's voice cut through the crowd that had gathered around the tables. "Each contestant has their own section of the table and a basic tool set. The rest of the supplies, including the flowers, are shared on tables. *No hoarding.* You will have one hour to create your masterpiece, then the judges will get to work."

Holly held her breath. Luis would announce the theme next. As a contestant, she hadn't been allowed to know that part in advance.

"This year's theme is the Kentucky Derby, which means you'll be fashioning a hat made of flowers. What constitutes a hat is open to your interpretation. Are we ready?"

A few cheers and whistles came from the crowd that had gathered around the twelve contestants.

Luis blew an air horn, and Holly jumped into action. She quickly tuned out everything around her, even Ash, who was on her right. She got to work reaching for materials: bendable willow branches, tendrils of ivy, and flowers of reds, pinks, and purples. She could feel the magic vibrating through her hands as she worked, completely consumed in the activity.

The hour passed in the blink of an eye, and Holly jumped when the air horn sounded, signaling that time was up. She dropped her supplies immediately but noticed Ash shove one last delicate yellow flower onto his hat.

She smiled as she looked at it. He'd used netting that was common in fascinators and some yellow tulle to create a small beehive. White and yellow daisies were glued into the netting and on the tulle, and a few yellow petals had been carefully mixed with some black material to imitate little bees. Her heart swelled. The execution wasn't perfect, but the idea was clever. She absolutely loved it and, despite her competitive streak, found herself hoping with all her heart that Ash would win.

They stepped back from the table, where the judges would spend the next hour making their decision. Ash took her hand. "That was stressful. I felt like I was on one of those reality shows. Like where they're making a cake under a time crunch."

Holly, who had never seen these shows, let out a soft laugh. "Oh, cakes would be fun. Maybe I'll challenge you to a cake-decorating contest next."

"When it comes to decorating, it's really not a contest. How about I challenge you to..." He thought for a moment, looking around the clearing. His eyes lit up as an idea came to him. "A fishing competition. Fishing season is going to be in full swing here soon. We'll see who can land the biggest fish."

Holly made a face. "Fishing?"

"Not so confident now, are you?" Ash asked with a grin.

"Okay, you're on. But only if the fish stock is high this season. And only if you promise to cook it for me afterward."

Ash looked positively thrilled at that. "You drive a hard bargain." He leaned in closer. "But you've got yourself a deal."

Chapter Forty-Nine

SOFIA

Day one of the tulip festival was winding down, and there were only two major events remaining: the Dutch dance and the lantern boats. Both were evening activities and would occur after the craft vendor stalls had closed. Sofia and Isaiah had been working nonstop at her booth, and when six o'clock rolled around, they both began to do the light teardown to store the materials for the second and last day of the festival.

Holly and Ash approached her booth, and Sofia's heart swelled, all her anxieties about the "expert" they were going to introduce Isaiah to the next day forgotten. Luis had announced the winner of the floral design contest about an hour ago, and no surprise to Sofia, Holly had been crowned the Flower Queen. The contestants could sport their creations for the rest of the night.

Ash had only agreed to take one picture with his fascinator on then quickly ditched it. Holly, however, was effortlessly wearing a large woodland wonderland: coiled branches laced through with greenery and stunning bright flowers. Sofia thought she looked like a woodland sprite.

197

Holly approached Sofia and slipped the smaller flower crown she'd been wearing earlier in the day onto Sofia's head.

"Congrats on your win, Holly. Maybe I should take you on as a business partner, and we could add flower hats to my jewelry collection."

Holly laughed. "Don't think these would fare well in the mail. How was business today?"

Isaiah feigned falling over against the table, and Sofia rolled her eyes. "Drama king over here. But we *were* slammed. I feel like I didn't take a breath all day."

"We brought you some food," Holly said.

Sofia finally noticed the paper boxes Ash was holding. Holly's hat had completely distracted her. She nabbed the boxes. "You are lifesavers. I'm starving." She opened both to see what was inside then handed one to Isaiah.

He took the plastic fork and began to eat immediately.

"Italian?" Sofia asked. "Is this from Enzo's booth?"

Ash nodded. "Did you know his son Luca is in town? He was working at the booth with Enzo."

Sofia raised her eyebrows. "He hasn't been back in years. Doesn't he live in some big city? LA?"

"San Diego," Ash replied.

Sofia nodded and began to eat.

"Are you two doing the Dutch dance?" Ash asked after Sofia had had a few bites of her salad. "Starts in thirty minutes."

Sofia turned and raised an eyebrow at Isaiah, who shrugged.

"We're in," she said.

They ate the remainder of their dinner then rested their legs in the camp chairs, chatting with Ash and Holly, until the Dutch dance was announced.

"So, who's leading this thing?" Isaiah asked as the four of them gathered with the rest of a large crowd of all ages near the stage.

"This will probably come as a surprise to no one, but Holly

has been to the tulip festival in Holland and apparently learned some dance steps while she was there," Ash said.

"I saw those dancers when I attended years ago. That's so funny. I wonder if we could have been there at the same time. Do you know what year you were there?" Sofia asked.

Something that Sofia couldn't interpret flickered across Holly's face before she said, "I've been a few times. Can't place the years exactly. Did you learn the steps? Do you want to help me lead?"

Sofia laughed loudly. "No way. I don't remember them at all. Lead the way, Flower Queen."

THIRTY MINUTES LATER, THE WHOLE CROWD WAS performing some simple movements and trotting arm-in-arm with their partners then moving in a large circle together and executing perfect klompen kicks. Sofia wasn't sure how Holly was doing it, but the crowd was picking up on her instruction the first time around, and everyone from kids to adults was moving like pros in no time.

As Sofia and Isaiah coupled up once more, moving from side to side with his arm on her back and hers on his shoulder, Sofia nearly imperceptibly broke pattern and stood on her tiptoes to kiss him. In the crowd, someone whistled.

"What was that for?" Isaiah asked as the song finally came to an end and everyone began to clap then slowly disperse. He slipped his arms around her waist and pulled her close.

Her cheeks were flushed from the dance, and she smiled coyly. "I didn't know the next time I'd have the opportunity to kiss you during a Dutch dance, so..."

Sofia's heart melted at Isaiah's smile. Behind him, the sun was rapidly setting, and the swaths of orange and red were a perfect imitation of the massive field of tulips around them.

Then she thought about the next activity, and her stomach tightened.

"Are you going back to the Emerald House now, or do you want to come to the lantern release?"

Isaiah pulled back slightly and studied her face. "Do you want me to come to the lantern release?"

"I just wasn't sure if it would be weird for you. Some people will place a wish in their lantern..."

"And you think I don't have a wish because I don't have any memories?"

"It's not that," Sofia said, struggling to put her feelings into words. The memory specialist was coming the next day, which she should feel hopeful about. Instead, what she was experiencing was a lot more like guilt.

Isaiah didn't make her finish her thoughts. His eyes softened. "Some people place a wish in the lantern, but for others, it's a memorial, right?"

She looked up at him, her eyes wide.

"Ash told me about what you were doing on the day you found me. I'm sorry I interrupted that."

Sofia pulled back ever so slightly, but she didn't let go of his hands. "Yeah, well, this lantern thing... I think my mom would have liked it."

"Then I like it too. Let's go."

They followed the group of people who were beginning to exit the clearing and walk toward the river. It was about half a mile away, and those who weren't participating headed back to their cars or to the Emerald House.

A not-unpleasant shiver ran across Sofia's arms in the cooling night air as she walked hand in hand with Isaiah to the small, calm river. She didn't have to do it alone.

Chapter Fifty

SOFIA

Sofia scanned the scene at the river as if she were seeing a fairy-tale setting come to life. The lanterns Holly and Ash had crafted were made of colorful paper and fashioned into the shape of bright, open flowers like tulips.

Sofia placed her candle in a pink tulip, said a silent prayer, then placed the lantern on the flower boat and laid it gently on the water. She watched as it mixed with dozens of others and didn't take her eyes off of it until it passed so far down the river that she could no longer identify it.

As she watched the river, Sofia felt as connected to her mom as she had when the hummingbirds had paid their visit, as if the flickering flame slowly making its way across the water was her mom's presence waving a soft "I love you." *Is this how I should feel when I do the memorial hike for Mom on New Year's Eve? Is this what it feels like to have a tradition of remembrance I can look to with hope instead of dread?*

"What are you thinking about?" Isaiah asked gently, coming up by her side.

"I was thinking that my mom would like me honoring her this way. We did the hike on New Year's Day when she was alive because she enjoyed getting out in the crisp winter air for some exercise, but I've never enjoyed it the way she did. And whenever I do the hike now, it's just so apparent how she isn't there with me. I wonder…"

Isaiah surprised her by picking up on her line of thought. "You wonder if she would be okay with your forming a new tradition and leaving behind one that you shared with her?"

Sofia swallowed the lump that had formed in her throat and nodded.

"I didn't know your mom, but I'm fairly sure she would have wanted whatever way you choose to remember her to be one that brings you comfort. If that's lighting a candle and sending it down the river rather than hiking a trail, wouldn't that be okay?"

Sofia didn't have to think about it for long. Isaiah was right. Her mom had always wanted her to be happy and to blaze her own trail. Maybe she didn't have to hold on to traditions for the sake of tradition but could forge new ones for the true sense of peace and remembrance they gave her.

The soft winking colors continued to dance in the corners of her vision as more flower boats were placed in the river. Isaiah placed a candle in a yellow flower and sent it down the gently flowing water.

"What did you wish for?" she asked once she was able to look away from the glistening water.

He mimed zipping his lips. "Isn't it like birthday wishes? If you say it aloud, it won't come true?"

"Oh, come ooon," Sofia moaned, though she was smiling. "Is it really that embarrassing?"

"Nope. I'm not breaking the magic. The wish stays in here." He tapped the side of his head.

Sofia threw her head back and dropped her shoulders slightly in defeat. "Fiiine. But you're not getting any of my tulip ice cream tomorrow."

Isaiah raised an eyebrow. "Tulip ice cream?"

"Okay, it's just sherbet, but you know, we're still leaning into the theme."

"So what *is* the plan for tomorrow?"

"Vendors are selling for only half a day on Sunday, so I'll only be doing that until about one. Then I'm serving ice cream at the Emerald House booth for an hour, then I clean everything up and go home."

"I can't believe you still have inventory after today. That was intense."

"Yeah, I've been making the jewelry in every free moment since Ash decided to host this thing."

Instead of responding, Isaiah took her hand and tugged her back from the riverbank into the trees, where they were out of sight of the other festival-goers. "Hey, there's something I've been wanting to talk to you about."

Sofia met his eyes and was surprised to see that he looked serious, all his usual playfulness gone. "What is it?"

"Before, when we were at the rental house in Ashland, you said you thought if I got my memories back, you would realize I didn't deserve someone like you. That's been bothering me ever since. Don't you know how amazing you are? Who... Did someone... tell you otherwise?"

Sofia inhaled sharply and looked up at the sky. She hadn't been planning to ever tell Isaiah about it, but since he'd asked, and she'd committed to trying things out with him, she realized she wanted to share.

"There was... someone. Noah. He was my superior officer when I was stationed in Germany. I told you I was enlisted right?"

Isaiah nodded, and Sofia thought she saw a strained tick in his neck. She hurried on. "We started dating. It was against all advisement, but he was the most romantic person ever, told me he loved me, blah, blah, blah. The classic cliché." She let out a mirthless laugh, remembering how naive she'd been. "We'd been together for nearly a year when I found out he had a fiancé back home."

Sofia thought she could hear Isaiah grinding his teeth, and his eyes were dark. She looked away, to where she could still see lights glistening as the flower boats drifted down the river with their lanterns. "Of course, somehow, everyone in the squadron knew about it but me. So I turned out looking like a real peach. It was all a scandal. I ended up getting a phone call from a screaming fiancé I hadn't known existed. You can imagine how that felt." Sofia sighed, remembering the embarrassment and heartache.

"Then Noah put all the blame on me, convincing me I'd been some irresistible enchantress, and it was all my fault his engagement was nearly ruined. Yep, I said nearly. They still ended up getting married. It was easy to decide to separate from the military when my mom got sick. There wasn't much for me to leave behind."

Isaiah was quiet for several moments. Then he tugged her firmly to him and cupped her face in his hands. "None of that was your fault, and he lost out on the best woman he's ever been lucky enough to lay eyes on." His voice was fierce, and Sofia nearly stepped back at the fire she saw swirling in his eyes.

But he pulled her closer, tucked a hand under her chin, and slowly lifted her face to his. After they kissed, he let out a deep breath and ran a hand through his hair. All the anger was gone, and his mischievous grin was back.

"What?" she asked, pulling back slightly and feeling a hundred pounds lighter than she had in years.

"I guess I can tell you now. My wish just came true."

Chapter Fifty-One

HOLLY

Holly moved quickly, working out her nerves as she and Ash walked Comet through the forest trail outside the Emerald House. The first day of the tulip festival had been magical, everything Ash had envisioned it to be, and Holly had felt an incredible sense of peace when she'd sent two lit candles in miniature boats down the river in honor of her parents. There were many human traditions she'd never fully appreciated until she experienced them for herself.

But concerns crept back as she thought about the next day. "We must disguise Auryn somehow, and we need a plausible reason for him to approach Isaiah to reverse the memory loss. But that's not the worst part." She took a deep breath, and Ash squeezed her hand. "If our plan works, how are we going to explain that Isaiah suddenly has his memories back? Sofia was so suspicious of him at the beginning. I worry that those suspicions will return."

She glanced at Ash and saw an expression of deep concentration on his face.

"Maybe there is a way we can make it seem medically plausible. Like he saw something that suddenly triggered his memories to come back. Isn't that how it happens in the movies? Someone sees something familiar, and it all comes flooding in?"

Holly let out a breath. She hadn't seen many movies, so she wasn't sure what Ash was talking about, but that didn't sound medically plausible to her. It sounded more like magic. "But how would we know what's familiar to him that could be the trigger? We won't know what his memories are until he gets them back." Her stomach was tied up in knots. "I hate how manipulative this feels, Ash. Sofia is our best friend."

He ran a hand through his hair. "I don't like it either. But we both agree that Isaiah needs to get his memories back. We know that Sofia and Isaiah want that too. It's the only ethical thing to do. So the main issue is that we can't tell them how he lost his memories in the first place or how he got them back. We're just going to have to trust their minds to fill in the gaps, I guess. Maybe they will think there was a minor head injury that wasn't caught by the machines, and it healed over time."

"And all his memories came rushing back, just like that?"

"Unless Auryn knows of a way to make the memories come back slowly."

Holly shook her head. "Auryn doesn't know much of anything. If he did, Isaiah wouldn't be in this situation in the first place. Thank the stars for Lumi Kringle. At least we know how to reverse it."

"Maybe we can get Dr. Margo involved somehow," Ash suggested, squinting slightly.

"I'd like that, but I don't want to have to manipulate her. My magic won't stand for that, and neither will I."

"That's it!" Ash said, stopping and turning to look at her.

"What?" Holly asked, startled.

"Your magic. It always seems to interfere when it's beneficial. It brought us together." He slipped an arm around her waist and pulled her close to him. "And it's possible that all this happened to bring Isaiah and Sofia together too."

Holly raised her eyebrows. The thought had never crossed her mind. "So what are you saying?"

"I think that magic has to be the solution. There must be a way it can smooth things over for Sofia and Isaiah, right? Make it more believable that he got his memories back suddenly. Maybe we just need to trust it."

Holly thought about it for a moment. Her stomach still churned, but it relaxed ever so slightly. "So you think we just go with it? Cure Isaiah and take things from there?"

"Without coming up with a more deceitful ruse, yes. I think this is one of those situations where we just have to let things shake out and hope for the best."

Holly couldn't help but smile. The Ash she'd met in the fall would never have just left things to fate. He was a bit of a control freak, as Sofia would call it. *Maybe the North Pole magic is rubbing off on him.*

"Okay. You might be right. We get Isaiah his memories back and let magic take care of the rest."

"It's still really strange, talking about magic," Ash said with a smile. He shook his head as he took her hand, and they began to walk the path again.

"But strange *good*, right?" Holly asked, something tugging at her chest.

"Strange *very* good," Ash replied, and he pulled her in for a kiss.

$\sim$

"I'm so nervous," Holly admitted to Ash as they walked toward the outskirts of the festival, where Lumi and Auryn were going to meet them. Her stomach had been in anxious knots the whole morning as the plan with the elves and Isaiah loomed closer.

It was similar to the feeling she used to get when her Cheer meter sensed a powerful negative emotion that threatened to sap all the Cheer she'd collected. She was grateful she didn't have to worry about that anymore, but relationships with humans weren't completely stress free, especially when the situation had been caused by someone from the North Pole.

"It'll be okay," Ash assured her, pausing to rub her arms. "Trust the magic, remember?"

"Trust the magic, yes." Holly took a deep breath and walked to the bench where she saw Lumi and Auryn waiting.

Auryn's eyes were downcast, and Holly tried to relax her face.

"Hi, Auryn. Are you ready for this?"

"Ms. Claus, I'm so sorry. If I'd known anything like this could have happened, I would never have—"

"Shh," Holly said gently. "It's okay, Auryn. You didn't know. We're going to fix it, all right? Has Lumi walked you through the process?"

"She has." Auryn nodded, still not meeting Holly's gaze.

"The only issue I can see is that there's no snow around here. We need it to create the tunnel," Lumi said.

Holly turned to Ash. "Do you think there's still snow up at the higher elevations?"

"I think there's a good chance, especially outside the city limits. This hyper-early spring tulip bloom seems to have only affected Emerald Hollow."

Holly nodded. "Okay, so we need an excuse to bring Isaiah out of town. Maybe say we're taking him to where we think he first started hiking."

"That should work. Auryn, you're posing as a memory-loss expert for now, so you'll need to lead the conversation."

Auryn's eyes widened, and Holly thought she noticed movement under his hat, which was hiding his prominent elf ears.

"It's okay. We'll walk you through it."

They spent about ten minutes practicing, then Ash walked away to get Isaiah.

Holly took a deep breath as she watched him. *Here we go. Magic, don't fail me now.*

Chapter Fifty-Two

ISAIAH

Isaiah had been helping Sofia at her booth through the nonstop morning rush, which didn't seem to be any less intense on the second day of the festival. It seemed that everyone wanted some Emerald Hollow Artisanal tulip jewelry as a souvenir.

At the sound of his name, Isaiah stood quickly from where he'd been searching through a box under the table. Ash was standing there with his hands in his pockets. "Hey, man. You ready?"

Isaiah had almost forgotten that he'd agreed to see the memory specialist that day. "Oh yeah, sorry. Lost track of time. Let me just…" He moved toward where Sofia was currently ringing up a customer.

"Hey, Sof. Ash is here, so I need to…"

"What?" Sofia glanced over her shoulder and caught sight of Ash. "Oh right. Yeah. Of course. Um—" She seemed flustered, and he waited for her to finish her train of thought. "Just a second. Don't go yet." She finished ringing up the customer, then she knelt under the table, pulling something out of her purse. She passed him a white box the size of a book.

Isaiah looked at her in confusion. "What's this?"

"Something I wanted to give you before you go. Open it." She pushed the box closer to him.

He pulled up the lid, and his breath caught when he saw a sophisticated belt buckle inside. The buckle had been painted with a gorgeous scene of a sunset over a river. His chest constricted. It looked like the scene from the previous night. *But she couldn't possibly have...*

"I made it for you last night. Just something to—" She seemed to change her mind on what she wanted to say.

Isaiah pulled her in and kissed her gently for several moments. "It's perfect," he said and was happy to see her beautiful smile light her face. He never wanted her to feel the way Noah had made her feel ever again and vowed not to take her for granted.

"Go on, then," she said, inclining her head toward Ash.

Isaiah thought there was something strange in her voice, and he experienced a twinge of guilt in his stomach that he was leaving her, even if it was for a short amount of time. He couldn't imagine how she had managed the booth on her own at previous festivals.

"Ready?" Ash asked again.

Isaiah turned away from Sofia and followed Ash across the festival clearing, dodging groups small and large who were posing for pictures with the tulips, exploring the vendor stalls, or purchasing food. He spotted someone eating pink cotton candy in the shape of a tulip.

"This thing really came together," he said. "Sofia said it was a quick turnaround."

"Yeah, way too quick. But the finished product seems to be worth it. How's Sofia's booth doing?"

"Great, from what I can tell. We've barely had a breather all day."

Ash stepped out of the clearing to where three people were

gathered near a bench. Holly was the only one he recognized. As he drew closer, he thought there was something strange about the other two, but he couldn't put his finger on what.

"Hi, Isaiah," Holly said. "This is my friend Lumi, and this is Auryn, the one who wants to... help with your memory."

Isaiah reached out a hand, and the small man glanced at Holly with an expression of panic on his face. Holly gave him what looked like a reassuring smile, and Auryn took his hand. A small jolt of energy seemed to pass through Isaiah then, similar to what he had felt when he returned to the trailhead. He shivered and frowned.

Holly looked anxious, but she put on a comforting smile. "We'd like to take you back to the woods, to a trailhead where it's possible that you started your hike."

Isaiah noticed she spoke slowly, as if she were choosing her words carefully.

"It could be useful for recovering your memories," Auryn said.

"If that's what you think is best," Isaiah replied, though he was doubtful. Aside from the weird feeling he'd experienced at the spot where Sofia had found him, it hadn't done anything to jog his memories.

Ash and Holly began to walk toward the parking lot, and Isaiah fell in next to them, Lumi and Auryn following a few paces behind. Sofia had told him Holly was from Canada, and he wondered if her friends were as well.

They all got into Ash's truck, with Isaiah in the front seat and Holly and her two friends in the back. The three were silent as they drove, and Isaiah noticed that they sat stiffly in the truck, as if they weren't sure if they were allowed to move. Ash quickly began to make small talk with Isaiah and Holly, and the tension broke.

Twenty minutes later, they were at a trailhead outside of

Emerald Hollow. All the brilliant tulips that had lined the road on their drive to the city limits were gone.

"What made you choose this trailhead?" Isaiah asked as they climbed out of the truck.

"Closest one outside of Emerald Hollow," Ash said but didn't elaborate.

The group hiked up the trail a ways.

"Wow, there's still snow here," Isaiah said. "Hard to imagine coming from the tulip festival."

"We'd like to recreate the original scenario as much as possible," Auryn replied, and it came out in a bit of a squeak.

Is the man nervous? Being a memory specialist, he probably worked in an office or hospital and didn't make a lot of house calls. He wondered how Holly had convinced him to come.

"Okay, go ahead and stand there," Holly said to Isaiah while the others took a step back.

The elderly woman, Lumi, stepped closer to Auryn and whispered something in his ear. Isaiah shifted his weight uncomfortably.

"Do you mind turning away from us? Just look around the trailhead, as if you were on a normal hike," Auryn directed quietly.

Isaiah did as instructed. There was a very soft whooshing sound, as if the wind had picked up.

He started to turn around, but Auryn stopped him. "Not yet. Try to visualize the day you were found."

Isaiah closed his eyes and tried to focus on the snowy trail in January, but the only thing that came to mind was Sofia and the look of concern and trepidation in her eyes as she'd helped him. A cold sensation rushed over his skin, just like he'd felt at his return to the trailhead. The cold, jittery feeling passed over his whole body.

Moments later, the feeling was gone.

His eyes flew open, and he turned to where the four of them

were watching him anxiously. Holly was leaning forward slightly, and Auryn appeared to be sweating.

"Isaiah, are you okay?" Holly asked, taking a step toward him.

Then it all came rushing back, a flood of images, names, and places.

Isaiah sank to his knees and blacked out.

Chapter Fifty-Three
SOFIA

The tulip festival was still in full swing, but Sofia and the other craft vendors had already shut down their stalls for the day. As the evening's music began to play and people wandered toward the enchanting notes, the main hustle and bustle was concentrated around the food vendors.

After she finished cleaning up, Sofia slunk into the little folding chair she always kept in her booth but rarely got a chance to use and glanced at her phone. It had been nearly three hours since Isaiah had gone off with Ash. *Are they still meeting with the memory specialist? What is he doing? Hypnotizing Isaiah?*

Sofia wandered to the Emerald House booth to buy something called a "wild tulip bowl," which appeared to consist of chicken, wild rice, and a few vegetables of vibrant colors that matched the field of tulips.

When she couldn't take it anymore, she picked up her phone and dialed Ash's number. After three rings, he answered.

"Hey, Sof." There was something odd in his voice—the slightest bit of reluctance—and she caught onto it immediately.

"Ash. What's going on? You guys have been gone for hours. Is Isaiah still with you?"

A pause followed, and Sofia repeated herself. "Ash? Is everything okay?"

"Yes, everything's fine. We took Isaiah to Dr. Margo to get checked out just in case." Ash hesitated.

Sofia gripped the phone tighter. "Just in case what?"

"He passed out," Ash's voice was calm, but Sofia was suddenly dizzy.

"What?" she asked, her voice high-pitched, as she jumped to her feet.

"He's okay, Sof. He's already been released, and we're heading back to the festival. I was just about to call you."

Sofia calmed slightly, but her mind was racing with questions, concern, and a sense of dread she didn't want to face. "Ash, why did he pass out?"

After a pause in which Sofia wanted to reach through the phone and grab Ash by the shoulders, the response came. "Sofia, his memories are back."

When Isaiah emerged at the entrance to the tulip festival, Sofia's heart jumped into her throat. As soon as he caught sight of her, he started in her direction, a slightly bewildered smile on his face.

"Isaiah, Ash told me what happened. Are you okay?"

"What? Oh, passing out." He looked mildly embarrassed. "That was weird. Dr. Margo thinks it's from the influx of so many memories returning at once like that. She's never heard of anything like it."

"So it's true? All your memories are back?" Sofia asked softly. She had a million questions for him, but she wanted to let him process everything first.

"Yeah, at least, I think so. Dr. Margo thinks some will continue to come trickling back as needed. Where do I even start? My name is Isaiah Perez, and I'm from Phoenix, Arizona. But currently living in San Francisco, California." He paused, as if deciding what to tell her next. "I did geospatial imaging in the army. I started as enlisted then commissioned. That explains why I was so comfortable with digital maps."

Geospatial imaging. The army. A military member. An officer—a profile she'd sworn off ever dating again. Her mind flashed to the moment in the frozen yogurt shop when Ash had broken up the near fight. The teenage boy had responded with a straightened posture and a "Yes, sir."

Sofia had had a strange sensation then, and suddenly, it all made sense. Her subconscious had been trying to show her something, and she'd ignored it.

Her warring emotions must have shown on her face, because Isaiah put an arm on her waist. "Sofia, are you okay?"

She shook her head then nodded. "Yeah, yeah. I'm fine. This is all just... a lot to process. For you more than me, I'm sure." He hadn't said he was married or in a relationship or had children, but she was still incredibly nervous. She'd avoided dating military men after the disaster with Noah, and she'd inadvertently fallen in love with one.

The thought caused her to stiffen. *Love.* She put a hand to her mouth, but Isaiah spoke again.

"It's weird. It's just kind of like everything feels normal again but also... not. Everything I was doing here in Emerald Hollow now feels like it was done in a vacuum or something. Like two different versions of me. It's strange."

Sofia's stomach clenched again. *Two different versions of me.*

"So does this mean you'll want to go home now? To California?"

"I mean, California's not exactly home, but it's where I was living when all this happened. Now I remember that I was in the early stages of wanting to start a veteran-owned coffee business. I was planning to design the bags with interesting maps of the local areas I wanted to sell in. Nothing was off the ground yet, though. I can't believe I forgot about all that. I think some details are still coming back to me. I can pick up where I left off with it now."

"Uh-huh," Sofia said, her heart sinking more and more with every word. Isaiah had a whole life somewhere else, a good one, from the sounds of it. *So what does that mean for us?*

"I called Willow, and she's going to drive up here tomorrow to get me. We can all grab dinner. I have a few calls to make from the landline at the Emerald House, but dinner at six tomorrow, okay?"

Before Sofia could ask who Willow was, Isaiah squeezed her hand and walked away.

Sofia sat on her couch that night with her laptop out but was unable to focus on work. Not even the success of her booth at the tulip festival could help ease the nerves she was experiencing. *Isaiah Perez. From Phoenix, Arizona. A former officer in the US Army. Preparing to start a coffee business in California.*

She'd really thought that Isaiah had grown fond of Emerald Hollow, but she wondered if it had been something like Stockholm Syndrome. He was from Phoenix and lived in San Francisco, both massive cities compared to rural Emerald Hollow.

San Francisco. She could hardly imagine him there. If that was the type of place he'd chosen to live when he got out of the military, he certainly wouldn't be interested in Emerald Hollow as a place of residence.

And who is Willow? He'd said her name so casually, as if he'd known her forever. *A best friend? A girlfriend? Certainly, he would have said if that were the case, right?* She took a sip of her wine then rolled her shoulders, trying to calm her anxieties about the next day.

Two different versions of me. Isaiah's words rang in her head like a morning alarm. If there were two different hims, it meant the Isaiah before the memory loss was the real him, and the Emerald Hollow Isaiah had just been someone his brain had clung to in order to function during the trauma of the memory loss.

Maybe *she* had been someone he'd clung to for the same reason, and he didn't need her anymore. *Be reasonable,* she told herself. *He hasn't said any of that. Maybe it can still work out.*

She drained her wineglass and turned on the TV. The movie *50 First Dates* was playing. *Great, a movie about a couple falling in love despite a traumatic memory loss.* She scowled and quickly changed the channel. It was going to be a long night.

Chapter Fifty-Four

HOLLY

Holly strolled through the woods behind the Emerald House, Comet at her heels. She was trying to prepare herself for a conversation with Ash. The incident with Auryn and Isaiah had given her an idea. If she was right, it could lead to healing for a family. But if she was wrong, if could cause bitter disappointment.

She'd experienced enough human emotions through her Cheer meter to know that getting one's hopes up only to have them crushed was not something she wanted a person she loved to go through.

And if I were the cause of it? Holly shivered.

She reached the small clearing where her reindeer liked to roam, and Comet ran over to greet his friends.

Holly tapped her watch anxiously. *To tell or not to tell.* There was always the option of pursuing the idea without telling Ash first, but she felt a strange twisting in the pit of her stomach when she thought about that. She'd already told Ash who she was and all about her magic. He'd even been to the North Pole.

But this feels different. This is about his *family.* And Holly thought it was possible that someone from the North Pole had accidentally destroyed it.

Chapter Fifty-Five

ASH

Ash finished closing up the kitchen for the night, flicking off the light switches as he left the restaurant. He was oddly calm. The tulip festival had been a success by all accounts, Isaiah's memories had been restored, thanks to Holly and her elves, and he was starting to wonder if the magic that seemed to seep out of Holly and into the town was going to continue to benefit its residents for years to come—as long as there were no more snow tunneling incidents.

The knowledge that Holly was a Claus and that North Pole magic ran through her was still astounding, but it had never been impossible to accept. He'd known from the moment he met her that something was different about her. The explanation, once he'd received it, had come as a confirmation more than anything. Still, it was difficult not being able to share any of that with their best friend, Sofia.

Ash made his way slowly through the lobby, where brilliant, bold, fabric tulip decor was still covering all free surfaces. He smiled. *Holly and her decorating.*

He shook his head and decided not to worry about Sofia. She and Isaiah had hit it off, and though he knew that Isaiah's getting his memories back might change some things between them, he was sure they would work it out in the end, if their relationship was meant to be.

He smiled as he walked down the hall toward his rooms. He'd never seen his best friend as happy as she'd been these past few weeks. She was a firecracker, and Isaiah seemed to handle all that personality with ease. It was like they were built for each other.

And Ash liked the idea that Holly's magic had somehow brought them together, just like it had for the two of them.

Ash opened the back door across from the entrance to his apartment and glanced out at the forest. Holly had said she was taking Comet for a walk while he closed up, and he hoped to catch sight of them on their way back. He waited a few minutes then spotted his gorgeous woman emerging from the forest trail, Comet at her heels. Though it was dark, he thought he caught a worried expression on her face.

Has something gone wrong with Isaiah? Have there been some side effects she didn't tell me about?

A frown creased his face. He never wanted Holly to be stressed. No matter what unintended consequences came from her magic and her being in Emerald Hollow, it was never her fault. But he was pretty sure from the look on her face that she disagreed.

Chapter Fifty-Six

SOFIA

Sofia got to the Emerald House a little early for once, anxious about her dinner with Isaiah and Willow, whoever she was. She and Isaiah hadn't had a chance to talk since he'd left the tulip festival the previous afternoon. She caught sight of him in the lobby and walked toward him.

She reached for his hands, but he angled himself away. It was subtle, masked to appear as if he hadn't noticed and was shrugging on his hoodie, but it stung. Sofia took a step back.

"Everything okay?" she asked.

"Willow will be arriving any minute. Just gonna go out to meet her," Isaiah said. His voice was normal, but Sofia didn't miss that he had avoided her question.

What's happened between us since yesterday? He'd squeezed her hand before he said goodbye at the tulip festival, and she thought that meant things were okay.

Isaiah went outside, and her eyes zeroed in on a black car as it pulled into the parking lot. Isaiah was out there, ready and waiting, while Sofia watched through the window.

A woman who Sofia guessed was a few years younger than her with gorgeous shiny auburn hair jumped out of the car and ran to Isaiah. He hurried to meet her, and the two hugged for a long time.

Sofia continued to watch as the two pulled apart and said a few words to each other, both grinning. Sofia had known all along that once Isaiah figured out who he was, his other life would come crashing down around them with full force. She just hadn't expected it to be in the form of that pretty-as-a-picture woman. The two walked into the Emerald House.

"Sofia, this is my sister, Willow," Isaiah said, grinning, as the two walked toward Sofia.

Sofia tried to rearrange her expression, but the sinking sensation in the pit of her stomach didn't fully ease. *Sister.*

Sofia didn't have any siblings, and neither did Ash or Holly, but Isaiah had at least one. The knowledge made her uneasy. It was just another aspect of his life that was so different from hers. She wondered how having a sister had shaped Isaiah growing up.

She forced herself to sideline the dozens of questions that had jumped into her mind upon meeting Willow. Those could wait. Instead, she stuck out her hand. "Welcome to Emerald Hollow."

Willow gently shook her hand then pulled her in. "Sorry, I'm a hugger." Willow's shiny auburn hair swished around her face as she pulled back. She kept her hands on Sofia's arms. "But seriously, I can't thank you enough for everything you've done for Isaiah. I couldn't believe any of this when he first called me. I'm so glad he's okay."

Sofia really wanted to jump in with questions, but Ash emerged from the restaurant and invited them all to the table.

"Why don't we talk over food?" he suggested.

Isaiah and Willow accepted eagerly, Isaiah following Ash without saying a word to Sofia. She still didn't know what to think. Willow had greeted her so warmly, but Isaiah was obviously keeping her at a distance. *Why?*

"Are you okay?" Holly whispered to her as they began to take their seats in the largest booth in the restaurant.

"Not sure yet," Sofia said.

Isaiah had barely met her eyes, and the worry in the pit of her stomach was growing.

Holly nodded and squeezed her hand under the table. Sofia sat between Holly and Isaiah. Willow was on Isaiah's other side, with Ash next to her.

To Sofia's surprise, Luca, Enzo's son, slid in next to Ash.

"Luca was here getting coffee, and I invited him to join us. It's been a long time since he's had an Emerald House meal. I thought we could welcome him and Willow both to Emerald Hollow. Hope that's okay with everybody?" Ash looked around the table, and they all nodded.

"Of course," Isaiah said. "Luca, you've just walked into the most hospitable place in the country. They've been taking care of me for the past few months."

Sofia watched him closely, wondering what was going through his brain. His words to Luca, a complete stranger, seemed normal enough. But he couldn't even say two words to her. *Getting all his memories like that had to have been a shock. Maybe he is just adjusting to everything.*

Luca gave an easy smile. "Oh, I remember. I haven't been here in years, and the Emerald House has grown a lot, but this restaurant feels exactly like it was."

Ash did a quick round of introductions—everyone was new to Luca except for Ash and Sofia—then turned to Willow. "So, Willow, tell us everything. What happened when you got the phone call? Had you been looking for Isaiah?"

Tyler, their server, began to fill their glasses with water.

"It was the craziest thing," Willow said, gesturing with her hands. "I had been expecting to hear from Isaiah within a few weeks, so the call itself wasn't a surprise, but when he told me where he was and what had happened, I was shocked. We all thought he had been hiking the Pacific Crest Trail all that time. He was supposed to be nearly to Canada by now."

"The PCT?" Ash asked, his eyes widening. "So that explains why you weren't marked as a missing person."

"I'd mailed him a few packages at prearranged points for him to pick up at post offices along his trip, but he'd told me he was going fully off-grid and likely wouldn't be calling. So I didn't think anything of it. I feel terrible about that now. Maybe if I'd insisted on checking in..."

"It's fine, Will. That was the plan. I remember it all now." His voice dropped an octave.

Sofia angled her body toward his, concern creasing her brow. But he still didn't look at her.

Willow's expression softened as well. "It was an important trip to you. I'm sorry it took such a turn. But I'm so grateful for everyone here." She gestured around the table, her eyes lingering on Sofia's for a moment then going back to her brother.

"It's the strangest thing." Willow paused, as if she wasn't sure she should say what came next. "Isaiah and I are half-siblings, so we didn't live together growing up. Izz, do you remember when I lived in Oregon for a year in elementary school?"

Isaiah's eyes went distant, then they opened wide. "I do remember that. You were in what? Third grade?"

"Yep. And guess where I was living."

Everyone watched her, waiting to hear the response.

"Here, in Emerald Hollow."

Ash let out a surprised laugh, and Sofia's jaw dropped. Beside her, Holly stiffened a little and glanced at her watch.

"No way," Sofia said.

"Isn't it crazy? What are the chances?"

"Wait a minute..." Luca spoke up, his brow knitting. "Willow. Willow Moss?"

Willow nearly jumped out of her seat. "Yes! Wait... Do we know each other?"

"I'm not sure how I could forget a name like Willow Moss. You were in class with my sister, Ellie. You came over to our house once or twice. I'm Luca Moretti."

"Luca Moretti!" Willow clapped once. "I remember you. Wow, what a small world."

"And years later, your brother ends up losing his memory and spending two months here," Sofia said slowly, struggling to process her thoughts. Despite the joyous reminiscing that was happening around her, her hands were numb as she clenched them together under the table.

"Life's weird like that," Willow said, shrugging as if the coincidence didn't bother her in the slightest.

"It certainly is," Holly agreed, and Sofia detected a hint of confusion or possibly even concern in her voice.

But she didn't have time to wonder about it more because just then, Tyler began to bring out their food. There was a break in the conversation as the group ate. Nausea twisted slightly in Sofia's stomach, and she pushed her food lightly across her plate.

"This situation kind of feels like something from *The Twilight Zone*," Isaiah murmured in her direction, and Sofia jolted when she realized he was speaking to her. He looked tired. She wondered if getting his memories back had affected him physically.

"It really does," Sofia said, her stomach unclenching slightly.

"Hey, are you okay? You didn't eat anything," Isaiah observed, glancing down at her plate.

"I'm fine. But is everything okay with—" Sofia couldn't put her question into words. She should be thrilled that Isaiah had rediscovered his identity. *Two different versions of me,* she thought, her stomach sinking once more.

Isaiah shifted his attention to something Willow was saying when Sofia didn't finish the thought.

Next to her, Holly leaned in close. "Is there anything I can do?" she asked softly, her eyes green lakes of understanding.

Sofia shook her head but gave Holly a forced smile. She knew what was going to happen next by the way the conversation was going between Isaiah and Willow.

The fun and games were over. Isaiah was going home.

Chapter Fifty-Seven
SOFIA

When the meal ended, and Luca, Ash, and Holly were preparing to leave, Sofia grabbed Isaiah's arm. "Can we talk?"

Something flashed across his eyes. *Fear? Regret?* But he nodded and slid out of the booth. "Will, we'll be right back."

His sister nodded and smiled at Sofia.

They walked out of the restaurant, through the lobby, and out the front entrance. The smell of flowers hit Sofia immediately, but they didn't make her inhale deeply like they usually did. Instead, she crossed her arms and looked out toward the town.

"Isaiah, what's going on?" she asked after a few moments of silence.

"What do you mean?"

"Ever since yesterday, after you told me you got your memories back, we've barely spoken. You haven't even looked at me. I'm sure this is all overwhelming, but I feel like I at least deserve to know what you're thinking."

Isaiah took a deep breath and ran a hand through his dark hair. His tall frame cast a large shadow next to her. "You're right.

It was intentional. I just... A lot came flooding back when my memories were restored. At first, it was okay, but... more kept trickling in last night."

A million thoughts ran through Sofia's head—a million scenarios, none of them good. *Is there another woman after all? Does he realize he isn't interested in women like me? Has he decided he isn't truly charmed by this small town?*

Sofia's insecurities flared, her emotions a mix of sympathy for him and a particular anxiety she hadn't experienced in years. Instead of firing all the questions at him like she wanted to, she forced herself to boil it all down to the bare bones. Only one thing mattered. "Okay. I'm sure that was all really overwhelming. But once you've had more time to process... What does that mean for us?"

Time froze as she waited for his answer. She wanted him to scoop her into his arms, take her face in his warm hands, and tell her nothing was changing. But even before he spoke, she knew what was coming. She saw the fall of his shoulders and the tension in his jaw.

"Sof, I..."

She jerked back, taking a step away from him. "So that's it, then?"

"I'm not the person you thought I was." His expression was pained, his mouth twisted slightly downward.

The sight made her stomach plummet. She wanted to see a smile pulling at the corners of his mouth again.

"You deserve so much better."

It was the opposite of what Noah had said to her, but somehow, it cut her just as deeply.

"Shouldn't I get to be the judge of that?" She was forcing back tears, and her words came out sharp.

"Sof, I'm so sorry."

He tried to reach for her, but she pulled her arm away and shook her head.

"Don't."

She didn't let him or herself say another word. She turned on her heel and hurried to her car, hurt and furious with herself that things had gone exactly the way she had once expected. She'd only prayed it would be different.

Chapter Fifty-Eight

ISAIAH

The drive to San Francisco was uneventful. Willow had chatted nonstop, sharing memories of the year she'd spent in Emerald Hollow as a child, as if she thought of it as the most enchanting place on earth. She was still in complete disbelief that it was where he'd been all that time.

"That place is exactly as I remember it," she said as they carried their take-out Chinese food up the outdoor stairs to her third-floor apartment. Willow twisted the key in the lock with one hand and pushed the door open with her hip.

Isaiah wasn't that excited about returning to San Francisco. When his exit from the military had corresponded with Willow's current roommate moving out, she'd suggested he rent the room. It had really just been a landing station for his possessions while he hiked the Pacific Crest Trail for a few months and figured out his next steps.

"Main Street maybe has fewer shops, but who knows? I was only eight when I lived there. I do remember this old-fashioned candy store, though. I didn't see it when I was driving through. Do you know if it's still there?"

"Huh?" Isaiah asked. His mind had been on one particular

person in Emerald Hollow and the look on her face the last time he'd seen her. He felt nauseated every time he replayed it. He'd vowed never to make her feel like Noah had, and he hoped he hadn't. He hoped he'd portrayed how much she was worth and that it was *he* who wasn't good enough for *her*, not the other way around. *But the look on her face...*

"An old-fashioned candy store. I can't remember the name of it. They had all the classics like bubble gum tape, gummy cheeseburgers, the works."

He tried to focus on what Willow was saying. *A candy store...* "I don't remember seeing that."

"Darn. Probably closed. It's hard for little stores like that to make it these days. It seems like the place where you were staying, the Emerald House, was doing well, though. The owner and his girlfriend look like they could be models for a Macy's catalog. Those are some beautiful people."

Despite his cloudy mood, which matched the San Francisco weather, Isaiah let out a short laugh. "There is something different about them, her especially. That whole place, really. Did you notice the tulips?"

"Yes! That was unbelievable. I thought that sort of thing only happened in movies. It looked like a dream. The tulips were popping out of every nook and cranny in the town as soon as I entered the city limits. I definitely don't remember that happening the year I lived there."

Isaiah's mind flashed to the tulip festival and to Sofia's quietly proud face as she showed him her finished display. He remembered her snarky comments whenever he reached for the wrong pair of earrings for a customer. He reached into his pocket and felt the belt buckle she'd crafted for him there. Instantly, he was full-body tired.

"You didn't forget where the plates were, did you? We should probably get you in with a follow-up specialist here to make sure there aren't any lasting effects from the memory loss."

"What? Oh, no," Isaiah said, realizing he must have missed her asking him to get plates for their dinner. He walked to the cabinet where he knew they were and grabbed two then took some chopsticks out of the silverware drawer. As his hand brushed the countertop, he pictured Sofia on New Year's Eve, slicing and dicing in that stunning dress as she prepared the sandwich.

He quickly shook the image away and took the dishes to the table, where Willow immediately began to serve herself. "I was starving. That's a long drive. I'm probably going to pass out right after dinner."

Isaiah nodded and continued to half listen and give short replies as Willow chatted throughout their meal. Despite her comment about being tired, Willow could still talk nonstop. He smiled a little at that. At least one thing hadn't changed.

After they finished eating and his sister went to bed, Isaiah changed into some comfortable shoes and left the apartment. He needed to clear his mind, and a green forest seemed like the only place to do it.

Chapter Fifty-Nine

SOFIA

Sofia awoke much earlier than she preferred the next morning, but she couldn't go back to sleep. Her eyes were raw from crying and her body deeply exhausted.

She crawled out of bed on autopilot and went straight for the coffee maker. Once it was running, she went to the front window and peered outside, hoping her tulips would cheer her up. She squinted into the still-dark sky, trying to make sense of what she saw.

Her tulips and the entire yard, from her porch out to the street, were covered with a light dusting of snow.

Sofia let out a mirthless laugh. "I was right," she said, wishing she could see the look on Isaiah's face in reaction to the late-spring snow. But she cleared that from her mind like plucking a rotten tomato from the vine, turning her thoughts to the impacts. A freeze at that point would kill the tulips as well as the garden she'd given in and started early in her backyard.

It felt like a slap in the face. She'd been expecting the late snow—knew it was coming deep in her bones, even—yet she'd let herself dive in as if it weren't. It was exactly what she'd done with Isaiah. And the consequences of both dives were going to haunt her.

After she finished her coffee, gulping down the hot drink too quickly, she went to her computer and pulled up her online store. Without more than a moment's thought, she delisted her entire WanderLost collection. She didn't want to make those designs anymore.

She flipped open her sketchbook, intent on planning a new line, but after nearly an hour, she hadn't produced anything she liked. Tears welled in her eyes, and she ripped the page of scribbles out of her notebook and tossed it across the room.

I'm acting like a heartsick teenager, and I'm not going to let myself do that a second time. She took a deep breath then stood, got dressed, and slipped on her hiking boots.

~

SOFIA PARKED AT THE TRAILHEAD AND BEGAN HER hike, just as she had a few months before. She still didn't like hiking. Isaiah hadn't changed that. No, she was just letting off some steam, resetting all that had occurred since she'd been on the trail that New Year's Eve.

It all felt a bit eerie to Sofia. There had been snow that New Year's Eve, and despite the weeks of blooming tulips they'd had, there was snow on the ground again. For a second, it made her wonder if she'd dreamed the past few months, but that would be too easy.

What she'd had with Isaiah—whatever it was—couldn't have hurt so much if it had all been a dream. *No, I'm not letting my mind go there today. I'm a grown woman, these are different circumstances, and I am equipped to handle this.*

She put her headphones in and turned on a podcast for women entrepreneurs. Despite what had happened with Isaiah, she had big goals, and that year, she was going to reach them.

Her business was hers to build and to control, and no one could take that away.

The minutes passed quickly, and soon, she was hiking near the spot where she'd found Isaiah that cold day in December. As she walked by it, an icy prickle ran over her skin. She shivered.

What on earth was that? She shook her arms out and turned up the volume on her podcast, determined not to think about Isaiah again.

When she reached the vista point where her mom had always liked to stop and look out over the woods sloping down below, she paused her podcast. Not for the first time, she thought how nice it would be to have a bench there.

She made a mental note to look into making that happen. It could be a memorial for her mom, like she'd seen in parks. Even if Sofia did enact a new tradition of connecting with her mom through a candle-lit boat launched onto the river, other visitors who enjoyed hiking could remember her mom as they passed through the area and found an unexpected place to rest.

Her mind flashed to Isaiah then—to him gently tugging her into the woods that night by the river, to the feel of his lips on hers. As she turned away from the vista point, she allowed a single tear to slip down her face before lifting her chin and turning toward home.

Chapter Sixty

ISAIAH

Golden Gate Park was lively by day, but a few hours after sunset, the normally busy fields were nearly empty, the cars that lined the streets on weekends all gone. The chilly overcast evening weather, the dark, wispy trees... Isaiah thought all of it matched his mood.

He hated how he'd left things with Sofia. But as his memories had continued to come back over the course of the night after the tulip festival, too much had come flooding in—the reason he'd left the military and why he'd wanted to hike the PCT. He'd done all that to forget, and oddly enough, some strange mishap in the woods outside of Emerald Hollow had temporarily made him *literally* forget it all.

Isaiah rounded the corner, and his heart rate increased as he felt something icy touch his face. *Is it... snowing?* He reached toward a falling white flake, and a pinprick of cold met his finger. He was not a native to the area, but even he knew that wasn't typical.

He found a bench and took a seat as the snow began to fall in earnest. Though he pulled up the hood on his jacket, he didn't feel the need to keep moving. The snow and the woods reminded him of the trail where he'd first met Sofia, and he didn't want her image to disappear. He wondered if she would ever go hiking on that trail again. *If I did the right thing by leaving her, why do I feel so wrong?*

He stuck his hands in the pockets of the jacket he'd slipped on for the walk and felt a thin round object there. He pulled it out and realized he had forgotten all about the coin he'd found while geocaching in Emerald Hollow. He read the inscription again. "Not all who wander are lost." Something constricted in his chest, and he let out a deep breath, oblivious to the cold.

And there he sat on a bench in Golden Gate Park as the first snow in San Francisco in more than fifty years fell around him.

Chapter Sixty-One

SOFIA

Sofia slunk into her usual bistro chair next to Holly in the Emerald House Café. With the sudden snow, the fireplace was roaring, and the café was crowded with locals and guests escaping from the cold.

Holly had her hands wrapped around a white mug, and she passed a second one to Sofia. *Good gracious, Holly's still drinking hot chocolate in March.* Sofia wanted to laugh, but her friend was so endearing that she simply couldn't.

Just because she was miserable didn't mean she wanted everyone else to be. That was another thing that had changed since her first heartbreak. Besides, it *had* snowed that morning. Maybe Holly had the right idea. She took the mug and gave it a little sip, instantly feeling warmer.

"Yours is spiked with a little rum. Ash thought you might want it. Sofia, I just feel so bad about all of this."

"What? Why? It's not your fault."

An expression somewhere between guilt and despair passed over Holly's face, but Sofia didn't linger on it. Holly experienced things deeply, and she could only hope that it would pass.

"It's just that, well, things have been a little different around here since I arrived, and I can't help but wonder if I've set the town... off-kilter?"

Sofia was so surprised by the comment that she let out a genuine laugh despite her mood. "Off-kilter? If you have, it's in a good way. Ever since you arrived, we've had the best harvest fest and Christmas Faire the town has ever seen. The tulips have seemed to bloom like Mary Poppins is in town, and..." She grabbed Holly's hand. "My best friend Ash is the happiest I've ever seen him."

Holly blushed, and Sofia smiled before it slipped off her face. "So there you have it. You're the best thing that's happened to this town in a while."

"But what about Isaiah? How does he factor in? You two seemed so *good* together."

Sofia sighed and took another long drink of her hot chocolate. "We really were, weren't we?" A spark passed through her at the words. They *had* been good. *So why doesn't he see that? Maybe I truly am the problem, just like Noah said.*

She turned toward Holly again. "Holly, you're a big-city girl, right? Traveling all over the world for work? Was it hard to settle down here in Emerald Hollow?"

Holly paused, seeming to know where Sofia was going with the question. "When I got here, it wasn't long before this place started to feel like... well, like home."

"So it wasn't totally off-putting and boring to someone like you?"

"Quite the opposite. I found Emerald Hollow to be charming and full of life. Because of the people here. People like you. You're the life of every party, Sof. Don't let that dim."

Sofia sniffed and clinked her mug against Holly's, both of which were nearly empty. The rum was taking effect, and she was a little more relaxed than she had been when she'd walked in. "You know what? You're right. I *am* the life of the party. Thank you for noticing."

Holly laughed. "It's hard not to."

Sofia's phone dinged, and she opened the social media app where she did most of her business advertising. As she registered what was on the screen, she let out a gasp.

"Is everything okay?" Holly asked, concern clouding her huge green eyes.

Sofia looked back down at her phone and sighed heavily. "I recently took down my new WanderLost collection, and people are not happy about it."

"Why'd you take it down? Oh..."

Sofia knew she didn't need to explain. "Yeah. Except it was my most popular line. I really didn't think people would notice, but..." She held out her phone to Holly to show her the dozens of comments and messages that had come through.

Holly squinted at the phone, not seeming to understand what she was seeing.

Sofia sighed and put the phone back in her purse. "I suppose I'll have to put the line back up. I was hoping to replace it with something better, but..." She paused and looked out the window. "I've never had my work resonate with people this much. Maybe you can't capture lightning twice, you know?"

"If anyone can, it's you," Holly said so confidently that Sofia thought she just might be able to believe it.

~

"CANDY CANES," SOFIA MURMURED AS SHE SURVEYED her front yard the next morning. As soon as the expression slipped out of her mouth, she scowled. *Why am I using one of Holly's Canada-isms?*

Ash had dropped her off at home after a few hours of girl time with Holly, and the spiked hot chocolate had assisted her in sleeping soundly, something she couldn't say for the previous night.

She scanned the yard again then quickly crossed the house to check the planters in the back. The snow had all melted, but the tulips and garden veggies she had started didn't seem the worse for wear. In fact, they looked healthier than ever.

It was almost as if, instead of being a killing frost, the snow had served as a fertilizer. She shook her head. *Nothing makes any sense these days.* She thought of Ash's words a few weeks ago about a rare soil event that was allowing the tulips to bloom earlier and for a longer time. She'd been meaning to research it but had been too sidetracked spending every free minute with Isaiah.

No. She quickly crushed her hands into her eyes and twisted them before stretching her arms over her head and doing a little shake. Sofia was not going to think about him that day. She had enough to deal with to get her clients back to being happy. Emerald Hollow Artisanal had to be her sole focus.

While Holly's confidence had nearly convinced her that she could recreate the magic of the WanderLost line with a new concept, sometime during the ride home, she'd realized she didn't want to. The WanderLost line had been her creation, no matter who had inspired it. She'd made something that connected with people, then she had deleted it like it was nothing. That wasn't fair to them or to her.

For the next few hours, she worked on a new piece for the collection, something she could share with her customers to announce that the line was back. She let all the emotions of the last few weeks run through her as she worked—suspicion, fear, and unease, which over time had given way to interest, care, excitement, and something she was pretty sure had been love.

She stopped her mind there before letting in the feelings of confusion and loss.

Sofia let her hands work rapidly, and by dinnertime, she had what she needed.

Chapter Sixty-Two

HOLLY

Holly spent some time with her reindeer and Comet in the forest that morning before going to find Ash. The surprise snow that had fallen the previous day was completely gone, and spring was back in full bloom, as if the ground had not been covered in a blanket of white mere hours ago.

Holly had been nervous when she'd first seen the snow. She didn't know what it meant, but she sensed deep within her that North Pole magic was somehow at work. But what it was up to, she didn't know. Ever since the moment in the restaurant, when Luca and Isaiah's sister, Willow, had realized they'd known each other from childhood, Holly had started to wonder if the North Pole's connection to Emerald Hollow was even more embedded than she realized.

Is there more to the goings-on in Emerald Hollow than my presence and the snow tunneling of the past? Or is it merely a coincidence that Willow lived here as a child? That seemed highly unlikely to Holly, and she wondered how much else there was to North Pole magic that she didn't understand.

That conversation combined with the little flash of snow—

and the magic she thought it indicated—had finally convinced her to do what she'd been putting off. She took a deep breath and walked back toward the Emerald House, Comet trotting happily beside her.

She'd even stayed up late after Sofia left the café concert, creeping into the dark kitchen to distract herself by baking. Automatically, without realizing what she was doing, she pulled out the ingredients for her North Pole-famous jingle pops and got to baking.

She wanted to give one to Auryn to express that she forgave him for the incident with Isaiah. While he had been at fault, it hadn't been intentional. If anything, she felt it was her fault for not keeping a closer eye on what was happening at the North Pole. It had been her asking Lumi about snow tunneling that allowed Auryn to overhear the conversation in the first place.

Ash walked into the kitchen just as Holly pulled the jingle pops out of the oven. He scratched his neck sleepily. "What are you still doing up?"

Holly moved so that her body blocked the jingle pops. She remembered what had happened when humans consumed them the previous year, and she didn't want a repeat of the situation. "Just doing a little baking. Something for Auryn."

Ash glanced at the oven, and his eyes widened. "Jingle pops? Yeah, you don't have to worry about me sneaking one of those. I don't want to be found line dancing in the café."

Holly choked out a laugh then relaxed as she saw the twinkle in Ash's eyes. "And what are *you* still doing up?"

"Felt like a late-night snack." He reached for a pan, set it on the stove, then began rummaging around in the large commercial fridge.

While Ash made them some omelets, Holly placed the jingle pops in Tupperware and stashed them deep in the kitchen cabinets—safely away from humans—with the intention of delivering them to the North Pole within a day or two, hoping they would cheer Auryn up.

Holly studied Ash as he prepared then plated their omelets. Everything about the man radiated a good-natured peace that she didn't see often in humans, and an icy fear gripped her heart as she thought about what she needed to do.

"Do you want a hot chocolate?" Ash asked, already moving to the pantry where he kept the secret recipe.

"Sure. That sounds great."

Ash expertly prepared the cocoa then passed it to Holly, joining her at the restaurant counter. She sipped it gratefully, letting the delicious, familiar flavor calm her.

The hot chocolate took her back to how their story began, with her trying it at the Emerald House on her first trip to Emerald Hollow and noticing it tasted exactly like the hot cocoa at the North Pole. The memory gave her the courage to pursue the thing that was nagging at her.

"So, Ash, there's something I've been wanting to discuss with you."

Ash paused eating and looked at her expectantly. Holly's chest squeezed. If she could sweat like a human, she guessed she would be perspiring at that moment.

"It's about—" She looked around and lowered her voice, even though the restaurant had been empty for hours. "It's about my magic."

"You don't think the elves have been snow tunneling again, do you?" Ash asked, his voice still completely casual, as if they were discussing the weather. Then his eyes widened. "Is that what that surprise snow dusting was about?"

Holly shook her head. "I don't know. Maybe. But that's not what... well, not *exactly* what I wanted to talk about."

Ash must have sensed her anxiety, because he took her hand. "Are you okay?"

"It's not me I'm worried about. It's you." Her voice was barely above a whisper.

"Me? I'm fine, Holly. What's bothering you?"

She took a deep breath and knew it was time to get it all over with. "I think possibly... I don't know for sure, but I have a suspicion—" She paused to take a sip of her hot cocoa, letting it fortify her. "I think it's possible that your mom disappeared through a snow tunnel years ago." The words came out in a whoosh, then she held her breath.

Something strange happened to Ash's face then. First, he looked confused, as if he couldn't comprehend what she was saying. Then his eyebrows rose with understanding and surprise, and finally, his face tightened, and he shook his head. "Holly, I don't think so."

"How do you know? She disappeared during a snowstorm. You and your dad never heard from her again. That was around the time that Lumi said snow tunneling was getting out of control. There have been so many signs of magic being connected to Emerald Hollow. It's possible..."

He shook his head again, and she quieted, wanting to give him the space to think or speak.

"My dad said they'd been fighting that day, and they'd been unhappy for a while. It wasn't like everything was perfectly fine and she just disappeared. It's not like with Isaiah."

"That's true," Holly said, not wanting to push. "I've just been having this weird feeling about it, and I wanted to tell you. We don't have to discuss it anymore if you don't want to."

Ash looked across the dark restaurant toward one of the large windows, his eyes cloudy.

"I'm sorry," Holly began, "I didn't mean to—"

He stopped her by getting up from the counter. Drawing her up and into his arms, he planted a warm, sweet kiss on her forehead. "I'm glad you shared what was bothering you."

Holly leaned back to study his face, still worried that she'd upset him.

"I've got to get back to bed, but we can talk more tomorrow, okay?"

Holly nodded and gave him a smile, but as he walked away, she experienced a crushing sense of failure she hadn't encountered since the time she'd almost ruined Christmas for the entire world.

Chapter Sixty-Three

ASH

Holly's words in the kitchen followed Ash all the next day, and he worked at an even quicker pace than normal, diving into every project with the intensity of a blizzard.

She disappeared during a snowstorm. He grabbed a heavy box and heaved it onto a shelf in the pantry.

You and your dad never heard from her again. He expertly sliced open another box and began to unpack the cans of tomatoes.

That was around the time Lumi said snow tunneling was getting out of control. He refocused intently on the inventory sheet he was filling out then closed his eyes as he processed her words again.

You and your dad never heard from her again.

Is that true? He'd always thought that was the case, but his dad had finally told him the previous year that he thought he'd received a postcard from her. He'd said it had turned out to be the wrong address. *But what if...*

He set the clipboard with the inventory sheet on the pantry shelf and pulled out his phone, his hands shaking.

Chapter Sixty-Four
HOLLY

Holly was working on putting away decorations from the tulip festival when Ash burst into the storage room. She stood up quickly upon seeing the harried look on his face, her chest tightening.

"Ash, what's wrong?"

"I'm heading out to my dad's. Will you come with me?"

Holly's eyes widened with surprise, but she stepped away from the boxes she'd been organizing, moving toward Ash, and said, "Of course."

Lately, Holly had been doing all the driving, since she'd learned the new skill and fallen in love with it. But that day, when Ash jumped into the driver's seat, she didn't protest. A fire had been lit under him, and she wasn't going to do anything to slow him down.

"I don't know if I ever told you this, but last year, when you were gone and I called my dad, he mentioned something about a postcard he'd received when I was a kid."

"A postcard?" Holly turned to look at him as they raced down the highway toward the outskirts of town, where she knew

Ash's dad lived. They'd been there once for dinner a few weeks earlier.

"He thought it was from my mom because of the handwriting but dismissed it as junk mail when he didn't recognize the name or return address."

Holly gasped. "So you think...?"

Ash shrugged, his face tight. "I don't know. But it's worth a shot."

Fifteen minutes later, they were sitting at the small round kitchen table in Michael's cabin.

After some brief small talk and Michael's telling Holly he was delighted to see her again, Ash got down to business.

"Dad, do you still have that postcard? The one you thought was from mom?"

Michael ran a hand through his thinning hair and quirked his lips, thinking. Ash had warned him why he was coming with a phone call. The man, who was in his sixties and still quite fit, walked to a china cabinet and began to search through drawers. "If I kept it, I probably would have tossed it in here."

He continued to sort through the stacks of papers, and Holly slipped her hand into Ash's under the table.

"Well, I'll be darned. Here it is." He held out the postcard to Ash, who released Holly's hand and took it anxiously.

Holly watched as he studied the writing for a moment then flipped it over to see the image on the front.

"Greetings from..." He paused, and Holly thought he was barely breathing. He turned to her, his eyes wide. "This postcard is from Finland."

Ash's mind was whirling as he tore his eyes from Holly's and looked back at the postcard.

"It says it's from a woman named Helena. Her address is on here." Ash's hands trembled slightly, and he set the postcard on the table.

Holly quickly picked it up. "This can't be a coincidence."

"Is one of you going to tell me what's going on here?" Michael asked.

Ash let out a breath. They had to tread lightly. Like everyone else in Emerald Hollow, his dad didn't know who Holly really was or that North Pole magic ran through her. He turned to Holly, and they locked eyes for a moment, having a silent conversation.

After a few seconds, Holly spoke. "Michael, I don't know if Ash ever told you this, but the reason I came to Emerald Hollow in the first place was because of something I saw in Finland. I was at a café in Helsinki, and there was a flyer for the Emerald Hollow harvest festival. I was going to be in this part of the world in October anyway, so I decided to drop in. Ash and I were both curious as to how a poster for a festival in Oregon ended up in Finland, since no one here seems to have any contacts there."

She took a deep breath as Ash studied his father. For the moment, his face was calm, with just a slight pull of confusion in his lips.

"Recently, there's been a man in Emerald Hollow who suffered memory loss in the woods. When we were researching what had happened to him... we started to wonder if something similar could have happened to..."

Ash knew she wasn't sure if she should say the words *your wife*.

"To Mom," he said just as Michael's features widened with shock.

"Why on earth would you think that?"

"We can't really explain it, Dad, but as we were talking about it, I remembered the postcard you mentioned. How you thought it was in mom's handwriting, but the name wasn't familiar. If she had lost her memories, maybe there was a time where she still felt some connection to us and sent the postcard. Almost as if by..." Ash couldn't use the word that described the situation most accurately.

"That's as implausible as anything I've ever heard, Ash. If that were true, how'd she wind up in Finland? Wouldn't she just turn up a town or two over?"

Ash cast his eyes to Holly, who said, "I know it sounds impossible. But sometimes there are things we can't explain. This may turn out to be nothing, but I think... I think Ash and I should go to Finland. If he wants to, that is." She turned her gaze toward him, those bright-green eyes searching his.

Ash squeezed her hand then nodded. "I'm in."

Chapter Sixty-Six

SOFIA

"Finland? I rarely see you leave Emerald Hollow for a vacation, and now you're heading across the world?" Sofia asked, incredulous. Despite her surprise at the abruptness of the announcement, she was happy for them. Ash never took vacations, and he deserved a break. Still, she couldn't help thinking that their timing wasn't the best. Isaiah had left a little over a week ago, and with Ash and Holly going, too, part of her felt like she was being left behind.

"It should be a quick trip. We think Ash may have some roots there, and it's one of my favorite places, so why not now?" Holly had her arms wrapped around Ash's waist from the side and was leaning into him.

Sofia's heart squeezed at how happy they looked. She tried not to think about how Isaiah's arms had felt around her.

"Well, you two have an amazing time. And bring me back some chocolate."

Holly laughed. "We will. I'm going to go load the car."

As Holly left the room, Ash turned back to Sofia.

"Are you sure you're okay with our leaving right now? I know that it might not be the best timing..."

That he'd read her mind made her feel instantly better. "Of course I am. You deserve this. But I was serious about the chocolate. There will be consequences if I don't get to try some Finnish chocolate."

Ash grinned and gave her a quick hug. "Thanks for holding down the fort and watching Comet. See you in a few days."

Sofia watched through the restaurant window as they drove away, headed to the airport a few hours from Emerald Hollow. She had a suspicion there was something about the trip—and the spontaneity of it—that they weren't telling her. But she didn't have the mental capacity to dwell on that.

Between relaunching the WanderLost collection, trying not to think of Isaiah, and keeping up with her suddenly thriving garden, Sofia was busier than ever. And while Ash and Holly were off to Finland, she had the Emerald House to run.

SOFIA WAS CLEANING UP THE KITCHEN AFTER THE morning breakfast rush when she found a Tupperware container in the cabinet. It was full of Holly's cake pop creations. Sofia knew what they were on first sight because they were identical to the ones Holly had made at her home the previous year for the ugly sweater Christmas party. *What did she call them?* The festive name came back to her. *Jingle pops.*

Sofia realized Holly must have made them then forgotten about them in their rush to head to Finland. They would be bad by the time Holly returned to Emerald Hollow. Sofia took one out of the container and ate it in two quick bites. She had fond memories of the ugly-sweater party and suddenly pictured herself there later that year with Isaiah.

Instead of the thought causing a deep sadness like she'd expected, Sofia felt surprisingly relaxed, like she could conquer anything.

She ate another jingle pop, the feeling of relaxation increasing.

St. Patrick's Day was coming up the next week, and an idea came to her like a butterfly landing softly on a flower.

SOFIA PASSED THE JINGLE POPS OUT TO THE OTHER employees of the Emerald House who were on shift. She'd had four of the cake pop treats already, and she had decided they were the best things she'd ever tasted.

The rest of the workday flew by in a whimsical rush, Sofia feeling like Cinderella as the birds helped her get dressed in the morning. All her regular tasks of serving and cleaning were delightful and easy that day, and all the employees were working in sync. She'd been nervous about being in charge while Ash was gone, but now she wondered why she'd ever worried.

When she mentioned the plan that had formed in her mind for St. Patrick's Day, each of the other employees agreed fervently. Sofia's shift ended at three, and she met with a few of the other employees in the café. They spent the next few hours creating colorful posters, preparing riddles, and crafting displays, even breaking into Holly's décor-supply closet.

By the time everyone was ready to go home, they had a huge load of supplies ready in the storage room and a large pile of colorful printed flyers.

"Spread the word," Sofia said in a singsong voice, handing them each a stack. "The hunt starts at noon on St. Patrick's Day."

Chapter Sixty-Seven

SOFIA

As Sofia sipped her coffee the next morning, events from the previous day began to creep into her memory. She nearly spat out her coffee when she remembered what she had done.

Maybe it was all a dream. She immediately picked up her phone and called her young coworker, Tyler, who was working the morning shift that day. He answered on the second ring.

"Tyler? Please tell me I'm wrong about something. Did we all... plan a St. Patrick's Day treasure hunt yesterday?"

Tyler laughed. "Yeah, we did. Usually, Ash is the one to come up with those kinds of ideas, but that was all you. Everyone was really into it. I think it's going to be a blast."

Sofia grimaced. *So it wasn't a dream. What came over me?*

"Maybe no one will sign up," Sofia said hopefully.

"Nice try. We've had people coming in or calling to add their names to the list all morning. We already have thirty participants."

Sofia sat up straighter and took a deep breath. St. Patrick's Day was on Saturday, and Holly and Ash were not likely to be back by then—which meant she was running the thing.

"Okay. Thanks, Tyler. Call if you need anything today."

They hung up, and Sofia sat in open-mouthed astonishment for a moment.

What took over me yesterday? She had a fuzzy memory of gobbling down jingle pops. *Did Holly spike them or something?* She shook her head. There was no way. Holly didn't even drink. She could only chalk it up to a temporary loss of mind because of everyone abandoning her at once.

Sofia pushed thoughts of abandonment out of her mind. She still didn't know what had caused Isaiah to leave. She hated having things be so unfinished between them, but she'd taken the lessons learned from her breakup with Noah seriously.

And she missed Isaiah—fiercely—but she wouldn't let his presence or absence dictate her happiness like Noah's had, not entirely. Her mom wouldn't want that for her again, and she didn't want it for herself.

So Sofia poured a second cup of coffee and went to her fabric box. *If I'm going to run this treasure hunt, I'm going to look darn good while doing it.*

Chapter Sixty-Eight

ASH

The reindeer landed in a large field in Helsinki. Their "drive" to the airport had only been for cover. The reindeer were a much more efficient form of transportation, and the creatures were always ready to flex their flying muscles.

Holly led him to the café where Lumi, the oldest elf, worked part time, blending in seamlessly with the humans. He tried to take in the beauty of the city around him despite his nerves over what might or might not be coming. Compared to Emerald Hollow, it still felt cold in Helsinki, and he took Holly's hand.

When they arrived at the café, they paused.

Holly turned to him. "Ash, if this doesn't turn out to be what I thought..."

He shook his head. "I'm prepared for that. I'm glad you brought your suspicions to me. If it turns out to be nothing, I'll know for sure that she left of her own accord, and I can live with that now."

Hand in hand, they entered the café. Lumi, whom Ash recognized from the tulip festival and witnessing as Auryn restored Isaiah's memories, came out from around the counter to greet them. She smiled, but wariness showed on her face.

After giving them each a hug she said, "I'm guessing this isn't a social call."

Holly shook her head. "Not exactly." She explained everything they knew about Ash's mom and her disappearance so many years ago, Lumi listening intently. Then Holly shared something Ash hadn't heard yet.

"Lumi, I know that you're an expert snow tunneler now. But is there any chance that back then, you could have left some traces of magic in Emerald Hollow? You're the only elf I know with a connection to Finland."

Lumi shook her head. "I told you last year, Holly, I'd never been to Emerald Hollow. The tulip festival was my first visit."

"I know you'd never been into the town, but what about the woods outside? If you'd been visiting a nearby city and had used the snow there as a tunneling point..."

They watched an expression of concern creep across Lumi's face.

"It wasn't me," she said.

Both Ash and Holly seemed to deflate, their shoulders falling.

"But I think it could have been my sister."

Chapter Sixty-Nine

HOLLY

L umi, Holly, and Ash had coffee and pastries in the café as Lumi explained how the Kringle elves had snow tunneled often when she was younger. Lumi's favorite place was Finland, and she mainly went from the North Pole to Finland and back.

"But there were some Kringles who had the travel bug. They went anywhere there was snow. My sister was one of them. She was generally careful and in control of her snow tunneling, but she did it so often that she started to get careless. And she wasn't the only one. This was all about twenty years ago, and the elves and your father, Holly, decided we needed to put an end to the snow tunneling. We didn't ban it completely, but it had to be done much less frequently and only by trusted, experienced elves. My sister, Luna, is the only other elf I knew around that time who was also coming to Finland. So if there's a connection between Emerald Hollow and Finland, I think it could have been through her."

Holly's heart sank as she listened. "With Isaiah's memory loss, Auryn had to be the one who restored it, since he was the elf who opened the tunnel. If Luna did have a connection to what happened to Ash's mom, and Luna has since passed on..."

A look of devastation washed across Ash's face as he realized what that meant. Holly took his hand under the table.

Lumi was quiet for a moment. "I'm quite strong, Holly. And Luna was my sister, so our magic was very similar. I think there's a chance that if we found Ash's mom, and if she truly did pass through a snow tunnel made by my sister, I could serve as a substitute and restore her memories, at least in part."

Holly gasped, and Ash looked at Lumi in relief.

"So I guess the next step is finding Ash's mom, Eleanor, and determining whether any of this is even true." Holly pulled out the postcard and slid it to Lumi. "It was sent years ago, so we have no idea if the address is even accurate. But we're looking for a woman named Helena—"

"Helena Laine," Lumi said. She gave a wry smile. "Well, this shouldn't be too difficult. I know a woman by that name. And she lives right down the street."

Chapter Seventy

SOFIA

Sofia arrived at the Emerald House predawn, dressed in a formfitting Irish barmaid costume she'd sewn, her hair in loose curls falling to her shoulders. She failed to suppress a yawn as she looked around at the rest of the volunteer treasure team who were trickling in the front door.

Despite the sadness that was hovering under her skin at the realization that Isaiah wouldn't be there to tease her about her costume, Sofia couldn't help but grin as she looked at the group. Tyler and the other Emerald House employees were all wearing shades of green. Some wore flashing shamrock necklaces. Tyler was sporting a long orange beard.

"Okay, so it looks like things are all set here," Sofia said, motioning to the few boxes they'd assembled during their feverish planning. "We just need to drop the coins at the various checkpoints and get the treasure ready at the end of the rainbow."

The group formed pairs and selected checkpoints to set up. Tyler paired with Sofia to do the treasure box. They filled it with chocolate coins and four golden tickets to the summer's carnival.

"All right. Let's do this," Sofia said, picking up the ornate box. Tyler followed and helped her load it into the trunk of her car.

"It was pretty brilliant to have the clues lead out to Jewel's Meadow," Tyler said as they pulled away from the Emerald House.

Sofia blinked. "I hadn't even thought of that when we set it up."

"It was strange, right? How everything was just flowing for us?" Tyler's lanky frame was relaxed in her front seat as he looked out the passenger window.

Her heart squeezed as she realized Isaiah was the last person who had sat there.

"I have no idea how we created that map and the clues so quickly."

"Neither do I," Sofia said, not wanting to admit how much it bothered her that she couldn't explain what had happened that night.

"It felt like something that would happen when Holly was around, but she was out of town."

Sofia frowned. "What do you mean?"

Tyler shrugged. "Things just always feel... different when she's around. Somehow relaxed and exciting all at once. Like anything could happen, and it would be okay if it did."

Sofia turned toward him, surprised. *Does he have a crush on Holly?* But the more she thought about it, she realized she knew what he meant. Holly had brought something unique to the town that she couldn't explain. Maybe she and Ash weren't the only ones who had benefitted from her presence.

She eased the car down a dirt road and parked at the end of it. At the edge of the trees was a tiny wooden sign battered with age, which read Jewel's Meadow.

Sofia retrieved the treasure box from the trunk and followed Tyler through the thin woods. As they emerged into the clearing, the early-morning sun sent streaks down to the ground, casting an enchanting look over the blades of grass and vibrant flowers that encompassed the field. The tulips were still blooming around town, but in the clearing, there was a stunning assortment of wildflowers in all colors. Butterflies flitted from bloom to bloom as if they'd found the perfect sanctuary in the meadow. Sofia's breath caught as she looked around. For a moment, she wondered if she'd ever seen anything more beautiful.

"Right in the middle?" Tyler called, snapping her out of her moment of wonder.

"Sure," she said, helping him carry the treasure box to the center of the meadow.

They nestled it into the ground, and Tyler sprinkled some gold tinsel from the bag he'd been carrying across the grass and wildflowers around it.

Just as they prepared to leave, the sun disappeared, and a dark cloud rolled overhead. *Great. It's going to storm today,* she thought glumly, the magic of the dawn in the meadow fully dissolved.

"May the best leprechaun win," Tyler said, seemingly unaffected by the change in the air.

Sofia cast one last glance at the ominous sky as they turned their backs to the treasure box and left Jewel's Meadow.

Chapter Seventy-One

SOFIA

After returning to the Emerald House for a quick breakfast, Sofia headed back to the meadow. She'd volunteered to man the final destination, the treasure box, during the hunt. Tyler, whom she was realizing more and more was an extremely capable young man, had volunteered to kick off the event.

Sometime within the last hour, he'd passed out the maps they'd created to the leprechaun groups, as they'd decided to call them during their feverish planning. The treasure hunt was well underway. Other volunteers from their treasure team were posted at the other stops with water, snacks, and the special coins that needed to be collected before they reached the final stop.

Sofia sat in a camp chair at the edge of the meadow, hidden by the trees. She pulled out her laptop to edit some of her product photos while she waited for the winners to arrive.

It wasn't lost on her that her feverish planning of the treasure hunt might have been subconsciously inspired by Isaiah and the geocaching they'd done together. She just hoped she could get through the day without constantly thinking about him.

Sofia had been working for half an hour when the dark clouds finally let loose. But instead of a heavy downpour, it was a soft sprinkle, as if the clouds were holding something back. Sofia adjusted her camp chair so that she was fully protected under the dense branches of the pine trees and continued to work, emptying her mind of anything else.

THE TIME PASSED QUICKLY AS SOFIA WAITED FOR A leprechaun team to come claim the final prize, the soft mist falling around her as she worked. Eventually, a slice of sunlight streaked across her computer screen, and Sofia looked up as the sky brightened, and she smiled in surprise. The clouds were moving away, the mist dissolving, and to her delight, a massive rainbow formed in front of her.

She stood, barely able to believe her eyes. She'd seen rainbows many times throughout her life, but she'd never seen the end of one. But on St. Patrick's Day, during the middle of a treasure hunt, a rainbow had landed in Jewel's Meadow, right over the treasure box.

Sofia set down her laptop and began to walk toward the rainbow, feeling as if she were in another world, in complete awe of the sight before her. It was as if the light were dancing around her from every direction. She experienced a sense of surrealness similar to when the two hummingbirds had appeared on her porch late at night. Time seemed to slow down as she marveled at the natural world, and she wanted to stand in the exact spot where she thought the rainbow met the ground.

Halfway to the treasure box, she noticed she wasn't alone. Two figures emerged from the trees on the other side of the meadow. Sofia realized that one of the leprechaun teams had finally deciphered the map and found the treasure box.

As they moved closer, Sofia tried to make out who it was.

Along with a man was a boy who, based on height, was probably elementary school aged. With a sharp intake of breath, she recognized them. The boy was Henry, son of Matilda and Ben, who ran the museum.

But the man wasn't Henry's dad. The tall, devastatingly handsome man striding toward her through a real-life rainbow was Isaiah.

Chapter Seventy-Two

SOFIA

"Did I really just find you at the end of a rainbow?" Isaiah asked, a wicked gleam in his eyes, as Henry ran to the treasure box.

Sofia was so shocked to see him that her usual snarkiness didn't immediately flare. Instead, she just stared at him, disbelieving.

"You're pretty cute as a bar maiden," he said, and that broke the spell.

Sofia rolled her eyes. She threw up her arms in exasperation, though she was still stunned at seeing him. Her legs were slightly shaky. "What are you doing here, Isaiah?"

"You didn't think you could put together a scavenger hunt with clues and a map that led to you and not have me be the one to get here first, did you?" His eyes were sparkling, forming heart-melting lines at the corners.

Sofia pursed her lips. "It wasn't supposed to lead to me. It's leading to the pot of gold."

Isaiah snorted. "You think that's what I came back for?"

Sofia tried to ignore how that comment made her feel, but tingles spread from her chest through her limbs. She narrowed her eyes as something occurred to her, and she studied his face carefully as she asked, "How did you hear about the treasure hunt anyway?"

For once, Isaiah didn't have a quick retort. He seemed to struggle over what to say. Finally, his shoulders relaxed, and he shrugged. "Okay, you caught me. I was already in town. I got here last night and saw the flyers for the event."

"Last night? Why were you in town? Did you forget something?" Her tone was more accusatory than she'd intended. Her heart was beating too quickly, a tiny bubble of hope mixed up with the hurt and confusion floating just under the surface of her question.

Isaiah, whose right hand had slipped into his pocket, moved it in front of him. A small raffle ticket that Sofia recognized as being from Groundhog Day was clasped between his fingers. A smile tugged at the corners of his mouth. "You owe me an Italian dinner date, remember?"

Chapter Seventy-Three

ASH

Ash's heart pounded as he and Holly followed Lumi down the street, blood rushing in his ears. He couldn't hear anything around him. Then a small, warm hand slid into his, and Holly's presence greeted him like a calming fireplace. He squeezed her hand, and together, they watched as Lumi knocked on the door of the apartment that belonged to Helena Laine.

The plum-colored door swung open, and a woman appeared. She had dark-blond hair that was naturally blended with gray in a way that made her look like a gracefully aging film star. She beamed when she saw Lumi.

"Lia! What brings you here today?" Helena asked.

Ash's chest constricted. *Is her voice familiar?* He couldn't tell. It had a warm tone to it that he thought he remembered, but she spoke with an accent he didn't recognize.

"Hello, Helena. These are my friends Holly and Ash. They're visiting from the United States. We were hoping you'd take a walk with us."

The woman looked over Holly and Ash curiously. When her

eyes landed on Ash's face, her expression changed slightly, and her eyebrows rose. "Do I know you?"

Ash was about to speak when Lumi touched Helena's arm. "Can we talk on the way to the park?"

Helena turned back into her house and emerged with a coat, which she slipped on as the foursome began to walk down the road. She kept casting glances at Ash, and he wanted so badly to tell her everything. But they'd agreed they didn't want to shock her, so he let Lumi take the lead.

"Helena, when we met many years ago, you told me you'd come here on an exchange program in college and decided to stay. Was that true?"

Helena's forehead creased. She glanced back at Holly and Ash. "Lia, I—"

"It's okay," Lumi said. "You can talk freely in front of them. I've known Holly all her life."

Helena nodded, Lumi's words seeming to have soothed her. "To be honest, Lia, I made that up about the exchange program." She wrung her hands then continued to speak. "I woke up in the heart of Helsinki on a snowy winter day and just... didn't have any memories of what came before. I went to a nearby church, and they helped me to see a doctor, but we couldn't find any explanation for it. I suppose there are better treatments for it now, but at the time, they told me that I should just wait for my memories to come back."

Ash's heart was racing again, and Holly still held his hand tightly.

"I made friends at the church who gave me a job, and soon, I became roommates with another young woman. Eventually, I grew comfortable in my life here, though I always knew something was missing. I wondered if I had family somewhere looking for me. It's hard to explain what it feels like, not having a past. At times, I felt almost like an alien who had dropped out of the sky." She laughed, and the sound hit Ash with force.

Her laugh was a sound he'd carried with him his entire life. He wanted to reach out, but he forced himself to wait a little longer. They had just reached the park, which was thick with trees and a spattering of snow.

"There were times when I had little inklings about my past, like hobbies I enjoyed." Helena's brow knitted. "There was one time when I had a strong feeling about a place that came up when I was browsing tourist destinations on the internet. I did that, sometimes, wondering if I would stumble across anywhere that would spur my memory. It was a town in the United States, actually."

She glanced in the direction of Ash and Holly before continuing. "In Oregon. A cozy-looking inn appeared on the town's website, and I sent a postcard there. I can't even remember what I wrote on it. Probably just 'Season's greetings' or something silly like that. I never heard back, so I figured it hadn't meant anything. Or that whoever I'd left there preferred to leave things with me in the past." She sounded sad, and Ash's heart broke.

"Helena, I'm so sorry I didn't know about this earlier, but I think there's an explanation for your memory loss. I can't explain it completely, but if I told you I could help you restore your memories, what would you say?"

Helena gasped, and her arms were shaking. Lumi clasped his mother's hands.

"Lia, none of this makes any sense, but I've known you a long time, and I trust you. But how can I get my memories back?"

"I just need you to stand right over here and close your eyes."

"What on earth?" Helena asked, but then her eyes shot to Ash's, and she nodded decisively. "Okay, I'll do it." She walked a few feet away from them and locked eyes with Ash before closing them.

Holly and Lumi glanced around to make sure they were

alone, but he couldn't take his eyes off the woman in front of him.

As he stared at her openly, he could see all the little features he'd forgotten over the years—the slightly upturned nose and the long, light lashes. He inhaled sharply.

Lia moved her hand, and the snow around them began to swirl. He watched in awe as, just like with Auryn and Isaiah in the woods, Lia seemed to form a tunnel of snow that swirled around his mother. After a few seconds that felt like a lifetime, the snow calmed, and Helena opened her eyes.

For a moment, she just stood there, her body stiff. Then she looked at Ash and ran to him as she said, "Oh, Ash, my boy!"

Chapter Seventy-Four

SOFIA

"You're taking me to an Italian restaurant on St. Patrick's Day?" Sofia asked skeptically as Isaiah climbed into her passenger seat. Isaiah and Henry had been crowned the winners of the first annual Emerald Hollow St. Patrick's Day Treasure Hunt, then Sofia had gone home to change out of her barmaid costume.

She hadn't hesitated when Isaiah asked her to dinner. Yes, he'd left with very little explanation after an overwhelming experience of getting all his memories back. But while she'd been hurt by the abrupt way he'd left things, what he had done was nothing like what Noah had done. He deserved a chance to explain, and she craved an explanation. After months of only knowing the limited-memory Isaiah, she was desperate to know what he was like with his history back.

And seeing him there, under the rainbow in Jewel's Meadow, had sparked a feeling in her like the one she'd felt when they were wrapped up in the kites together or when the hummingbirds visited her porch, as if some magical essence she'd never encountered before was nudging things along. Sofia wondered if those feelings were what people meant when they spoke of fate. But no matter what had led him to that meadow, it had been too magical of a moment to say anything but yes.

Before dinner, she'd changed into a sleek black dress and heeled boots but left the shamrock earrings on. Some traditions, she preferred to keep.

"Don't you worry. The owner was advertising some kind of Italian-style corned beef special." He winked at her then ran his eyes over her outfit. "You look stunning."

"Don't start flattering me now," she said, though she glanced over and gave an appreciative look at the svelte suit he had donned. "Though you do clean up all right."

"Just all right? I broke out the big guns for tonight. I don't usually wear this unless I'm going to a wedding or a funeral."

His voice changed on the last word, and silence rang throughout the vehicle for a few moments. Sofia kept her eyes straight ahead as she drove to the restaurant. She was suddenly uncharacteristically nervous to have dinner with him.

They parked on Main Street then entered the Italian restaurant together, Isaiah holding the door open for her. As she passed by, she noticed he smelled like expensive cologne, something he'd never worn in Emerald Hollow before, and it had the desired effect. Part of her wanted to pause and kiss him right then, but she wasn't sure if they would ever be kissing again or if Isaiah had come to give her an explanation then say goodbye for good.

They made small talk about the treasure hunt until they ordered, then they both seemed to sense that it was time to get down to business.

"Okay, let's do this," Sofia said, after taking a gulp of her wine. "Why did you leave like that?"

Isaiah nodded as if he had anticipated her question. "Things were... strange when I got my memories back. It was good at first. I was excited to share everything with you. Then as I started to remember more and more, I just sort of... panicked."

Sofia watched him closely but didn't speak. She resisted reaching into the bread basket to give her something to do with her hands.

"The truth is a lot different from how I made it seem at first. Yes, all my memories came rushing back, but there were many things about my life that I hadn't processed yet." He took a deep breath, and Sofia watched him carefully.

"The reason I was hiking the Pacific Crest Trail this spring was in memory of a fallen comrade. A good friend from my hometown who joined the army around when I did. He was killed in action a year ago and—"

Sofia sucked in a deep breath and reached across the table to put her hand on his. "I'm so sorry, Isaiah." She knew the pain of losing someone, and she couldn't imagine what it would be like to have that memory come crashing down on you suddenly.

Isaiah squeezed her hand. "I was doing the hike as a memorial to him. I was his commanding officer, and I felt responsible and useless when he died. It was like everything about my identity disappeared in an instant, and nothing felt right anymore. His death was the reason I got out of the military. Too many constant reminders. But I'd been struggling with my next steps. That's why I went to stay with my sister until I could figure out where I wanted to settle down. I figured I would decide all that after I hiked the PCT."

"That makes a lot of sense, Isaiah."

"The truth was I'd been trying to make the pain disappear. I couldn't work through it, as much as I tried. It was so hard to carry—"

His voice caught, and Sofia wanted to walk around the side of the table and put her arms around him. But she didn't. She wanted to let him get it out.

"I think I would have done anything to forget it all. I tried lots of things, none of them healthy. Hiking the PCT was kind of a last resort. But then all this happened. I lost my memory, and I *actually* forgot about my friend's death. I forgot my friend completely. When it all came back... it felt like an anvil smacking into my chest."

He paused and took a sip of his wine, and Sofia mirrored him, a thick lump in her throat.

"But when I went back to San Francisco, I realized something. I couldn't forget my friend's death. I couldn't block out what had happened. And I didn't want to, because forgetting the things you cared about—the things that make you who you are—I realize now that that is worse than anything."

"Oh, Isaiah," Sofia began, but he continued.

"But something good came out of it. Two things, actually. I realized that having those memories, even the ones that hurt, are better than having none at all. It means I've lived and loved, you know?"

Sofia nodded, tears filling her eyes. She would never want to forget her mom, despite all the pain that losing her had caused.

"And the second thing..." He met her eyes and took both of her hands. "Is that I met you. You, Emerald Hollow, starting a business here, honoring my friend's memory how I can—that is what I want. More than anything."

Sofia swallowed and tried to smile, but she still had a lump in her throat. "Really? You don't want a fancy life in the city?"

"I never wanted that. I didn't *know* what I wanted. But now I do. And I have you to thank for that. I have no excuse for running out on you so suddenly. I can't explain it other than to say I thought that sparing you from the onslaught of my emotional mess was the right thing to do. But I don't believe that anymore. You are the smartest, strongest, sexiest—" He paused, and Sofia's mind flashed to that night in the Emerald House kitchen, when he'd overheard her calling him a "sexy stranger." "Woman I've ever met. And you get to make your own judgments."

A smile crept over Sofia's face, and she clenched her bottom lip between her teeth.

Isaiah continued, "I know you don't think you're the best judge of character, but that's not true. Whoever made you feel that way, that says everything negative about them, and the only thing it says about you is that you're kind, open, and willing to find the good in your world. There's no one I would rather see who I am than you. Even if you didn't believe me about the amnesia and called me a malingerer that one time."

He grinned, and Sofia barked out a laugh. *So he did hear the word correctly.*

After she'd let him sweat for a moment or two while she collected her thoughts, she finally spoke. "I thought you were gone forever. Then when you showed up today, with that stupid crumpled raffle ticket, of all things..." She let out a laugh and rolled her eyes, and the genuine smile that she loved so much came out for the first time since they'd sat down.

"You thought I'd forget about the dinner you owed me, Wrecker? Not in a million years."

Sofia couldn't help herself. She pushed back her chair, walked around the table, and plunked herself onto his lap. Before he could say anything, she wrapped her arms around his neck and kissed him.

<h1 style="text-align:center">Chapter Seventy-Five</h1>

ASH

Ash was nervous for the reunion of his parents. He had flown commercial back to the United States with his mom, while Holly had flown back with the reindeer, claiming to take a different flight.

He'd called his dad and warned him of what was coming. It wasn't the type of thing you just sprang on a man. They pulled up to his dad's cabin, and Holly and his mom followed him up to the porch.

His dad opened the door and stepped out. His eyes went to Ash first, then he turned, and they landed on Helena. He sucked in a breath. "Eleanor," he whispered.

"Michael."

They walked toward each other and immediately hugged. Seconds later, both burst out laughing.

"Ash told me you lost your memories. And you just got them back?"

"It's impossible to explain, Michael. I don't even understand it myself."

"So you didn't leave us all those years ago?" A kind of cautious hope sat behind his eyes, and Ash could barely watch.

"I was just going for a drive to clear my head, and I decided to walk in the woods, out toward where we'd set up that old birdhouse geocache. Remember that? Then the storm seemed like it came out of nowhere, and the next thing I knew, I was in Finland, with no memories of who I was or how I got there. The only thing I could remember was that my name was Helena, and somehow, I spoke English and Finnish."

"Helena is the Finnish equivalent of Eleanor," Holly said quietly.

Ash's dad looked at Ash then Holly and back again. "You two know how crazy this sounds, right? How did she get to Finland?"

Ash was saved from lying when his mom spoke again. "Something must have happened in between. Maybe I fell and bumped my head. Probably, I got disoriented and walked out of town. Maybe I got on a bus? I'm not sure at what point I lost my memories. Somehow, I ended up in Finland."

"With no identification? How'd you get on a plane?" Ash's dad's voice was filled with compassion, but his confusion was palpable.

Ash glanced at Holly and noticed her staring at his dad, a strange expression in her eyes. The next thing he knew, his dad seemed to relax.

"Well, like Ash said on the phone, some things can't be explained. And it's ancient history. I know Ash is glad to have you back in his life again."

Ash let out a deep breath, wondering what kind of magic Holly had just worked on him.

"Maybe we can all have dinner. I'll cook," Ash offered. He realized that there wasn't going to be a magical love-at-second-sight reunion for his parents. They both needed time to process what had happened, and he wasn't sure how possible that was when neither had the full explanation. *Will he always be suspicious of Mom's story?*

But then he glanced at Holly, and a sense of peace washed over him. As usual, her presence was calming both the situation and him. Hope flared in his chest. Maybe they could all get past it in time, with a little help from magic.

Chapter Seventy-Six

HOLLY

"Wow, this hot chocolate tastes just like I remember it. I've never had anything as good since," Helena said.

She, Holly, and Ash sat in a booth at the Emerald House after closing. Ash's dad had opted to stay home. The situation was a lot to take in for all of them, and they agreed to take things one day at a time.

Holly leaned forward, energy pulsing through her veins. Her Cheer meter was buzzing rapidly. "I noticed the same thing when I first came here. Do you... Do you happen to know the history of the recipe?"

Helena, who had decided to keep going by her Finnish name for the time being after the familiarity of using it for so many years, sat back and was quiet for a moment, as if trying to remember. "I think my mother was the first one in the family to make it. But now that you mention it, she learned it from a friend. When she was a teenager and just starting to follow her passion of baking, someone came to town for a little while in the winter. She visited my grandmother's bakery. I miss that place."

Her mind seemed to wander in her newly returned memories for a moment before she continued the story.

"They quickly became friends, and the other young woman shared a hot chocolate recipe with her. My mom became obsessed with it, and they started selling it at the bakery about a year later, long after her friend had gone back home."

Holly's pulse quickened, suspicion crowding her thoughts. She tried to relax her expression when she asked, "Did your mom mention anything... special about this friend?"

Helena pursed her lips then smiled. "You know, she did, actually. She mentioned that her friend wore glasses with a slight tint—which was uncommon in those days—but there was one time she'd seen her with her glasses off, and she could have sworn her eyes were golden."

Ash whipped his head around to look at Holly, and she let out a deep breath, her watch vibrating and warming her wrist. *So the recipe came from an elf.*

Helena laughed again, not seeming to notice their reactions. "I can't believe I remembered that, but there it was. Locked away with all the other memories I didn't have access to all these years." She turned to Ash, her large eyes full of love. "I'm going to need you to fill me in on everything I've missed over the years. But first, I want to know how the two of you met."

He turned to Holly, their eyes locking, and he grinned as he launched into the story. "Actually, Holly was sitting in this booth the first time I saw her."

Chapter Seventy-Seven

SOFIA

"I heard there were some fireworks at Enzo's restaurant last night," Ash said as Sofia slipped an apron around her neck in the kitchen of the Emerald House.

Sofia smacked him with a towel but grinned. "Oh really? Where did you hear this?"

"It's the talk of the town. So Isaiah's back, huh?" Ash studied her face, and she knew he wasn't sure whether to be concerned or relieved about her and Isaiah's current status.

"He is. He wanted to explain... well, everything."

"And it's all good now? Or was that a farewell kiss?"

Sofia rolled her eyes. "I think he wants to move to Emerald Hollow. Maybe start a coffee business and incorporate some kind of bonus geocaching maps on their packaging. And create a little geocaching club for local kids. He's such a nerd," she said with a smile. "You might have a little competition."

"Bring it on," Ash said, "as long as his shop is on the other side of town."

Sofia laughed. "I'm really happy, Ash."

"He's a good guy. I'm really happy for you too. So's Holly."

"About that... Why did you two run off to Finland so quickly? Believe me—I'll be the first one to say you were overdue a vacation. But is that really what it was?"

Sofia thought she saw Ash tense, but it was gone a second later. "Actually, no. There's someone I'd like you to meet."

Chapter Seventy-Eight

HOLLY

"Holy crap!" Sofia exclaimed later that night as she, Isaiah, Ash, and Holly sat in the café of the Emerald House. "I can't believe I just met your mom."

"Me either," Ash said, a slightly dazed look on his face. But Holly saw something else there too. There was a light in his eyes that hadn't been quite so bright before. A missing piece of his life's puzzle had fallen into place.

"It's weird that she also suffered from amnesia, though. What is it about this place?" Isaiah asked.

Holly tensed.

Sofia, who had just finished her second glass of wine, answered before Holly or Ash could think of anything to say. "*Super* weird. But I'm not complaining." She leaned over and gave Isaiah a long, lingering kiss, making Holly blush.

When they broke apart, Sofia turned to Ash and looked pained. "Sorry, Ash. I didn't mean that like it sounded. It was good in Isaiah's case, but your mom, all those years..." Her face looked sad.

Ash shook his head and gave her a soft smile. "That's life,

right? We don't get to control everything that happens. But she's here now. That's more than I'd hoped for in a long time."

"So what happens now? Doesn't she have a whole life in Finland? Is she going to stay there, or is she thinking about moving back here?"

"She's still figuring that out. But she never married or had children there, and her printing business can be mobile, so maybe..."

"Printing business?" Sofia asked.

"She prints things for small businesses. Pamphlets, business cards, T-shirts, bags... You name it. She has some fancy printers. Apparently..." He glanced over at Holly, whose stomach fluttered at his gaze. "She printed the posters for the Emerald Hollow fall festival last summer. Those are the posters Holly saw and what inspired her to come here."

Sofia's eyes widened, and she leaned forward. "Well, that's quite the coincidence. Why did she print that poster? Was it a client request?"

"She said she came across it online when doing some research for a new design. She'd stumbled across Emerald Hollow in research before, and on a whim, she printed it out. She ended up putting it on the events board at her friend Lu—Lia's café."

"Then I stumbled across it and came here," Holly said, her heart full. She'd been wondering for months about the poster and how her and Ash's paths had intersected. To know that his long-lost mom had unknowingly been involved felt serendipitous to her in a way that had her bursting with gratitude.

"Huh. That's absolutely wild. But I watch enough rom-coms to know that, sometimes, fate exists," Sofia said. Her eyes shifted back to Isaiah's and lingered there.

"And I think that's our cue to go," Ash said, taking Holly's hand and helping her up. "See you later, love birds."

"Back at you," Sofia said, but her eyes didn't leave Isaiah's.

Ash whistled to Comet, then they headed outside for their nightly walk. As the moon shone brightly over the still-blooming tulips, Holly wondered if it was possible for her heart to be fuller.

Chapter Seventy-Nine

SOFIA

"I think it's time," Isaiah said, lifting her by the waist and easily plucking her down from the stage.

They had just belted out three songs together, and Sofia had never felt so energized. When Isaiah pitched the idea for Karaoke Thursdays, Ash had given the green light.

Sofia had been surprised to realize that over the last few months, Thursday had become her favorite night of the week. As long as Isaiah sang with her, she wasn't nervous to go on stage. He was just too much fun when he had a microphone in his hand.

"Time for what?" Sofia asked, tossing her curls over her shoulder. She was still breathless from their high-energy duet.

"Time for you to tell me why you used to be afraid of karaoke."

Sofia groaned. "I told you. I'm taking that secret with me to my grave."

"Come on. It can't be that bad," Isaiah teased as they made their way through the small sea of people who high-fived them as they walked away from the stage.

"Easy for you to say. The whole town agrees you're a Grammy-worthy singer. I'm sure you've never hit a wrong note in your life."

Isaiah laughed. "Fine then, Wrecker. Take that one to your grave. But then you'll never get to hear the story of why I don't play volleyball."

Sofia gasped in delight at the new information. She wanted to know absolutely everything about Isaiah since he had his memories back, and that included every embarrassing little story. Willow had told her a few on her most recent visit, but no one told stories like Isaiah. She couldn't resist.

"All right, fiiine." She heaved out a sigh. "Where to begin?"

Isaiah's eyes sparked. "Wait. Let me go get Ash."

Sofia grabbed his arms to stop him. "Nope. He still owes me one for letting slip about my karaoke phobia to you in the first place. This one's for you and only you."

Isaiah leaned against the desk in the lobby and crossed his arms, grinning.

Let's get this over with. She needed to get on with it before she got too distracted by that smile and went on her tiptoes for a kiss.

"So, the story starts in elementary school. You know how we used to all have roles in those little class plays?"

Isaiah nodded, and she continued, "I used to love those. I'd audition for the starring role, and most times, I got it."

Isaiah looked as if that fact didn't surprise him.

"Then in middle school, I joined the drama club, and we put on a production of *Grease.*"

He rubbed his hands together like things were about to get juicy.

Sofia gave him a little shove. "Isaiah, this is a core embarrassing memory!"

"Sorry," he said, putting up his hands placatingly. "Continue."

"I didn't get the role of Sandy, but I was cast as her understudy."

"I'm sure that girl had a target on her back because of that." Isaiah smirked again.

"Apparently, you don't want to hear this story after all." Sofia started to turn away.

But Isaiah tugged her back. "I'm sorry. I'll be quiet this time."

Sofia raised her eyebrows, not believing him, but she was determined to get it over with.

"So anyway, rehearsals had been going well, and I was killing it in my smaller role while also keeping up with all my understudy duties. But on opening night, the girl who was supposed to play Sandy got a wicked case of food poisoning, and I had to step in. Everything was going fine, but toward the end, when we were performing the final number and I was wearing those tight leather pants..."

Isaiah covered a laugh with his hands, and Sofia groaned.

"We were similar in size, so they didn't make a spare costume for the understudy. But the original girl was a bit less curvy than I was, and I was doing a dance move when the pants split right down the middle, exposing my hot-pink underwear to the entire gymnasium."

"Nooo," Isaiah said, playing along with her horror.

"Yep. It was all anyone could talk about for at least a month, until the next middle school scandal came along."

"So the embarrassment didn't have anything to do with singing? It was all about a costume malfunction? And all this time, I thought you were afraid you had a terrible voice and had been booed off the stage as a child." Isaiah's eyes were sparkling, his grin devilish, and Sofia smacked him.

"Honestly, ever since, I had no idea if I had a good voice or not. Performing live and showing my underwear to half the town were basically synonymous events in my brain."

"Until Valentine's Day," Isaiah said, grabbing her hand and tugging her toward him.

"Until Valentine's Day," she said with a grin. Then she stood on her toes, wrapped her arms around his neck, and kissed him.

Epilogue

In a boutique curio shop in Ashland, Oregon, a Kringle elf stared out the window after closing the shop for the night. As a couple laughed and crossed the street, her thoughts drifted to a different couple who had visited that spring. She hadn't been able to stop thinking about the incident since, and the scene ran through her head once again.

A couple paused outside her window, seemingly eying a pink kite that she had collected years before. After a brief conversation, the two stepped inside. The man did a quick look over the shop, but the woman went straight to the window, her eyes drawn instantly to the kite.

The Kringle elf watched as the young woman picked up the old fuchsia kite, wondering with a surprising sense of melancholy if she was going to sell it at last. The woman had freckles spattered across her nose like beautiful constellations, and the man looked at her as if she were the brightest star in the sky. A smile touched the elf's lips, then surprise jolted her.

An old, familiar prickling rushed through her veins, and she suppressed a gasp as the kite glowed with the type of magic that only elves could see. The elf gripped the edge of her cashier's counter, letting the feeling of the magic wash over her.

The kite had been sitting on her shelf for years. It had been picked up by a child or two, and it had never given any indication of containing traces of magic. So why is this happening now?

She studied the man and woman more closely, tapping into the intensified elf eyesight she'd been cut off from for years, and thought she detected the faintest trace of magic in the air around them.

It's not possible, *she thought as she watched the woman cling to the kite. She had lost her ability to detect and use magic years ago.*

Before she could contemplate what she was doing, the Kringle elf swiped another kite from her shelf and approached the couple.

"Take it," she said, the words sliding out of her mouth.

The woman with the freckles and caramel streaks in her hair turned toward her, her eyes wide.

The elf held out the white kite to the man, who accepted it without hesitation.

"Take them both. Those kites have been sitting on my shelf for far too long." It was a relief to say the words, as if she had been waiting for that opportunity her entire life.

The young woman reached toward her purse, but the elf shook her head. "It's my treat. I'm just glad to see them going to a good home after all this time." Again, the words seemed to flow out of her as naturally as the brook bubbled in the park just up the path.

"Are you sure? That's very generous." The young woman turned toward her, and the elf thought she saw a flash of surprise pass across her face. She quickly turned away, wondering if she'd forgotten to put her contacts in that morning. She didn't wear them all the time anymore. Most people skimmed right over her golden eyes, their gazes drawn instead to the bejeweled bright silver strands she wore in piled curls to obscure her too-long ears. But this woman... The elf was pretty sure she had noticed.

Just then, another customer entered the shop, and she quickly turned to greet them, not giving the woman a chance to take a second look at her eyes. She let out a breath of relief a few moments later when she heard the bells over the door chime again and saw the couple slip back onto the street.

The elf had no idea who the couple was or where they had come from. All she knew was that for the first time in years, she had experienced North Pole magic once again. And for the first time in as many years, the Kringle elf was filled with hope.

Acknowledgments

I am incredibly grateful to all who believe in the Magical Emerald Hollow stories and this cozy genre of small towns with magic.

Mom, for loving these stories, the characters, and the world, and always having a positive word just when I need it.

Chelsea, for all your valuable feedback and your eagle eye.

Shirley, for being such a supporter of my work and life this year (and for all the dog sitting!).

Bethanie, for being along for the ride with me on this author journey. Your support and friendship are so encouraging!

Zach, for being my partner in everything, and for the memes that keep me laughing.

To the book clubs and community of Nellis Air Force Base, you all have been so supportive of me as a local milspouse author, and I can't tell you how much I appreciate it.

To my ARC team and those of you who interact on my social media reader communities, every time you comment, share, squeal with excitement through a GIF, or simply give a 'heart' inspires me to keep creating.

To my cover designer, Kylie Sek, thank you for creating another magical cover for the Emerald Hollow stories!

To the editors and proofreaders at Red Adept Publishing, thank you for all your care with my work.

And lastly, to everyone who reads my books, recommends them to others, reviews them, and places them lovingly on your shelves, thank you for making my dreams come true!

About the Author

Heather Schneider is an author of young adult and women's fiction novels.

Heather lives with her husband and their Chiweenie, Toby. When she's not writing, you can find her reading, listening to podcasts, traveling, or spending time with family.

As an indie author, Heather would love to hear your feedback on *Finding Cheer*!

Please connect with her on Instagram or Facebook @heatherschneiderauthor and leave a review wherever you review books.

You can visit her website and subscribe to her newsletter at heatherschneiderauthor.com.